Martha McLeod, Head Mistress of Rowan House, Skye's most exclusive pleasure house, is heartbroken.

Frustrated and lonely after a bitter split with her lover, she departs Rowan House for Lake Como, Italy to seek solace at the feet of Madam Givernay, keeper of Martha's deepest secret. Lake Como and Madam's attention is the perfect balm for Martha's broken heart, until she meets Mistress Lucia Coruso.

Captivated by Lucia's regal elegance and cool demeanor, Martha is torn between her desire for Lucia and the fear her secret will be revealed. When an extortionist threatens to destroy Rowan House, Martha and Lucia must join forces to save it.

KNOTTED LEGACY

Brenda Murphy

A NineStar Press Publication

Published by NineStar Press
P.O. Box 91792,
Albuquerque, New Mexico, 87199 USA.
www.ninestarpress.com

Knotted Legacy

Printed in the USA
First Edition
September, 2018

Print ISBN: 978-1-949340-71-6

Also available in eBook, ISBN: 978-1-949340-67-9

Warning: This book contains sexually explicit content, which may only be suitable for mature readers, and depictions of hot wax play, blood play, rope play, collaring, kidnapping and forced captivity.

To C, always.

I am forever grateful to my friends at Templeton's, the best tea shop ever, for the endless pots of tea and support. Alison, Stuart and Jennifer, thank you.

Chapter One

"BLACK SUIT? WEDDING, or funeral?" Elaine shifted her weight on the bed and plumped the pillow with her fist.

Martha tilted her head and looked at her sister. "Madam has a thing for suits." She folded her shirt and placed it in her packing cube. "I miss the way Sarah ironed my shirts. So meticulous."

Elaine snorted. "Another one that left us. Are you going to see Vivian? I wonder how things are going with Bridget. What a succulent little brat." She sucked her teeth.

"Miss her?"

"Do you miss Octavia?" Elaine smiled a sick smile, the one guaranteed to start a fist fight when they were children.

Martha frowned at Elaine. "Let's drop this. I'm not going to see Vivian. She messaged me last week. Something's come up. She won't be attending."

Elaine raised her eyebrows. "Something? She's never missed one. Even the year she lost Miriam."

Martha sighed. "She said the three of them were—involved, and she was not attending."

Elaine's expression changed, the teasing look on her face gone. "I'm sorry. Are you okay?"

Martha pursed her lips. "I will be. I love Vivian. I want her to be happy. I can't believe Bridget is okay with it. She's such a tight-ass."

Elaine left the bed. She moved behind Martha and hugged her hard before she released her. "I'll get out of your hair and let you finish packing. Anything special you want for lunch?"

"Is Myfanwy busy?" Martha chewed her lower lip, longing for the comfort of Myfanwy's sweet submission.

"She's scheduled with a client until tomorrow night." Elaine rested her hand on her sister's forearm. "Should I have Robin bring it to you? You haven't even looked at her since I hired her."

Maybe something new. Who knows? It might fill this empty place inside of me. Martha patted her sister's hand. "That sounds delightful. Is there any of the soup we had last night?"

Elaine squeezed her arm. "Yes. I'll send her up in an hour."

Martha,

I hope this letter finds you well. I expect you will attend me for what will be my last occasion. I will explain more when you arrive. G.

Martha folded the scented notepaper and placed it in her journal. *The last?* She swallowed on a dry throat. *The rumors must be true. What will become of the Onyx?* She sat back and looked out of the window. The last of the sun highlighted the drive and reflected off the white stones surrounding the center fountain. Her thoughts folded back in on themselves. *So many years. No decisions. No worries. Submission. Obedience. Pain. And love. Madam's love. What will I do?*

A tap at the door interrupted her melancholy thoughts. She slid her journal into her desk drawer and sat back in her chair. "Enter."

The door opened, and a small woman in a short black skirt and simple white blouse pushed a meal cart into the room. She was thin, her face defined by sharp angles. Her makeup was professionally applied, the cherry-red lipstick contrasting with her pale skin and overbright blue eyes. A cap of bleached blonde curls covered her head.

"Your soup, Mistress." She met Martha's gaze briefly and looked down. Her voice was soft. "Where would you like me to serve you?"

Elaine did well. Tasty indeed. "My bed."

"Pardon, Mistress?"

Martha stood up and crossed the room to stand over to the small woman. She hooked her fingers under her collar. "Robin, isn't it?" She leaned down, watching her response, and cupped the back of her neck. "My bed."

Robin stilled in her arms. Desire coiled in Martha's gut.

"Me, Mistress?" Robin's voice was tremulous.

"Look at me." Martha pinned her with her gaze, assessing her true feelings. She ran her thumb over Robin's plump bottom lip, smearing her lipstick. *No fear. Acting. Enticing but not real.* "You can refuse. I won't hold it against you."

"Oh no, I'm not refusing, Mistress. I didn't expect you would want me." She spoke in a well-practiced voice, the facade of innocence mildly annoying to Martha as they moved through the dance of permissions. Robin lifted her chin and held Martha's gaze.

Martha studied Robin's face. Her self-deprecating words didn't match the hard edge reflected in her eyes. *Practiced. Not innocent. But she plays it well.* "I won't ask for your permission again. You're free to refuse me as is anyone who works here."

Robin pushed into Martha's arms. "Oh no, Mistress. Please." The breathy quality of her voice and the way she pressed her body into Martha's embrace signaled her willingness to serve. "Don't send me away. Let me serve you."

Willing. Truth. Not innocent but willing. Martha kissed her, letting herself get lost in Robin's well-acted surrender. She broke their kiss, and Robin lowered herself to her knees. "Bed. Now. Face up."

Robin crawled across the floor. She stood up and toed her shoes off before she climbed up. She lay in the middle of the large bed, dwarfed by the king-size mattress.

"Hands over your head." Martha stood next to the bed, her thighs slick with want in spite of her depressed mood. Or maybe because of it. "Spread your legs."

She kicked off her shoes and shed her pants and underwear before she mounted the bed. Martha kneeled between her legs and shoved Robin's skirt up; then she grabbed the waistband of her panties. She stripped her sheer underwear off and tossed them over the edge of the bed. The scent of Robin's excitement made saliva pool in her mouth. She slid one finger over her clit. The small gasp from Robin made Martha press her legs together to relieve the ache. She thrust her thumb into the liquid evidence of her desire. *Can't fake being wet. At least she's into it.* She gathered Robin's wetness before she leaned over her and pushed her thumb into her mouth. Robin opened to her and sucked hard. She moaned on cue, and the mechanical sound of her response threatened to derail Martha's plans.

"You like that, don't you? You look like sugar wouldn't melt in your mouth, but I see the slut in you." She pulled her thumb free and slapped her face. "You want to suck my clit, don't you?"

Robin's eyes were bright. "Oh yes please, Mistress. Let me. Let me please you. Please."

Martha moved her hand down and entered her, fucking her slowly. Robin arched up to meet her thrusts. "Do you want to be my little fuck-toy?" She ground the heel of her hand against Robin's clit, watching pleasure play across her face.

"Oh. Oh please, Mistress. I. Oh please. Just for you. Please, Mistress." Robin twisted her hands in the sheets above her head.

"Do you want to come for me?" *Well trained. Knows what I like.* Hot need wound through Martha's body. She thrust harder.

"Please, Mistress. Let me come for you. Just you." Robin thrashed her hips, welcoming Martha's deep thrusts. "Please."

"Give it to me. All of it. Now." Martha pushed hard and deep, sweeping her fingers over Robin's sweet spot.

Robin arched off the bed and groaned as she spilled her pleasure, soaking the duvet beneath her. Martha pulled her hand away and rose to kneel over Robin's face. She pinned her arms with her knees.

"Lick me." She settled on Robin's face, rocking herself on her tongue, rolling her hips. Robin lapped at her and thrust her tongue deep before she sucked hard on Martha's clit. Sharp spikes of pleasure shot through Martha and she came with a deep groan. She raised her hips and lay next to her.

Robin rolled to her side to face Martha. Her lipstick was smeared, and Martha touched her cheek and looked into her eyes. "That was lovely."

Robin smiled at her. "The pleasure was mine, Mistress." She reached out and rested her hand on the front of

Martha's shirt, toying with the buttons. "Is there anything else, Mistress?"

Yes. No. Good, and yet not what... No. Who I want. Will I ever stop missing her? Martha caught her hand and squeezed it hard. "No. Thank you. You may return to your duties."

A flash of anger passed over Robin's face before she smoothed her features. "Your soup will be cold. Should I bring you another bowl?"

Angry. At me. Interesting. "No. I'm not hungry." Martha shifted off the bed and picked up her clothes. She turned her back to the bed. She heard the bedsprings squeak, the rustle of Robin's clothes as she put her uniform to rights. She kept her back turned and listened to the cart wheels rattle as Robin left and pulled the door closed with a hard click. Martha let out the breath she had been holding.

She went to the bathroom and washed her hands in the sink, anxious to be rid of the reminder that what she had was not what she wanted.

TWENTY WOMEN STOOD before Martha in the main ballroom. She looked at each of their faces, favoring some of them with a smile. "I will be gone for two weeks. The house is closed to guests. You are all free to go or stay. Those of you who choose to go on holiday, please leave a copy of your plans with Millie. If anyone has any trouble while traveling, please call the main landline." She inclined her head at Elaine. "Cook is in charge while I am away." She didn't miss the small murmurs and one loud groan from someone in the crowd, or Elaine's expression of satisfaction. She would never understand her sister's desire to be the most feared Dominatrix in the house.

Elaine squared her shoulders and focused her gaze on one of the submissives. "You have something to say?"

Roxy had been with them since the start, and she never tired of pushing Elaine's buttons. "Oh no, Mistress. Nothing to say." She rested her hand on her hip and rocked back on her heels and dared to meet her Mistress's gaze. "Here."

Elaine's voice took on a warm tone. "Later then." She licked her lower lip and smiled a tight smile at Roxy. Martha looked away from their display, jealous of the obvious love between them. *Why doesn't she commit to her? She loves her. Has loved her for years. And Roxy would kill for her.* She scanned the faces of the rest of the crowd. Myfanwy stood close to Roxy. Her brows were knitted and her gaze fixed on Robin. The newest addition to Rowan House, Robin, was standing at the back of the crowd, a bored expression on her face. Martha watched her. The contrast between the woman who had served her at lunch yesterday, and the hard-faced woman she saw before her was disconcerting. Robin looked up suddenly and into Martha's eyes. The shift in her demeanor when she knew herself observed was startling, her face morphing from hardened whore to innocent woman in seconds. Martha looked away and waved her hand at the group.

"You're dismissed. See you in two weeks. Be well-behaved. Be sane. And for God's sake be careful."

MARTHA RESTED HER handbag on the foyer floor. "This may be the last time I make this trip." She buttoned her long gray wool coat. She pulled her black leather gloves on before she placed her fedora on her head and adjusted the brim. She checked herself in the mirror. Elaine picked up Martha's purse and handed her the large bag. Martha looped the strap over her shoulder.

Elaine met her gaze in the mirror. "Maybe not. You know it's not the first time she's implied it would be the last. She is dramatic."

"Yes, but the tone of her message is different than the other times." Martha opened the door and stepped out. The icy wind stung her cheeks. She flipped up the collar of her coat. The black car idled in the drive. Millie was loading the last of Martha's bags into the car.

Elaine pulled her thick blue sweater tighter, her hands red from the cold. "I envy you Italy this time of year."

"I'm sure Roxy will keep you warm." Martha hugged her tight. She released her and tucked a wisp of red hair that had worked loose from her braid behind her ear. "Go inside. I'll be okay. I'll text you when I get there. If you need me, I left the contact information on my desk."

"Don't worry. We'll be fine." Elaine stepped back.

She won't go inside until I'm in the car. Millie held the door of the car open, and Martha hurried across the drive. She entered the car, and Millie closed her door. She sat back and looked back at the house. Elaine had gone inside, but Martha could see her holding back the curtain and peering out of the foyer window. She waved, and Elaine raised her hand. As much as she treasured her two weeks with Madame Givernay, she hated to be away from her home and her sister. Not quite two years apart, orphaned young, they were as close as twins even if their looks could not have been more different. And yet. She longed to rest at Madame's feet, safe, cherished. Martha leaned back in her seat, settling her hips into the smooth leather. After buckling her seat belt in place, she blew out a long breath, ready to be away from the responsibility of running Rowan House. A nagging sensation of uncertainly tugged at her mind before she pushed it aside. *Elaine can handle it. They'll be fine. They always have been. I'm being silly.* She tapped her foot, anxious to be free, even if for only a bit.

"Are you warm enough, Mistress?" Millie met her gaze in the rearview mirror. "Should I adjust the heat?"

"I'm comfortable. Let's go. We're only one flock of sheep away from missing the ferry."

Millie laughed. "Yes, Mistress. I'll get you there in time."

She looked out at the gray clouds clustered over the distant mountains. *The ferry ride will be rough. And cold. Damn it.* She pulled her bag into her lap and rummaged through it, looking for her anti-sea-sickness bands. She slid them over her hands and pressed the button over the acupressure points on her wrists.

These things are fashion tragic. Ugh. At least they work.

THE LOUNGE ON the ferry was crowded. Not trusting her stomach, Martha found a spot along the rail, the cold wind quelling her nausea. She sighed as she looked back at Skye. Her thoughts worked in circles as she mulled over the message from Madame, Vivian's absence and new relationship with Octavia and Bridget, the way she had responded, or rather not responded, to Robin. She chewed her lip. The sound of a man's frustrated voice carried over the wind and disrupted her thoughts.

"You have to come inside. I can't leave your sister alone, and it's too cold for her out here. Please. We can stand near the door."

"No. Please, Dad. It's too hot in there. I don't want to throw up. Please."

Martha turned her head and saw a small boy. He looked about seven, red-haired, and thin. His face was pale. The man standing next to him had a diaper bag slung over his shoulder and a baby in his arms. The baby, wrapped in multicolored blankets, started to cry. The man looked as if he might join her any minute. He shifted the baby to his other arm and held out his hand. "I'm not going to ask again. I need to get your sister inside."

"I'll be sick, Dad. Please. I'll stay right here. Please don't make me go inside." The boy's voice was earnest, on the verge of tears. He held his stomach with one hand and belched loudly. Martha looked around for a bin just in case.

She walked along the rail and stopped bit away from the family. "Sir? I'll stay with him if you like." She pointed to one of the wide lounge windows. "You can see us from there."

The boy looked at her, his eyes wary. She smiled at the boy. "I get sick inside too." She looked at the man. "I'll wait here for you when we dock."

The baby's crying was louder. The man bounced her in his arms, and she settled for a moment. He met Martha's gaze, an uncertain expression on his face. The baby fussed again. "Thank you." He looked at the boy. "Mind her. I'll be right inside if you need me."

He hurried inside with the baby and took up a place at the window. The father waved at the boy and he waved back before he turned to Martha.

"I'm big enough to be alone out here, but Dad thinks I'm a baby." He looked up at Martha and cocked his head to the side. "You're really tall for a lady. I like your hat."

Martha laughed. "I suppose I am, and thank you."

"Do you really get sick too?"

"Yes." She held out her arms and displayed her wrist bands. "But these help."

The boy frowned. "How?"

"They press on a spot that helps keeps the sick feeling away. Hold out your arm."

He held out his arm, and she pointed to the gap between his glove and jacket sleeve and a spot on his wrist. "Measure down three of your fingers and press there with your thumb."

The boy did. "How long does it take?"

"It's not instant, and it works better if you put pressure on the spot before you start feeling sick."

His brow furrowed as he concentrated. After a few minutes he smiled. "It works."

Martha smiled back. She glanced back at the window. The man was focused on the baby, feeding her a bottle. *What is the story here? Why is he traveling alone, and how much farther do they have to go?*

The boy tugged her sleeve. "Where ya going, lady? We're going home. I'm getting a puppy. Do you have a dog? Do you like the ferry? I like it even if I get sick."

Martha numbered her answers on her fingers. "Italy. I have a horse and some cats but no dog. And yes, I like the ferry."

"You should get a dog. They're the best." He looked back and waved at his father. The man waved back.

"I'll think about it."

A gust of wind blew over the deck, and Martha held tight to her fedora. The boy pushed closer to her, leaning his body into her, and shivered.

"Are you cold? Do you want to go inside?" Martha looked down at him.

"No. I like it out here. Look at the clouds. Do you think we're halfway? Look, the gulls are following us. Do you like birds? I like birds."

They spent the rest of the trip with the boy talking and asking questions without waiting for answers. Martha was grateful for the distraction, marveling at the way seeing the world through the observations of a small boy made the excursion wondrous. They docked, and she waited with the boy until his father arrived. The baby was sleeping now.

"See, Dad. I told you I could do it." The boy's color had improved. His cheeks were a bright pink.

The man ruffled his hair. "You did. I saw." He looked at Martha. "Thank you. It was so nice of you to help. My wife does this by herself all the time. I don't know how."

The boy took his hand. "Look, Dad, there's Mom. Let's go. See ya, lady." He pulled his father through the crowd. A small part of her, the part that wondered what it would have been like if her parents had survived the accident, grieved for the normal life she'd never known. Boarding schools and caretakers had been her world.

She waited until the crowd cleared and made her way off the ferry. Millie was waiting for her. She opened the door, and Martha slid into the warm comfort of the car.

Millie met her gaze in the rearview mirror. "Do you want to stop at Fort William, Ma'am? For something to eat?"

"No. Unless you need something."

"I'm good, Ma'am." Millie pulled the car onto the road, and Martha focused her gaze out of the window and settled in for the ride.

Chapter Two

HER WOOL COAT, so practical on Skye, was ridiculously hot for Lake Como. Martha placed it beside her on the seat. The flight had been as rough as the ferry trip, and she wanted nothing more than to be out of a moving vehicle. The driver was quiet on the ride from Malpensa airport to Madame's villa. The limousine was appointed in white leather, impractical as hell but stunning.

The slight headache that had started on the ferry was now a ripping pain, and she wanted to curl into a ball in a dark room. *Great way to meet Madame. So stupid not to pack my medication. Or sunglasses.* She rubbed her neck, trying to ease the tight tendons along her spine. *I miss Octavia's hands. Damn if I don't miss all of her, not only her hands. Robin. Where did Cook find her? I'd have passed. Too whorish. We'll have to work on her demeanor. Our customers won't like it.* She looked out of the window, grateful to see the familiar unmarked drive of Madame's home. *Finally. I hope I can rest before I see her.*

The car glided to a stop in the formal drive. The white pavers leading to the front of the house gleamed. The housekeeper, Alicia, stood waiting on the steps. The driver opened her door, and she stepped out and pulled her hat down to shield her eyes from the glare of the sun. Her mood lightened as she walked up the familiar path.

Alicia smiled at her. "Buongiorno." She embraced Martha and kissed both cheeks. "*Madame sarà così felice di vederti.* I'm happy to see you too."

A tall woman in black slacks and a starched white shirt appeared. Alice pointed at the car waiting in the driveway and inclined her head at the woman. "Get her luggage." She clasped Martha's arm. "Let me take you to your room."

"Are the others here?"

Alicia looked down. "It is only you. Madame only asked for you and Ms. Abiola, who sends her regrets." She looked up and met Martha's eyes. "She is—Madame is tired."

The sadness in her voice undid Martha. She placed her hand on top of Alicia's hand. "Should I go to her now?" Martha wanted to see her, touch her forehead to her feet, let her command of her whatever she needed.

Alicia tilted her head, her lips pressed in a firm line. "No. She's napping and would never forgive me if I did not let you recover from your trip so you could present yourself properly." She guided Martha up the stairs to her room.

Alicia opened the door and pushed it wide. The room was bright. Fresh flowers graced the table, and the bed was turned down.

"I'll send Gia up with some coffee. Would you like something to eat?"

Martha's stomach turned at the idea of coffee and food. "Could I have some tea, please? Ginger tea if you have it."

"As you wish. Dinner is at eight. I laid out your gown and your collar."

Martha toed off her shoes. "Thank you."

Alicia smiled, her gaze steady, and she touched Martha's cheek. "Gia will bring the tea. If you need anything else, let me know."

She closed the door behind her, and Martha stripped out of her suit jacket. She opened her suitcase and retrieved her toiletries bag.

A sharp rap on the door made her jump. She opened it to find the woman Alicia had sent to get her luggage standing in the hall with a tray. "Come in." She stepped aside, and the woman placed the tray on the desk.

"You're Gia, yes?"

"*Sì.* Do you require anything else, Miss?"

Martha smiled at her. "It's been years since anyone has called me Miss."

Gia blushed. "No offense, Miss."

"None taken. Call me Martha."

Gia smiled back. "Will I see you at dinner—Martha?"

"Yes."

"See you then, Martha."

She closed the door softly. Martha sipped her tea. The ginger worked its magic and her stomach settled. She undressed, her nipples pebbling in the cool breeze from the window. She took her tea into the bath. The tub was deep, and she filled it as full as she dared. She added lemon-scented bath oil before she lowered herself into the soothing heat of the water. With a sigh she leaned back and closed her eyes. *Nap. Dinner. My collar.*

She thought over what Alicia had said, as the light citrus smell surrounded her, soothing her body but not her heart. *Why only me and Vivian? Fine time for Vivian not to show up.*

The water cooled, and she heaved herself out of the tub. She dried herself and brushed her teeth before she lay down on the crisp white sheets and pulled them over her. She closed her eyes. *I should text Elaine. Later. I'll text her later.* She turned to her side and gave in to sleep.

THE FORMAL DINING room was set for two places. Empty chairs greeted her, and a silence hung over the room like a shroud. Martha clasped her worn and faded collar tight in her hands to stop them from shaking. Her sheer gown hugged her curves. The fabric rubbing against her nipples kept them half-hard. She looked up when the door clicked open. Madame Givernay stepped through the double doors.

A wide white scarf covered her head. She had never been a large woman, but now her cheekbones stood out, her face all dark hollows and sharp angles. Her clothes hung loosely on her body.

So thin. So frail. No. Oh no. Martha bit her lip and suppressed a gasp. Gia stood next to Madame, letting her lean on her arm as she assisted her to the chair at the head of the table. Martha waited until Madame was settled and Gia had left them before she approached. She knelt next to Madame's chair. She lowered her head and held her collar out with both hands. The brush of Madame's fingers against her own as she took the collar from her made her shiver. Madame placed the collar around Martha's neck and buckled it. A firm hand on her chin pulled her head up.

"Eyes to me." Madame's voice, silk over steel, was loud in the quiet of their intimate dinner.

Martha raised her gaze and looked into Madame's deep-brown eyes. The light was there, her spirit strong, tempered but present.

"You look like you're afraid I'll break if you breathe." She patted her lap. "Lay your head here, pet. I've missed you."

Martha rested her head on Madame's lap, the soft folds of her skirt soothing on her cheek. Madame carded her fingers through Martha's hair before she traced her cheekbone with the sharp edge of her nail. Martha's tension melted away under Madame's touch. *She always knows what I need.* In her twenties and thirties, Martha would have been anxious for Madame to have her, to punish her, to beat her until Madame and her wishes were her world. But as Madame had aged, and Martha turned forty, she understood pacing, and the pleasure of serving, of simply sitting at her Mistress's feet waiting on her will, focusing all her attention on attending her.

Madame cleared her throat. "I'm dying, pet. I won't live to see the end of the year." She wrapped her hand in Martha's hair and tugged hard. The sharp pull on her scalp focused Martha. "No tears. I want no tears of pity, or of sadness."

Martha bit her lip, pushing away the emotion that dried her throat and made it hard to swallow. "Yes, Madame, as you command."

The hand in her hair tightened, and her head was pulled back. Madame grasped her chin. "I do. I command it." She kissed her forehead and took her mouth, kissing her, lips fierce and demanding. Martha trembled in her grip, surrendering herself to Madame's mouth. Madame released her before she rapped on the table with her knuckles. Martha knelt next to her chair, eyes down, hands resting on her thighs palms up. The sensation of Madame's kiss lingered on her lips and filled her body with longing.

The door opened, and Martha watched from under her lashes as Gia brought in the meal. Madame rested her hand on the top of Martha's head. "Rise, pet. Eat with me. I've not the strength to feed both of us."

Martha rose and took the seat next to Madame's chair. The delicate scent of saffron wafted from the soup placed before her.

"Eat." Madame took up her spoon and Martha did the same. They ate their soup, the silence heavy between them with unasked questions and answers Martha didn't want to hear. Martha shifted in her seat and rested her spoon on her soup plate.

Madame finished, and Gia cleared their plates. She returned with the main course.

Madame leaned back in her chair. "I am disappointed Vivian would not join us." She picked up her glass of water and took a sip. "I wanted you both to act as executors of my will."

Martha dropped her fork, and it clattered on the table. She raised her eyes to her Mistress's face. She held her gaze. No words passed between them. Madame pulled the scarf from her head. The sight of her bald scalp made Martha bite her cheek to keep her tears back and honor her promise to Madame.

"I've exhausted all treatment options." She turned in her chair and motioned to Gia. "Bring me the package on the sideboard." Gia brought an overstuffed folio to Madame and presented it with both hands. Madame took it, her arms trembling with the weight of the folder. She dropped it on the table.

Martha wiped her mouth and sat back. Grief stifled her appetite. She picked up her wine and gulped half the glass.

Madame eyed Martha's glass. "Go ahead, pet. I can't drink wine anymore, but I like to watch other people enjoy my cellar."

Martha picked up her glass and drained it. Gia moved quietly and refilled it with the bottle from the sideboard. She turned to go, and Martha grabbed her wrist.

"Leave the bottle."

Gia inclined her head at Madame, who nodded her agreement. She placed the bottle on the table and left them.

Madame rested her hand on the thick burgundy leather brief folio. "Here are my instructions. I want you to read them. We will discuss them tomorrow." She grabbed Martha's hand, her grip surprising in its strength. "Know if I could I would take you back to my room and spend the night listening to your sweet screams of surrender. I'm so sorry to not be able to attend to you as I should."

Martha leaned over and kissed the back of her Mistress's hand. "It is enough to be here with you."

Madame squeezed her hand. "You never disappoint me, my pet. My love." She pulled her hand free. "Eat. Drink. I want to watch your wonderful mouth while you eat. Everything has lost its flavor for me."

Martha ate because she knew her Mistress deserved her best behavior. Deserved her obedience. Deserved everything Martha wanted to give and more.

"YOU'VE READ THROUGH my instructions?" Madame looked at Martha from over the top of her glasses. "Are the directions clear?"

"Yes, Madame. Very clear." Martha knotted her hands together. "But there is one thing..."

"Out with it. I don't have time for chitchat. Imminent death focuses you as much as pain."

"Am I to understand you are giving me a person? A Lucia Coruso?"

Madame narrowed her eyes. "Not giving. I want you to provide a place for her. She has been with me for the last fifteen years. I want to provide for her."

Martha frowned. "I understand. But why do you think Rowan House is the right place for her?"

Madame sat back in her chair and raised her chin at Martha. "Are you questioning my judgment?"

"No. I just...I'm not sure I'm the right person to be her Mistress."

Madame laughed. "Whatever gave you the impression that's what I intended? Lucia will make her own decisions. I simply want you to provide a place for her to live. My house in Givernay reverts to my niece. Lucia inherits the bulk of my estate here. Everyone else will share in what's left after the sale of the house. They have families to return to if they choose. The Onyx ends with me, but for those who have developed a taste for what we have had here, there are very few places to go. Lucia has no family. Rowan House will be perfect for her."

"What if she doesn't want to go? Skye is a far cry from Lake Como. And our clientele tends to desire more physical forms of entertainment." Martha sipped her coffee. "Has she agreed to your plan?"

Madame pursed her lips, her eyes dark. "She will. Just as you will." She exhaled forcefully and sank back in her chair. She waved her hand over the documents. "Any more of my decisions you want to question?"

Chastised, Martha bowed her head. "No, Madame." She placed her cup on the table. "I'll do as you ask, Mistress. She'll have a place at Rowan House for as long as she desires. I will provide for her as you request."

"LUCIA CORUSO, THIS is Martha MacLeod." Madame sat back in her chair. "Lucia recently returned from Japan." She rested her hands in her lap, a half smile on her face as she observed them.

Madame's demeanor as she watched them raised the hairs on Martha's arms. The woman who stood before her was as tall as Martha. Her thick dark-brown shoulder-length hair hung in loose curls around her face and brushed the tops of her broad shoulders. Her skin was medium brown. *Corsican? Sicilian?* She was dressed in black trousers and a sharply tailored white shirt. The top three buttons of the shirt were unfastened, giving Martha an unfettered view of her collarless neck and ample cleavage. Martha caught herself staring, and she forced herself to look at Lucia's face. Her eyes were a bright blue-green. *Those eyes. Like the sea at Amalfi. Oh, Madame, you know me well.*

Lucia looked into Martha's eyes and inclined her head. "Madame has told me so much about you, Martha."

The cool edge in her voice cut through Martha's fog, and she extended her hand. "It's a pleasure to meet you." Martha caught the delicate scent of Lucia's perfume, sandalwood and jasmine, a subtle blend of spice and sweet.

Lucia took her hand and squeezed hard. Her grip firm, she kept her gaze on Martha's eyes. "And you as well."

The effect of her touch and the hard edge to her voice had Martha clenching her jaw. *Trying to top me? What the hell?* Martha returned the firm grip and her sharp gaze. *Does she think I'm a sub outside of here? She's a Mistress? What the hell is Madame up to?*

Lucia let go of Martha's hand and turned to face Madame. "I take it you've not changed your mind, Madame?" She pursed her lips. "You want me to go with—" she nodded toward Martha "—her."

It was the disdain in her voice and the failure to use an honorific that set off the Mistress in Martha. *Oh, fuck her. She doesn't want to go to Rowan House. I don't want her either. She and Elaine will be at each other's throats.*

Damn, this is awkward. That's all I need—another bitter, disgruntled Mistress in the house. Fuck.

Madame snapped her fingers. "Come here, Lucia."

Lucia lowered her chin to her chest and walked over to Madame's chair. She sank to her knees. Madame reached out and grabbed her chin. "You will not disrespect her. She was making subs beg for her touch when you were in grade school." She released her, and Lucia sat back on her heels. "It is my final wish you go to Rowan House. What transpires after you are there is your business. I won't be here to care."

Lucia's lip quivered for a moment before she firmed her mouth. "Yes, Madame." Her voice was soft, the tone one of respect. Martha watched. Not speaking, waiting for Madame to signal the meeting was over.

Madame fisted her hand in Lucia's shirt and pulled her face to within inches of her own. "Eyes to me." Lucia raised her head. "You came to me and asked for my ownership. I didn't force it on you. Trust me now. Honor my request. I will summon you to return here when I need you to attend me again." She pressed a rough kiss to her cheek and released her shirt. She looked away from Lucia. A fine tremor shook Madame's hand. She picked up the small hand bell by her chair and rang it once. Gia entered the room. "Take me to my room."

Gia assisted her to stand. Martha waited, trying to make sense of what had taken place between Madame and Lucia. Madame glared at Martha, her eyebrow raised and her gaze hard, daring Breng Martha to speak. Martha looked away from her Mistress and watched from under her eyelashes as Madame walked from the room, her fingers wrapped around Gia's arm and her head high, leaving behind the force of her will.

Lucia remained kneeling, her head bowed, her hand resting on her cheek where Madame had kissed her. Martha waited until Lucia rose. She kept her head down as she turned away from Martha and left the room, closing the door softly. Martha walked to the window and looked out at the garden. Bees hovered over the late September blooms, a riot of orange and yellow. She chewed her lip as she replayed her meeting with Lucia and Madame. *What the hell have I agreed to? This is trouble. She's trouble. And beautiful. What am I going to do? What are you up to, Madame?*

MARTHA STOOD IN the foyer. She watched Gia as she packed her bags into the trunk of the car. Her heart ached, but she held back the tears that had been a constant threat since her last dinner with Madame. She looked around the foyer, memorizing its detail, knowing the next time she stepped through the door it would be as executor of Madame's estate.

Alicia touched her elbow. "It's time to go."

Martha picked up her purse and settled the strap over her arm. She walked out into the early morning sun. Gia slammed the trunk closed before she moved to open Martha's door.

"Wait." Lucia's voice was loud and commanding.

Martha stopped and turned back. Lucia came toward her. She wore the sheer gown Madame preferred her submissives wear. A red collar graced her neck, and even though she wore the clothes of a submissive of Givernay, her strong posture and direct steps indicated to Martha even more strongly that outside of the Onyx she was a Mistress, as she had suspected. Martha did not look away from her ripe body on display. Lucia's nipples tented the sheer fabric.

Martha raked her gaze over her figure before she looked to her face. "Yes?"

"I'll be to you in one week." Lucia rested her hand on her hip.

"I'm aware." Martha raised her eyebrow. "Is there something else? I don't want to miss my plane."

Lucia cocked her head at Martha. "I don't know why Madame is sending me to you." She met Martha's hard gaze with one of her own. She lifted the edge of her collar and dropped it. "I only wear this here. I don't intend on wearing one ever again once Madame is gone."

Martha squared her shoulders. In her heels she was taller than Lucia, and she used it to her advantage. She stepped close, forcing Lucia to look up at her. "What you do, or do not do, is no concern of mine. I am honoring Madame's request. I do not expect you to be anything at Rowan House other than my guest. Madame asked me to provide a place for you and I will." She lowered her voice to a harsh whisper. "I don't like this any more than you do, but for now, it is how it is, unless you'd like to tell Madame otherwise." She pressed her advantage and stepped closer. "Understand this, guest or no. I will not tolerate anyone disrespecting me." She touched the edge of Lucia's collar with the tip of her finger before she trailed her hand down the front of her gown and flicked her nipple.

A flash of want shone in Lucia's eyes before it was replaced by an expression of shock and anger. She stepped back, putting distance between them. She clenched her fist in her gown and opened her mouth as if to speak before she closed it and pressed her lips in a thin line. She turned on her heel and walked back to the house, her steps loud on the stone path.

Martha watched her walk away, pushing away the desire stirring in her belly as she observed the sway of Lucia's thick hips under the filmy gown, and the way she held her head erect as she retreated into the house. *Her eyes. So like Octavia. And yet not. So much pushback. Her mouth is exquisite. Too bad she can't control it.* She waited until the door closed behind Lucia, then settled her fedora on her head before she turned and walked to the car. *What are you playing at, Madame?*

Chapter Three

THE THREAD OF desire for Lucia, begun on the path outside the Onyx, had expanded into a thick coil of want in Martha's body. She had replayed their last interaction in her mind in an endless loop with various endings, most of them some version of her taking Lucia back inside Madame's house to show her exactly why she shouldn't underestimate Martha. All her fantasies featured Lucia submitting to her in exquisite detail. She rearranged the pillows on the bed in the suite of rooms she had set aside for Lucia for the sixth time. She turned and looked around the room. *Flowers. I should have ordered flowers. No. Too much.* She chewed her lip as she paced the room.

"Are you sure you want her this close to you? Why not the Blue Suite? It was good enough for the princess we entertained last year." Elaine quirked her mouth at Martha. "I've not seen you like this in forever. Why are you making such a fuss? From what you said, she's a right bitch."

Martha tilted her head at her sister. "Yes. But Madame expects me to..."

"To what? Take her in? Make her your sub? You've been cagy since you got back." Elaine pulled out the desk chair and sat. She shoved the other chair out with her foot. "Spill it."

Martha left the pillow on the bed and took a seat across from her sister. She leaned forward and rested her arms on her knees. "Madame wants me to provide a place for her.

She asked me to care for her." She chewed her lip. "She was—unclear about specifics. I might have left things on a bad note with Lucia."

Elaine's laugh was loud. "I wish you could see your face." She reached over and patted Martha's arm. "We'll take her in hand. She'll not come here and disrupt what we have. And the fact she is still coming is something. You couldn't have been so bad."

"She's obeying Madame's request. She's a Mistress. We need to show her the proper respect."

Elaine snorted. "Respect is earned. I'll be respectful. Enough."

Martha rolled her eyes at her sister and huffed before she pulled her chair closer to the table. "Come on. I want to go over the menu with you."

"No. We've been over it twice." Elaine stood up and stretched. "You need to take the edge off. You haven't been with any of the subs since you returned, not even Myfanwy. Why don't you give Robin a try again?"

Martha pursed her lips. "No. Too whorish for me. It's not what I want."

"You mean who." Elaine frowned at her. "You've been a mess since Octavia left. I could kill her for leaving you."

"It was for the best. She wasn't happy. I could sense it. I choose to ignore it until it was too late." Martha leaned back in her chair and looked at the ceiling.

Elaine walked to the door. "Then let's take a walk to the stable. I've got my eye on Rachel. Her arms make me want to watch her work. She looks like she could bench-press a house. Or me."

Martha laughed. "She's built. I've seen her pick up a twenty-kilo bag of horse feed in each hand and walk to the other end of the barn without breathing hard." She stretched and shook out her hands. "Fresh air will do me good. Give me a minute to change. I'll take Bruno out for a ride, give you some time alone with her."

"You read my mind." Elaine led the way, and Martha closed the door behind them.

MARTHA TUGGED ON her black leather riding gloves and tightened the buckle on her hard hat. She gathered the reins in her hand before she climbed the mounting block and settled herself onto Bruno's broad back. She leaned down and adjusted her stirrup. She sat up and smiled at Rachel. "I'll be a while, but if I'm not back by eleven, search for me."

Rachel released Bruno's bridle and smiled up at her. "Yes, Mistress." Elaine lifted a well-worn crop and touched it to her brow in salute to Martha. "I'm sure we'll find a way to keep busy while you're gone." She rested her hand on Rachel's thick shoulder before she tugged at a lock of her hair. Rachel shifted her feet and inclined her body toward Elaine, leaning into her touch.

Martha rolled her eyes at her sister. She turned Bruno's head and urged him on with a squeeze of her legs. The morning was crisp, the grass a silver green with the morning frost. Not willing to risk a canter over the slickness of the wet grass, she guided him to the well-traveled path leading to the small stand of trees on the far side of the meadow and kept him to a fast walk. Thoughts of her visit with Madame, and Lucia's impending arrival, filled her head. *I wonder if she rides. It'd be nice to have a someone to ride with again.* She pushed away the edge of sadness cutting into her thoughts as she remembered times she had spent with Octavia riding the trails of Rowan House, and what would happen after.

She rode into the wood and Bruno's breath puffed out, visible in the chilly air of the forest. The trees were mostly bare. A few leaves remained behind, lone holdouts stubbornly clinging to the branches ready to be rid of them. As she rode deeper into the woods, the rhythm of the horse under her and the comforting smells of horse and leather mixed with the damp fall scent of the forest lifted her spirits and soothed her.

She came to the fire circle in the center of the woods. The neat stack of firewood and the tidiness of the turnout shed told her she had made the right choice in Rachel. She was as meticulous in her care of the horses and this area as Octavia had been. A vision of Octavia, bare to the waist, hands lashed to the top fence rail, back striped by Martha's lash, as she begged for the heavy pain she craved, pervaded Martha's thoughts. She straightened her posture, took a deep breath, and blew it out forcefully. *Let it go. Move on. She has. I need to.*

"Right, Bruno?" She dismounted and led the horse to the small fenced paddock. She knotted her reins and clipped a lead shank to his bridle before she tied him to the fence rail. "I won't be a minute. Behave." She patted his shoulder. He rubbed his head against her arm, leaning into her touch. She pressed her forehead against his neck, drawing strength from his simple affection. "Promise."

Martha stood next to the fire ring. She pulled the letter from her pocket and held it to her nose. The faded scent of Octavia's cologne clung to the note. She unfolded it, taking care with the brittle paper, and read the words Octavia had written to her when she had pleaded to be hers, to wear Martha's collar. She dug in her pocket for her lighter. With a steady hand, she rolled the flint and touched the edge of the lighter's flame to the paper. The thin stationery caught quickly, and she laid it in the fire circle. She watched the blue-and-yellow flame as it curled and burned the creamy white paper to gray ash. When it finished burning, she picked up the bucket of water standing by the fire ring and doused the embers.

Done then. It's time. Time to move on.

"THIS IS YOUR suite." Martha kept her tone even, wanting to put the tension of their last meeting behind them. She pushed the door open and handed Lucia the key.

Lucia took the key in her hand and walked ahead of Martha. She pulled her large-brimmed black hat off and set it on the bed. She shrugged off her suit jacket and placed it next to her hat. Lucia turned in a slow circle as she surveyed the room. "This is lovely. Thank you."

"I'll have Millie come and unpack for you." Martha stood in the doorway and rested her hand on the frame. "We've cleared your trunk and camera gear. I'll have them brought up. I'll return your phone to you once it's been cleared. We have the same rules for the staff and guests as the Onyx. Only you, my sister, and myself are allowed to have our phones. Everyone else has to check them out to use them and then return them. We don't allow any phones or photography equipment in any of the play areas, dungeons, or the stable."

"Understood."

"If you find you need anything, please let me know. The staff are all pledged to the house and available to you. Anyone with a collar is yours to command, if you—" she met Lucia's gaze "—have a need." She turned to leave.

"Wait. Please." Lucia called to her.

Her *please* and the soft tone in her voice fanned the flame of desire Martha had worked so hard to put out. She stepped back into the room and closed the door behind her. She walked over to Lucia and stopped in front of her. "Yes? Do you need something?"

"I need to apologize to you." Lucia lowered her chin to her chest.

"Not necessary. We were both not at our best. I'll leave you to get settled."

Lucia looked up and into Martha's face. "I was rude to you. I want us to start over."

Martha held her gaze. "I should apologize too. It wasn't right of me to touch you without your permission."

Lucia's mouth curved into a smile. "I can't say it didn't get my attention."

Martha looked into Lucia's eyes, letting her desire show, encouraged by Lucia's unguarded expression of interest. Her breath quickened, and a surge of desire stirred her.

Lucia stepped closer and lifted her mouth to Martha. *Her mouth. So close. Kiss her. No. Not yet. Not without her consent.*

"I hope in a good way." Martha stepped back, not trusting herself.

Lucia laughed and took a step toward Martha, her mien changing from one of contrite apology to predatory in an instant. Martha's stomach tightened when she heard the full notes of her laugh and observed the change in Lucia's demeanor. *Even more kissable when she laughs.* She curled her fingers into her palm to keep from grabbing her by the shoulders and kissing her. She fought the urge to push Lucia, to see what would happen if she challenged her.

"Yes. After I got over being angry." Lucia held her gaze a moment longer before she looked away. "You said all the staff are pledged to the house, not to you?" She walked to the edge of the bed and trailed her fingers over the brocade bedspread.

Does she know about Octavia? Did Madame tell her about Octavia? "No. They are contracted to the house. Sometimes there are personal arrangements between staff, but it does not relieve them of their duties to the house." Martha shifted her feet and shoved her hands into her pockets.

"How has it worked out? Any conflicts?" Lucia turned back to Martha and looked into her eyes.

Martha met her gaze. "Occasionally we have people who choose to leave, but I'd rather have them leave than be unhappy working here. Our guests deserve to have submissives and Mistresses who are emotionally present and like their work."

"And you?"

"What about me?"

"Do you like your work?" She closed the distance and stood in front of Martha, a teasing light in her eyes.

"Very much. I wouldn't do it if I didn't."

Lucia tilted her head and pursed her lips, her expression thoughtful. "Is the bath through there? I need to freshen up after my trip."

Martha wanted to linger, to continue getting to know this woman who challenged her. "Yes. Would you like me to send up someone to attend you?"

"No. I'm used to attending to myself."

Perhaps I could help you? Don't say it. Keep it together. "Would you like a tour of the house? After lunch?"

"I'd like that." Lucia unbuttoned the top button of her shirt and pulled the hem from her pants. She unbuttoned the rest of the buttons and stripped off her shirt. The saucy black-and-white polka-dot bra with black lace she wore matched the playfulness in her eyes. "Very much."

Martha studied Lucia's body, unable to keep herself from admiring her voluptuous curves. When Lucia reached for the button at the top of her trousers, Martha forced herself to turn away from Lucia's display. "See you at lunch." She left the room, her steps light, planning her tour.

THE HALL WAS empty, and Martha was grateful she didn't encounter any of the house staff on the way to her room. The thick ache of want between her legs drove her steps. She pushed through the door and leaned back against it to close it before she turned the lock. Her face was hot, and she tugged her shirt over her head before tossing it aside. After she toed off her shoes, she lay back on her bed and closed her eyes. She slipped her hand inside her silk tank top and pulled at her nipple until it was a hard point. Visions of Lucia's sultry curves and full body filled her mind. She moved her hand lower and cupped herself. She kept the other on her nipple and imagined Lucia's mouth on her, the way her nipples would harden and ache. A soft groan rumbled from her chest. She touched her clit and then lower, drawing the wetness between her legs over her clit. She rubbed faster as she imagined pushing Lucia to her knees and burying her hands in her hair. She moaned, thinking of Lucia's full lips on her, sucking her clit, as she knelt at her feet. She jacked her clit with slick fingers. She came quietly, her body shuddering as she brought herself off, her mind overflowing with she wanted to do with Lucia. She stroked her clit, riding out the aftershocks.

Does she want me? Would she submit to me? I want. So much I want with her. Please let her say yes. She looked at the mantel clock. *What should I show her first? The playroom? The dungeon?* She shivered as she imagined Lucia in the playroom. *Playroom first. Then the dungeon.*

Chapter Four

ELAINE SAT ACROSS from Lucia. Martha watched her sister closely from under her lashes. After Martha had introduced Lucia to Elaine and pleasantries had been exchanged, their conversation had evaporated. Martha's gut churned, anxious for their tour. Worried about Elaine's potential to offend, she was unable to manage more than a few bites of her lunch. She sat back and touched her napkin to her mouth. Lucia ate quietly, and Martha admired the way she was cool under Elaine's scrutiny. Lucia wore a simple black sweater set topped with a slender strand of pearls and khaki trousers. It was simple, elegant, enticing in its understated innocence, and Martha could not stop herself from wondering if she still wore the bra she had seen her in earlier beneath it.

"The juniper berries in this sauce for the venison is inspired. I am pleasantly surprised."

"Why?" Elaine stopped eating with her fork midway between her plate and her mouth.

"I didn't expect much by way of food here. Madame gave me the impression the strength of Rowan House was—" Lucia picked up her wineglass and looked at Martha over the rim "—its staff." She swirled the glass and studied the fall of the deep-red wine as it coated the inside; then she sniffed it. A grimace crossed her face, and she placed her glass on the table.

Martha leaned forward. "Something wrong?"

"The wine is off." She picked up her water glass and sipped.

"It's fine. I sampled it myself." Elaine's voice was sharp.

Martha picked up her glass and sniffed. The scent of wine leaning toward the edge of vinegar filled her nose. She forced herself to take a sip. "Ye gods, Elaine, it's off. She's right."

A thunderous frown crossed Elaine's face. She rested her fork on her plate and narrowed her eyes at Lucia. "And you could tell from the bouquet? Are you a sommelier? Where did Madame find you? A cellar?"

Martha made eye contact with her sister. "That's enough, Elaine. What the hell is wrong with you?" She tried to keep her voice even but failed.

Lucia cocked an eyebrow at Martha. "No need to defend me." She met Elaine's flinty stare with one of her own. "I met Madame in Dubai. Not that it's any of your business."

"Everything and everyone here is my business." Elaine pressed her lips in a thin line and leaned forward. She tented her fingers and rested her elbows on the table.

Lucia reclined in her chair and picked up her water glass. She looked up and shook her curls back before she brought her gaze to Elaine's face. "I was under the impression—" she inclined her head toward Martha "—Mistress Martha was in charge of the house."

"We own it together. I am in charge of operations, and the stable; Elaine oversees the kitchen and guest services. We both entertain clients and participate in hiring." Martha picked up her glass and took a long swallow of water, trying to clear the taste of the spoiled wine from her mouth.

Lucia tilted her head. "My apologies. However, it was my understanding I was here as a guest." Her sharp smile at Elaine did not reach her eyes. "Do you treat all your guests like this? Or is this your way of getting to know me?"

Elaine inhaled sharply before she opened her mouth to speak.

Got to stop this. Get her out of here before Elaine goes off. Martha stood up quickly and had to catch her chair before it fell over, drawing Elaine and Lucia's attention. "Are you ready for your tour?"

Lucia looked up at her. "Yes. I don't think I'm interested in dessert." She placed her napkin on the table and stood up, her gaze fixed on Martha's face.

Martha offered her arm, and Lucia rested her hand on her forearm. Neither of them looked back, leaving Elaine and the tension of the lunch behind.

"I'M SORRY ABOUT Elaine's behavior." Martha stopped with her hand on the door to the largest playroom in Rowan House.

"You're not the one who needs to apologize." Lucia flexed her fingers, squeezing Martha's arm. "Is your sister always so—forceful?"

"She is. She prides herself on being known as the harshest Mistress in the house."

"Hmm." She held Martha's gaze. "And you? What do you want to be known for?"

"I haven't thought about it. I follow Madame's philosophy. I'm firm but fair, harsh but never cruel. Unless a sub needs me to be." Martha opened the wide six-panel door to the main playroom, and held it open for her.

Lucia released Martha's arm and stepped through the door. She waited while Martha turned up the lights.

"We have the overhead lights set on dimmers." Martha pointed to the wall sconces. "We have it plumbed for gas also; it creates a nice ambience and lovely lighting. It has its own heating and cooling system so it can be fine-tuned for the needs of our guests. The larger pieces are designed to be moved so we can set up demonstrations in the ballroom. Any Mistress who wants to use this room has to complete a safety orientation."

"Madame told me you don't use safe words."

"They are not required. We pay a bonus to our employees if they choose to work without one. And our guests are thoroughly screened." Martha kept her tone neutral. She could only imagine what Madame had said. In all their time together it was the only thing they had ever argued about.

Lucia's face betrayed nothing as she turned and walked over to the wall of striking implements. Whips, floggers, crops, quirts, and canes hung on hooks. Next to the neat display, all manner of harnesses, collars, cuffs, and spreader bars were arranged. She tipped her fingers along the bondage equipment. "Where do you keep your rope play equipment?"

"We don't. I've not had any training. I've only had one or two Mistresses ask for it. I don't want to put any of our workers in danger. I can't supervise what I don't know."

A broad smile crossed Lucia's face. "I can train you if you'd like. I've spent the last five years traveling to Japan for *deshi*, instruction. I'm not considered a *nawashi*, a rope master, yet, but I'm qualified to teach you and your staff the basics of *shibari*, if you'd like. Enough for safe play."

Images of herself bound in intricate knots with Lucia holding on the end of the rope filled Martha's head. "I... Well." She swallowed hard. *Where did that come from? Get a grip.*

"If you're not sure, I could do a demonstration. I brought my personal supplies with me." Lucia's gaze was steady. Her voice, soft and laced with seduction, wrapped around Martha and slid under her skin. Her face flushed and she looked down.

Personal supplies. Her bonds. Get it together. Does she imagine me like that? "Um. Well, yes. I'm sure I can find a sub who will be interested in working with you." She looked up at the ceiling before she lowered her chin and met Lucia's gaze. *She's testing me. What does she want? She's a professional. Keep it professional.* "How long will you need to prepare?"

Lucia's half smile made Martha's belly tighten with want. "I'd need about an hour to organize my equipment and prepare mentally."

"We had planned a salon tonight for you to meet the rest of the staff. Would you be able to do a demonstration then?"

"I'd love to." She spun in a slow circle as she surveyed the room. "I see the standard accoutrements in this room." She trailed her fingers over the smooth wood of the Saint Andrew's cross. "Where do you do heavy pain play?"

"We have a soundproofed dungeon. It's next to the wine cellar."

"It sounds positively medieval and delightfully wicked. Would you show it to me?"

The heat in Lucia's eyes sent a rill of heat to Martha's clit. *I'd like to do more than show you. Easy. Get it together. When was the last time I wanted anyone like this?* "Yes." She held out her hand and Lucia clasped it, her fingers cool and firm. Martha waited a moment, savoring the sensation of Lucia's grip and the softness of her skin, before she transferred her hand to her forearm. They walked side by side, their hips brushing occasionally in the hall. Martha spent the walk to the back stairs trying to keep her mind on the tour instead of on the intoxicating woman at her side.

"THIS IS IMPRESSIVE. Even the Onyx didn't have anything like this." Lucia smoothed her hands over the whipping post set in the floor. "Is the stonework original? It is amazing."

"We copied the work at Dunvegan and added a few touches of our own." Martha pointed to the floor. "We installed a heated floor." She pointed to a dais, flanked by black velvet curtains. The dais held two ornately carved chairs with footstools. Dark mahogany wood contrasted with the crushed red velvet covering the chairs. Behind the chairs was a floor-to-ceiling tapestry with the Rowan House crest.

"How lovely. I can see why Madame thought I'd like it here. Do you have many guests who ask for this?"

"Enough. We are known for it."

"We?"

"Elaine has a reputation."

Lucia raised her eyebrows. "Why am I not surprised?"

Martha smiled at her before she moved a small rug back with her foot.

Lucia pointed to the round wooden trap set in the floor. "Where does it lead?"

Martha moved to the first chair and pressed a button under the armrest. The wooden panel slid open without a sound. She pressed a second button. Overhead lights spotlighted the open pit in the floor.

Lucia looked down into the pit then at Martha's face. "A pit? How deep is it?"

"Only fifteen feet but it looks much deeper from the bottom."

"How do you lower them?"

Martha pressed another button, and a panel slid over to reveal rungs set into the smooth walls. "Making them climb down is part of the headspace. It has its own heating system.

We never have to worry about cooling the space." She moved the tapestry and revealed a screen and pressed the button on the panel beneath it. The bottom of the pit came into view. "We can monitor them visually, and there is an intercom system so you can talk to your sub."

"Ingenious."

"Would you like a closer look?"

Lucia stepped away from the pit. A flash of panic crossed her face before she smoothed her expression. "Beg pardon?"

"Oh. No. I didn't mean like that. I... Oh hell. I wanted to know if you would like to see how we've outfitted it, in case you wanted to use it, with a sub, I mean." At Lucia's arched brow, she stopped. "I'm not making it any better, am I?"

Lucia laughed. "No, but it was fun listening to you trying to clear things up. And no, I wouldn't. I don't like small spaces."

Martha pressed the buttons, and the rungs disappeared and the spotlight shut off and the wooden trap slid back into place.

Lucia moved over to the brazier and pointed to the iron rack next to it. "Who makes your irons?"

"We have a local smith. We've not had a branding ceremony in years. I fear it's too permanent for the younger crowd."

Lucia moved her hands over her hips before she pulled her cardigan tighter. "It is a commitment." She looked away from Martha.

"Can I ask you something?" Martha stood with her hands clasped behind her back.

"Anything. I don't promise to answer, but feel free to ask."

"The first time we met, you were so angry at Madame's request, and dismissive of me. Why the change in your attitude?"

"At first I was jealous Madame chose you to be executor. I owe my life to Madame." Lucia kept her head down, avoiding Martha's gaze. "After she told me about your financial skills and qualifications, I understood why she chose you. I promised her to keep an open mind about the rest."

The rest? What did Madame tell her? This is not about me. This is about her promise to Madame. She's not interested. She's keeping a promise. And I'm a fool. "If you've seen enough, I can show you the rest of the house." The bitter taste of disappointment welled up in Martha's mouth. *She's being polite. That's all. What was I thinking?*

Lucia looked up and met her eyes. "I'm tired. I'd like to rest a bit before dinner, if you don't mind."

"Of course. I'll escort you to your suite."

Chapter Five

THE SALON PROGRESSED as each of the submissives in turn was introduced, along with their particular set of skills, kink specialties, and hard limits. Martha tried to keep her focus on her staff, but she was drawn to Lucia's face, the fine curve of her cheekbones, and the long line of her neck. She appeared to be focused as she watched. Her breathing never shifted, nor did she show any signs of excitement or interest. Robin was the last submissive to appear. Lucia shifted in her chair, her gaze settling on Robin's face.

Does she like her? Know her? A tendril of jealousy wove its way into Martha's head. *What is wrong with me? What if she does?* Robin kneeled before them, her palms up, head bowed. She listed her favorite kinks. Her voice had the quality of someone ordering fast food. Martha huffed her disappointment. *She has to go. I need to examine her contract, talk to Elaine.*

Lucia's voice cut into Martha's thoughts. "Do you have experience with rope play?"

Robin's head snapped up before she appeared to remember her place and lowered her head. "Yes."

Elaine's sharp voice echoed around the ballroom. "A Mistress has asked you a question. You'll answer correctly."

"Yes. Mistress."

Lucia looked at Martha. "I would like to use her for my demonstration, with your permission."

Martha pursed her lips, unsure why she wanted to say no. "Yes. Of course. Robin, eyes at me."

Robin raised her gaze to her Mistress's eyes.

"Are you willing to participate in the demonstration?"

A fine sheen of sweat shone on her face, but her voice was strong. "Yes, Mistress."

The other submissives waited against the wall. "The rest of you come here." The group came as one. "I would like you all to observe. Mistress Lucia is going to favor us with a demonstration of *shibari*. Pay attention. We will most likely offer this as an option for future clients." She gestured to the rug in front of her. "Sit."

The women sat on the rug on the floor in front of the chairs for Elaine, Martha, and Lucia. Myfanwy arranged her curvy body close to Martha, bending to press a kiss to the toe of Martha's boot before she took a position next to her chair. Her simple gesture of submission and the view of her beautiful full-figured body at her feet had Martha thinking of how much she had missed Myfanwy in her bed. *Tonight. I want total submission. Complete control of her lush body.* Martha rested her palm on the top of her head before she slipped her hand under her thick hair black hair and rested it on the back of her neck. The small sound of Myfanwy's satisfaction under Martha's touch and the way she leaned against Martha's knee-high boots sent a wave of want through her. Rachel settled her considerable frame on the floor close to Elaine's chair, taking the spot Roxy normally would have occupied. Martha noted Roxy's glower, directed toward Rachel, when Elaine wound a bit of Rachel's hair around her finger and toyed with it. *That's going to be trouble. Elaine needs to tend to her.*

Lucia rose. The low-cut inky-black gown she wore flowed about her legs. Robin waited on the stage. Lucia carried a white silk bag with a phoenix embroidered on the side of it in gold, red, and blue threads. She mounted the stage and opened the bag to withdraw a thick coil of white rope. She stood to the side of Robin and passed the length of the long rope through her hands.

"Passing the rope over my hands allows for me to make sure the rope is smooth and has no rough spots or bits of debris that could damage my submissive's skin."

Martha watched Robin's face. Her eyes held fear, and Martha considered stopping the demonstration.

Lucia gathered the rope in her hand. She grabbed Robin's chin and forced her head back. "What is your safe word?"

"Fig, Mistress." The tremor in her voice undid Martha, and her clit grew thick as she watched the interchange between Lucia and Robin.

She released her chin. "Stand."

Robin rose, and Lucia looped the rope over her neck. With quick hands she tied a series of knots in the rope, moving down Robin's body. She tied a final knot above the tidy pale-brown triangle of hair between Robin's legs. "Spread."

Robin spread her legs, and Lucia passed the rope between them. "Turn." Robin turned away from them. Lucia brought the rope up and passed it around Robin's waist. "Keep the rope smooth and flat and even. Uneven coils and twists can cause bruises and abrasions. Smooth coils with appropriate tension support the body. Turn again." Robin turned back, and Lucia passed the rope between the knots, pulling and weaving under the rope and making diamond shapes over her body. She passed the rope to the back again. "Turn."

Robin faced away from them, and Lucia finished binding her with a half hitch above the small dimple over her hips, leaving a loop to function as a handle. "Turn to the side."

Lucia stood with the loop of rope in her hand. "Put your hands behind you, one hand above the other, and clasp your wrists."

Robin obeyed, and the position thrust her breasts forward and arched her back.

Lucia bound her hands. She put her hand on her shoulder and turned her to face the crowd.

The beauty and sensual effect of the simple rope wound in smooth coils and intricate knots around Robin's body, her vulnerability, the way her lips were parted, and the needy look in her eyes made Martha squirm in her seat. Lucia reached between Robin's legs and worked them a moment before she pulled her fingers free. Liquid evidence of Robin's excitement covered her fingers. Lucia pushed her fingers into Robin's mouth, and she sucked greedily. Lucia pulled her hand from Robin's mouth. "Bend over."

Robin leaned forward and bent at the waist with her hands bound behind her. Lucia set her legs and held on to the rope binding Robin, keeping her from falling. She thrust her fingers in deep, fucking her roughly while holding her place with the rope. Robin panted and groaned. "Oh please. Mistress. I'm going to come. Please. May I?"

Lucia slowed her strokes. "You greedy girl. You want to come? What have you done to earn it?"

Robin twisted her head from side to side. "Please, Mistress. I... Please let me come. I'll do anything."

Lucia laughed and kept edging her. "You'll do that anyway."

Robin groaned as Lucia worked her, rocking back to try to obtain what she needed. "Oh. Please, Mistress. I can't. Stop. Please. Oh, I...can't."

"You will." Lucia stopped and pulled her hand free. She wiped Robin's wetness on her ass and brought her hand back and slapped her hard. The sound of her hand landing on Robin's ass was loud. Robin cried out. She lost her balance, and Lucia kept her from falling with the rope handle. She reached out and steadied her before she raised her hand and slapped the other cheek.

Myfanwy leaned into Martha's leg, pressing her breasts against the smooth leather. Martha smiled when she heard the soft moan she tried to stifle. She rubbed her thumb over the rapid pulse in her neck. Martha leaned down and whispered in her ear, "Soon, my pretty girl," before she returned her attention to the stage.

Lucia spanked Robin, holding the end of the rope in one hand, scattering her spanks over her ass until Robin's skin was bright red and tears streamed down her face. Lucia stopped spanking her and tugged the rope. "Straighten." Robin rose, and Lucia stepped behind her and wrapped her hand around her small frame and fingered her clit. "Now you may come for me."

Robin squealed and arched into her hand as she came. Lucia held her up as she leaned back against her body. The energy of their demonstration filled the room, and Martha found herself breathing hard as she watched the scene play out on the stage.

Lucia released Robin. "Kneel."

She kept her hand on Robin's shoulder, steadying her as she lowered her body. "As you witnessed, the sub is restrained, and the position provides access to their body. This is very basic but an excellent way to start." Lucia looked into Martha's eyes as she passed her hands over Robin's body.

Martha couldn't stop herself as she fell into Lucia's gaze and imagined herself under Lucia's hands, bound by her, at her mercy. She sat up and broke eye contact, but not before she caught the half smile and expression of triumph on Lucia's face. *What the hell is wrong with me? Fuck, she's dangerous. And gorgeous. And trouble.*

Lucia continued to stroke her hands over Robin's shoulders and down her arms. "You must check your partner's circulation. Submissives, if you feel any numbness or tingling, you must tell your Mistress immediately. Nerve injury is nothing to risk." She pulled a large pair of bandage scissors from her pocket. "You must always have a means to free your partner quickly if you need to."

The tone of her voice as she spoke and the direct eye contact had Martha shifting in her seat to ease the pressure between her legs. *What would it be like? To be bound. At her mercy. Fuck me. Will I ever have that again?* She swallowed hard and looked down, avoiding Lucia's gaze, distracting herself with the press of Myfanwy's body as she leaned against her leg.

Lucia shoved the scissors back into the pocket of her dress. "Stand." She began by unwrapping Robin's arms. "Remember pulling a rope over the skin causes friction and can result in burns. Know the burn speed of your rope to avoid unintentional injury." She worked steadily as she removed the rope. When she was finished she had Robin kneel. "Aftercare is important as always, but the extreme vulnerability and headspace of rope play make it even more important." She knelt next to Robin and brought her mouth close to her ear. Whatever she said was for Robin alone. She sat on the stage and pulled the smaller woman into her lap. Robin laid her head on Lucia's shoulder.

Martha's craving was a wild thing, clawing at her, and the small spark of jealousy, the one that had started when Lucia first put her rope on Robin, flared. *What is wrong with me? This was a demonstration. Nothing more. Or is it? And why do I care?* She tapped Myfanwy on the shoulder. "Water."

Myfanwy rose and poured two glasses of water. She kneeled and offered a glass of water to Lucia. She took it and gave some to Robin, holding her while she drank. Myfanwy waited until Lucia handed the glass back to her and passed her the second one.

Martha stood and turned her face away from the display on the stage. "You are all dismissed." She caught Elaine scrutinizing her with a raised eyebrow. Martha looked back at her sister and shifted her gaze to Robin and Lucia on the stage, the two of them oblivious to the room full of observers.

Elaine pursed her lips before she stood up. She dragged Rachel up by her hair. Roxy moved to leave, and Elaine caught her by her collar as she passed her. "Where do you think you're going?"

"My room." Roxy's tone was close to open insubordination. "Mistress."

Elaine drew her close and pressed a kiss to her mouth. Roxy kept her hands at her side, her hands clenched in fists. Elaine broke their kiss. "I think you misspoke. Look at me." She held Roxy's gaze. "My room. Now."

"If there's space for me, Mistress." Roxy frowned and looked at Rachel.

Elaine pressed a fierce kiss to Roxy's mouth. Roxy's hands unclenched and she raised them to grip Elaine's waist, pulling her hard against her. Elaine lifted her head from Roxy's mouth. "Always." She left, pulling Roxy by her collar and Rachel by her hair.

Martha sighed and looked away from the trio. Myfanwy came and kneeled next to Martha. She rested her forehead on the toe of Martha's boot, and wrapped both hands around her leather-bound ankle. Myfanwy's gesture of affection and desire made Martha desperate to relieve her need. She grabbed Myfanwy by the arm and dragged her to her feet. She kissed her, digging her nails into the soft flesh of her arms. She drank in her submission, savaging her tender lips as she yielded to her. Martha broke their kiss. "Did you hear my orders? You were dismissed."

"Yes, Mistress." Myfanwy panted and trembled in Martha's grip.

"And yet you are still here. Are you in need of a lesson in obedience?" She slid her hand up and clasped her thick nipple and twisted.

Myfanwy groaned. "Yes, Mistress."

Martha dropped her hand lower and shoved it between her slick thighs. She fingered her clit. Myfanwy shifted, opening herself to her Mistress's touch. Martha delighted in Myfanwy's willingness. "I don't have any elaborate tricks for you, no rope in my room," she whispered as she kissed her way along Myfanwy's neck.

"You're all I need, Mistress. I'm a simple woman. I don't fancy being trussed up like a Christmas goose." Myfanwy tilted her head toward Lucia and Robin. Her voice was defiant, and loyal, and what Martha needed to hear.

Honest. And real. My Myfanwy. Steady as the sun. Martha released her. "Follow me."

"Yes, Mistress."

Martha glanced back at Lucia and Robin. Robin had not moved. Lucia looked up and met Martha's gaze. Her predatory expression and the possessiveness in her eyes unsettled her. *Maybe she thinks I want Robin? That I would challenge her?* She turned away from them, respecting

Lucia, and the intimacy of the moment. Martha left them there, grateful for Myfanwy's willingness, anxious to have her under her, desperate to share her passion, to hear her cries of surrender. More than ready to unleash the side of herself that thrived on power exchange and pain. Her fingers trembled. She reached back and took Myfanwy's hand to ground herself as she pulled her toward her room.

MARTHA CLOSED THE door to her room and locked it. Myfanwy kneeled, head bowed, palms up resting on her thighs. Martha stripped off her shirt and her bra, leaving her fitted pants tucked into her knee-high boots. She studied the woman before her, remembering her likes and dislikes. The last time they had been together was the week after Octavia left. She crossed to her armoire and selected her favorite flogger and cane.

"End of the bed, face the bedpost, hands over your head, and clasp the post." Martha laid the cane on the bed. She pulled the tails of the flogger through her fingers as she watched Myfanwy rise with grace and follow her orders.

The broad expanse of her back was freckled. Her years of service to the house had left it scarred and beautiful, hard evidence of her devotion to all Rowan House stood for. Martha crossed to her and passed her hands over her skin, the map of her submission. She pressed kisses over the raised scars. Myfanwy groaned and shifted her legs, earning a slap on her thigh from Martha. "Be still."

Myfanwy stilled under Martha's touch. "Yes, Mistress."

Martha pressed her breasts against Myfanwy's back and trailed kisses along her shoulder before kissing the way to her ear. "You and I haven't played like this in a while. Do you still use the same word?"

Myfanwy's voice was clear. "Yes, Mistress. Cake."

"Cake." She moved her hand lower and pressed between Myfanwy's legs. She gathered the slickness there and spread it over her clit. She pinched and jacked her clit, reveling in the silky heat. "I look forward to hearing it." She thrust deep and hard before she pulled her fingers out slowly and thrust deep again. Myfanwy's deep groan made Martha's clit hard.

She trembled under Martha's touch. "Oh yes. Yes. Please, Mistress. Please. I've craved your marks."

Martha pressed her body flush against her back, forcing her against the bedpost. She kissed her shoulder, her neck, her cheek. "You'll have them, my sweet girl."

She stepped to the side and draped the flogger over her skin, measuring her distance. Myfanwy's body trembled. With a quick snap of her wrist she laid the flogger against her back. The sharp intake of Myfanwy's breath set Martha's blood on fire. She inhaled deeply to steady herself. With even strokes she worked the flogger over her body. Wide red stripes covered her broad back and her thick thighs. *So beautiful. Such a gift. Mine. My pretty girl. My pain slut.* Myfanwy squealed with each touch of the flogger's tails at the start, moving to deeper groans as Martha's excitement built and the force of her blows increased. The sound of leather slapping against Myfanwy's skin and her heartfelt cries made Martha ache with need. Sweat trickled between her shoulder blades and her breath was rough. *Easy. Enough now.* She stopped. Myfanwy sagged against the post, shuddering and gasping. Martha dropped the flogger on the bed and picked up the cane. She touched Myfanwy's cheek. "Eyes to me."

She opened her eyes. The haze of endorphins she rode gave them a glassy look. Martha drew her thumb over her lip. "Remember your word."

"Yes, Mistress."

She stepped to the side and rolled the cane over the red raised marks left from the flogger. Myfanwy groaned and wrapped her hands tighter against the post, her knuckles white.

Martha took a breath to center herself. She raised the cane and brought it down. It made a small whistling sound as it cut the air. It landed, and Myfanwy's skin rippled with the impact. She shrieked. And Martha closed her eyes, lost in the pleasure of Myfanwy's pain. Her clit thick, thighs slick, she swallowed on a dry throat, desperate to hear more.

She focused and raised the cane again and brought it down hard, a scant inch away from the first stripe. Another scream caressed her ears. Myfanwy's thighs gleamed with wetness and she pressed her thighs together and shifted her legs, and Martha allowed her the comfort.

She whipped the cane down and delivered two more blows. Two more screams. Martha panted with exertion and excitement. *My beautiful girl. My love. My heart.*

"More please, Mistress. Please. One more. Please."

Martha raised the cane and brought it down, and Myfanwy's skin broke and welled with blood. She dropped the cane and pressed her body against Myfanwy. The heat of her marks warmed her belly and her breasts. She reached around and thrust her fingers between Myfanwy's legs. Fucking her, grinding her clit with the heel of her hand, she rubbed herself against her wide, firm ass, pushing them toward the edge together.

"Oh please, Mistress. Please let me come for you. Please." Myfanwy's voice was husky, and she shifted her hips and pushed back against Martha.

Martha edged her, and herself, keeping them on the brink. Myfanwy's blood wet her skin, coated her nipples, and the slick slide of blood and sweat between them sent sharp spikes of pleasure through Martha and she sped up her thrusts.

"Please. Mistress. Please. Oh. I..." Myfanwy's pleas filled Martha's heart and she broke.

"Come with me. Now." Martha bit down, closing her teeth over the soft skin of Myfanwy's shoulder. Martha bought them both off, her deep groans mixing with Myfanwy's shrieks. She slowed her strokes, easing them down, as they rode out the aftershocks clinging to each other.

Myfanwy's body shuddered under her.

"Lower your hands and turn to me." Martha kissed and licked the deep marks her teeth had made on Myfanwy's shoulder.

She turned in her arms and Martha pulled her close. She bent and lifted Myfanwy, holding her to her chest and pressing her face into her hair and her lips against her damp temple.

"You'll hurt yourself, Mistress." Myfanwy clasped her hands around Martha's neck.

"Shh. Let me get you to the bed." She carried her over and placed her gently on the mattress. Martha poured a glass of water and handed it to her. "You'll be sleeping on your stomach for a bit." Martha kissed her forehead. "Let me clean you up." She went to her bathroom and gathered her supplies. She brought them back. Myfanwy lay on her stomach, her head pillowed on her hands. Martha sat on the edge of the bed. "This is going to sting." She wiped the wet, warm cloth over her skin, cleaning away the blood. Using a soft touch, she rubbed salve into the marks on her skin. Myfanwy sighed as Martha worked on her.

"I want to ask you something, not as Mistress to submissive but as—as whatever it is we are to each other."

Myfanwy turned her head and rolled to her side to meet Martha's gaze. "Friends? Lovers?"

"Lovers." Martha met her gaze. "Why have you never asked to be mine?"

"Because I said no the first time you asked me to be yours. Because now I'm a woman of a certain age and it would seem desperate if I asked for your collar now." Myfanwy smiled a tight sad smile. "I am yours. Even if I've never pledged as such."

"And if I asked again?" She pushed a lock of Myfanwy's hair behind her ear.

"Yes. And no. I wouldn't be able to keep working here if you asked me to be yours, to wear your collar." She touched the house collar she wore, and the tag jingled. "I want to pretend the door is open, even if it isn't, not if I'm honest with myself. I'm not as young as some of the new ones. I'm built for comfort, not speed. I'm real, not some silicon-injected Barbie-doll imitation." She smoothed her hand over her thick hips. "I love working here. If I said yes to your collar I'd feel like I was unfaithful to you any time I let another woman touch me. And I'd feel that way no matter what you said." She reached over and picked up Martha's hand. She pressed a kiss to her knuckles. "It's not because I don't love you, Mistress." She squeezed her hand and looked into Martha's eyes. "I could never give you what you need, truly need, if you're honest with yourself. If you couldn't get what you need from Octavia, you'd never be able to get it from me."

Martha let go of her hand and looked down, avoiding Myfanwy's eyes. "I'm so obvious?"

Myfanwy touched her cheek, drawing her gaze. "To me you are. I am ever yours, Mistress. I want you to be happy. To have what you need. Even if I pledged myself to you, it wouldn't fill the empty place inside you, the part that needs to submit as much as I do."

"What did I ever do to deserve you?"

Myfanwy sat up and cupped Martha's face with both hands. "You've kept me safe, you've sheltered me, fed me, loved me as I am, and made me feel like I am the most beautiful, precious woman in the world." Her grip and voice became fierce. "Pledged to you or not, I'm yours."

Martha kissed her, taking her time, drinking in the love that flowed from Myfanwy, drawing strength from her. She leaned back and looked into her eyes and sang softly, letting the words of the Welsh ballad say all the things she didn't trust herself to say.

"Myfanwy boed yr holl o'th fywyd,
Dan heulwen ddisglair canol dydd,
A boed i rosyn gwridog iechyd,
I ddawnsio ganmlwydd ar dy rudd.
Anghofia'r oll o'th addewidion,
A wneist i rywun, 'ngeneth ddel,
A dyro'th law, Myfanwy dirion,
I ddim ond dweud y gair "Ffarwél".

Myfanwy leaned her forehead against Martha brow. "You're going to make me cry."

"No." Martha kissed her lips gently and reached between them. She swept her fingers over Myfanwy's clit. "I'm going to make you come again. Eyes open, my pretty girl. Let me watch you come for me."

Chapter Six

LUCIA MET HER at the door. She wore a long black wool coat and the wide-brimmed hat she had worn when she arrived. Martha offered her arm, and she took it, resting her black-gloved hand on Martha's forearm. Millie opened the car, and Martha waited while Lucia entered first. She slid into the seat next to her, and Millie closed the door. The car was warm, and she opened the buttons on her coat.

Lucia took off her hat and placed it on the seat between them. She pulled her gloves off and tucked them into her handbag. "How long ago did you make this reservation?"

"Six months." Martha chewed her lip. *No need for her to know it was supposed to be an anniversary lunch with Octavia. Not going to let a reservation at The Stone Hearth go by.*

Lucia tilted her head at her. "Just in case you needed to take someone to lunch? Am I taking Elaine's place? She'll kill me. She's still not forgiven me about the wine."

Martha smiled at her. "No. Not taking Elaine's place. So no worries." *Don't ask. Please don't ask.* Lucia didn't press, and Martha was grateful.

"I've read so much about The Stone Hearth. I can't wait to try their marmalade pudding." Lucia unclasped the hooks on her coat.

"It's even better than you've read about. Everything is so fantastic. It is—" she lowered her voice and leaned close to Lucia "—the best food on Skye, but you didn't hear it from me."

Lucia's bright laugh made Martha's heart full, and she laughed with her. Lucia made her face serious and mimed locking her lips shut. "Mum's the word."

"You too, Millie." Martha tapped her driver on the shoulder, a mock-threatening tone in her voice.

"Aye, Ma'am." The chauffeur's broad shoulders shook with her laughter. "Even I'm not brave enough to carry a tale like that." She met Martha's gaze in the mirror. "It's good to hear you laugh again, Ma'am, if it's not too bold for me to say."

"When has being too bold ever stopped you from saying anything? And thank you, Millie, it feels good to laugh."

"I've got a podcast I want to listen to, Ma'am. Do you mind if I put the screen up?"

"It's fine."

The dark screen between the front seat and the rear of the limousine slid into place.

Lucia angled her body toward Martha. "If it's been so long since you've laughed, I am honored it is with me." Her gaze was warm.

When was the last time anyone looked at me like I'm the most interesting woman in the world? Like they wanted to know me. Martha let herself get lost in the deep blue-green of Lucia's eyes. "I'm pleased you wanted to have lunch with me. I only have one hard limit for our outing. No business talk."

"I think I can agree to your limit." Lucia rolled the edge of her coat between her fingers. "Have you lived on Skye always?"

"Other than university and graduate school, yes. And you? Where's home for you?"

Lucia looked out of the window before she brought her gaze back to Martha's face. "Anywhere and everywhere.

Other than my time with Madame, I've never settled anywhere long."

"Why?" Martha adjusted her seat belt and shifted in her seat, her knee bumping Lucia's leg. "Excuse me."

"Not at all. I'm one of those people who like to see what's around the bend. I blame it on my mother. We never stayed anywhere longer than three years."

"Was she in the military?"

"Foreign service." She frowned. "I lost her when I was sixteen."

"I'm so sorry. Losing a parent is hard. Losing one at such a young age must have been unbearable." She bit her lip. "Elaine was an infant and I was two when our parents died." She looked down at her hands. Martha had only wispy bits of memories of her parents, and for a moment she envied Lucia the time she had had with her mother. She brought her gaze back to Lucia's face and touched the back of her hand. "I'm sorry, this conversation took a very wrong turn. I wanted today to be pleasant, not stressful."

Lucia smiled at her. "It's okay. I started it."

Martha sat back and folded her hands in her lap. "What do you like to do when you're not working?"

Lucia met her gaze. "Travel. Read. Take photographs. Madame arranged a photography apprenticeship for me with Ms. Abiola. She was a wonderful teacher."

"Vivian is delightful. She captures the soul of whatever she photographs. Her work is incredible." Martha looked out of the window and pointed to the mountains in the distance. "She always says we have some of the best light and most dramatic landscape in the world."

Lucia's eyes were bright. "I brought my photography equipment with me. Do you think you could arrange a trip to the Storr for me? And the Fairy Pools?"

"Of course. Whenever you'd like. Millie is at your disposal. You only need to watch the weather; it can change fast this time of year. We might have a good view of the Minch today." She looked out the window at the clouds gathering over the mountains. "Why photography?"

"I spent a lot of my young life on the other side of the lens. I wanted to make my own images."

A model? Makes sense. "What is your favorite thing to photograph?"

"I like landscapes, and travel photography. I wish I were better at portrait photography. I studied with Ms. Abiola, but I've not the disposition for it."

"Why?

"No patience with the models." Lucia pressed her mouth into a thin line.

Martha laughed.

"What?" Lucia arched her brow.

"You've not patience for people?"

Lucia arched her brow. "I struggled with the models' limits."

Martha smiled at her. "Tell me more."

Lucia launched into a long talk about her photography, and Martha took it all in, appreciating her passion and imagining what else could make her so animated, enjoying their relaxed conversation. The ride was over too soon.

Millie opened the door and they exited the car. "What time should I be back to pick you up, Ma'am? Cook texted me with a request."

Martha smiled at her. "Later then. We should be done by half three."

She held out her arm, and Lucia clasped it. Martha steadied her as they walked to the door, the rough stones in the parking lot a challenge for Lucia's heels. Martha held the door open, and Lucia stepped inside. The dining room was crowded, the room warm. Martha helped Lucia off with her coat and hung it on the peg by the door before she shrugged out of her coat and hung it up next to hers. Lucia wore an emerald-green dress. Nipped in at the waist, it showed off her full figure to perfection. Her hair was fixed with silver combs and swept up in a mass of curls. Martha caught herself staring at Lucia and busied herself with tucking her gloves into her coat pocket. Lucia passed Martha her hat, and she hung it next to her own battered fedora.

The host greeted them, and Martha approached the small wooden stand where he stood. "MacLeod. For two."

The host nodded and made a note in his ledger. He looked at Lucia then brought his gaze back to Martha's eyes. "The occasion?"

Martha lifted her shoulders, straightening her posture, and forced a smile. "A free afternoon."

The host tilted his head at Martha. "As good a reason as any. This way."

He led them to a small table next to the fireplace. Located on the side of the dining room, it offered privacy. He held out Lucia's chair first then Martha's. "Matthew will be serving you today." He left them with the wine list and the menu.

Lucia picked up her menu. She studied it, and Martha took advantage of her distraction and studied her. Her loose curls were pulled back, displaying her long neck, and the low neckline of her dress showed off the swell of her breasts. Her brown skin glowed in the firelight reflecting off the white stone, making her blue-green eyes even more stark in her face.

"It all looks so good. Can we have the tasting menu?" She placed her menu on the table.

"Sounds perfect. It's what I usually order. They have a wine flight they serve with it. It's nice to let someone else make the decisions."

Lucia tilted her head and fixed Martha with her gaze. "It is. As long as you trust the other to make the right choices." Her voice was the same she had used with Robin, soft yet unyielding, quietly insistent, the voice of a woman so secure in her power she knew her words would be obeyed without question no matter the volume.

Martha's body responded to her tone. She took a sip of her water before she answered. "Indeed. It only works if it's so." Her clit was hard as she thought about the way Lucia had bound Robin. *What would be like to be so restrained, to have no choice but to obey, to trust another enough with your body and emotion? Like it is with Madame. But for how long? Would it go both ways? What would it be like to have her under me? Would she give over to me?*

The waiter arrived and took their order, and they passed over their menus.

Lucia looked around the dining room. "I want to memorize this room, all the small details so when I think of this meal I'll be able to close my eyes and remember it. I'll be right back here. A perfect day. A perfect meal." She brought her gaze back to Martha's eyes. "Perfect company."

Martha flushed. The sincerity in Lucia's voice fanned the tiny flame of hope in her chest. *Could this be more? Does she want more than lunch? I want it to be more. Please let it be more.* She held Lucia's gaze and let her desire show. Unguarded, she opened herself to Lucia.

The waiter arrived with their wine, breaking the moment. Martha stifled a groan. She sipped her wine. She met Lucia's gaze over the rim of her glass. "To more perfect days."

Lucia touched her glass to Martha's before she took a sip. She raised her glass. "To unexpected pleasures." She sipped her wine. She set her glass aside and slid her tongue over her lower lip.

Sincere? Or calculated? The hum of the dining room faded as Martha focused all her attention on the enchanting woman sitting across from her. She stilled and studied her. *Is it an act? To please Madame? Is this real? Is she playing me? What does she want?* "What are you doing?"

"Having a marvelous lunch." Lucia smiled a half smile. "Enjoying your company."

"It's more than that." Martha lowered her voice and leaned forward. "Are you trying to seduce me?"

"How am I doing?" Lucia swallowed the rest of her wine and placed the glass on the table. She smiled at Martha and fixed her with a gaze full of mischief and challenge.

Martha met her gaze. "I'll let you know after dessert."

SMALL PLATES OF deliciously fresh local food arrived at the table, each more luscious than the last. They devoured each course, savoring the perfectly paired wine and food, sharing the bounty of Skye. Their conversation drifted as they talked about everything, and nothing, as free as an unmoored boat. Martha let go of her Mistress persona and allowed herself to relax into Lucia's company.

The flawlessly plated dessert arrived. A marmalade pudding for Lucia and a Drambuie custard for Martha.

Lucia sat back in her chair. "It's so lovely. I hate destroying it to eat it." She picked up her spoon and dug into the pudding. She closed her eyes, and Martha watched as she ate, her face reflecting her enjoyment of the sumptuous dessert. *So beautiful. Her mouth. I've got to have her. Did you see this, Madame? Is it what you wanted? Does she want me? Or is she just honoring you?*

Martha plunged her spoon into the crisped topping of her Drambuie custard. The sweet, hot taste of the liqueur blended with the smooth-textured custard filled her mouth.

Lucia spooned up a bit of her pudding. "Would you like a bite? It is exquisite." She held the spoon out.

Martha observed Lucia's expression as she ate the offered treat from her spoon. She didn't miss the flare of desire as it crossed Lucia's face.

Martha finished her bite and wiped her mouth. "Perfect." She dipped her spoon into her custard and offered it to Lucia. "Would you like a taste of mine?"

"Yes. Please." Eyes wide, Lucia reached across the table and clasped her wrist, her fingers firm, holding her still as her mouth closed over the spoon. She released her and shut her eyes as she swallowed. Martha's pulse sped up as she watched, wondering what it would be like to kiss her plump perfectly shaped lips. Lucia opened her eyes and smiled at Martha. "So good. If we come here again, I'm going to order both for dessert."

"I'll share more of mine if you'd like." Martha moved the custard ramekin closer to Lucia. "Here."

Lucia smiled at her. "I don't want to be greedy. And I don't have anything to give you." She pointed with her spoon at the empty dish in front of her.

"Go on." Martha sat back in her chair. "I like watching you eat."

Lucia smiled at her, and Martha let herself get lost in her gaze. She pulled the ramekin closer to her side of the table. "Thank you. I confess to having a huge sweet tooth."

Martha's phone vibrated in her pocket, and she pulled it out and read the number on the screen. "Excuse me." She left the table and hurried outside to answer her phone. The cold air hit her as she stepped out into a thick drizzle. She flipped up the collar of her suit jacket against the cold and thumbed the screen to answer the call. "Millie?"

"Ma'am, I've had a bit of trouble with the car. I won't be able to make it back to pick you up." Her anxious tone set Martha's nerves on edge.

"Are you all right?"

"Yes. I'm fine, but the car's going to need some work. I hope Cook has a bunch of mutton recipes."

Martha breathed out the breath she had been holding. "Don't worry about the car. I'm glad you're all right." She shivered as the icy rain pelted her. "We'll be fine. When do you think you could be here?"

"Not until late, at least eight, Mistress. I'm waiting for the tow now."

"Don't worry, Millie. We'll find a way home. Or stay here."

"I'm sorry, Ma'am."

"The only thing that matters is you're not hurt. Stay safe till the tow truck arrives."

"Thank you, Ma'am."

She pressed the button, ending her call. The rain had turned to sleet, the icy pellets bouncing off the pavers leading to the door. She hurried back into the restaurant. Martha brushed the tiny bits of ice clinging to her suit to the floor. *We could wait in the lounge. Or stay. Would she say yes?* She stopped at the desk. "When I made my reservation, I originally reserved a room at the house over-by. I canceled the room a few days ago. Do you know if it's still available?"

"I'll check, Ms. MacLeod. We've had some cancelations because of the weather."

She returned to the table. Lucia looked up at her concern on her face. "Trouble?"

Martha sat down and took a sip of her wine. "Millie had an accident with the car."

Lucia frowned. "Is she all right?"

"She's fine, though I can't say the same for the sheep she hit. But she won't be able to pick us up. Just as well, the roads will be a mess. The drizzle has turned to thick rain and sleet."

Lucia picked up her wine. "I imagine taxis are sparse here."

"I asked if they would be able to accommodate us."

"Overnight? How could they? I've heard you have to make reservations a year in advance." A fine tremor shook Lucia's hand. She drained her wineglass and placed it on the table and lowered her chin to her chest.

Afraid? After all of her flirting? Martha tapped the table to draw her gaze. "When I made this reservation, I also reserved a room. I asked if it was still available."

Lucia met her gaze. "That's why he asked about the occasion. You'd arranged to come here with someone else. They couldn't make it and now anyone will do?" She frowned at Martha. "Of course. Why waste a reservation? Was it your plan all along? Bring me here assuming I'd want to pay for my meal in trade?"

Stung by her assumption, a flash of anger filled Martha. "No. Forget I asked. I'll call the house. Elaine can have one of the others risk their lives driving over wet, icy, single-track roads to pick us up. We can wait in the lounge." She sat back in her chair and looked away from Lucia's face. She twisted her napkin into a tight knot, trying to get her anger under control. *What the hell happened? From pleasant flirtation to this? Fuck me. She's playing me. It's a game to her. Not real. Why did I think it might be? Why did I let myself get caught up? She's playing a part to honor Madame. Fuck me.*

Their waiter appeared to clear the table. "Ms. MacLeod, the host wanted me to let you know we can accommodate you and—" he glanced at Lucia "—your friend."

"Thank you. We won't be—"

"Marvelous, thanks so much." Lucia spoke over Martha and flashed a broad smile at the waiter.

The waiter smiled back at her. "I'll let him know."

Martha waited until the waiter left them to meet Lucia's gaze. "Sudden change of heart? Or did you decide it's what Madame would want you to do?" She leaned toward Lucia and lowered her voice to a harsh whisper. "Let me make one thing clear to you. I don't want, or expect, anything from you. Not now. Not ever. I agreed to Madame's request out of respect for her. I will provide a place for you to work, if you choose to, and live, nothing more." She pinned Lucia in place with her gaze, letting her anger show in her eyes. "I'm not sure what impression you've formed of me, but I am not desperately seeking your attention. Do not mistake my kindness for weakness. I'm not easily taken in. Not anymore. I don't need this. Or you." She sat back in her chair and straightened her posture, willing her anger to subside, and failing miserably. "And if you think I have any plans on sharing a room here with you after your comments, you're drunk, or high. Fuck you. And fuck your ridiculous pitiful attempt at seduction."

She shoved her chair back. Her abrupt movement drew the eyes of some of the other diners. She ignored their stares and picked up the bill jacket. "I'll be outside. Wait in the lounge. I'll find you when the car gets here."

Martha kept her head down as she crossed to the restaurant. *What the hell was I thinking? Fuck her. Fuck Madame. She's a professional playing a part. I'm an idiot. Fuck me, why did I ask her to lunch?* There were other customers ahead of her when she arrived at the host stand. She clenched her jaw and crossed her arms as she waited while they took selfies before they collected their coats.

A hand on her shoulder made her turn. Lucia was close to her. She met Martha's gaze. "Forgive me. I'm sorry. So sorry. Could we stay?"

Her voice was contrite, but her eyes betrayed nothing as Martha studied them. The customers left, and a blast of sleet and wind spilled through the door. Martha chewed her lip. *If anything happened to anyone because of my anger, I'd never forgive myself.* "As you wish. But nothing's changed. The only reason I'm agreeing to this is because I don't want to endanger any of my staff in this weather."

Lucia lowered her chin, avoiding Martha's eyes. "Understood."

"Ms. MacLeod? Your room is ready. If you go down the hall to the left, the reception desk has your key."

Martha plucked her fedora from its peg and carried her coat over her arm. She stalked down the hall, her head high, jaw tight, not looking to see if Lucia followed.

Chapter Seven

MARTHA SIGNED THE forms at the reception desk.

"We'll have a table for you at dinner, Ms. MacLeod. It comes with the room reservation, and there will be a full breakfast in the morning." The clerk slid the key to the front of the counter.

"Thank you." Martha's stomach had gone from pleasantly full to uncomfortably anxious after her argument with Lucia. "After such a marvelous lunch I don't know if I could eat anything else today." She picked up the key.

"Our last seating is at nine, if you change your mind. You're across the parking lot, room six."

They crossed the wet parking lot, picking their way over the slick stones carefully. Even in her anger Martha held her arm out to assist Lucia, her boots giving her better traction than Lucia's pumps. With every step Martha was more convinced staying the night was the right thing to do, even if the idea of staying in one room with Lucia overnight made her stomach churn.

They entered the room, and Martha tossed the key on to the side table. "Oh hell."

The king-size bed filled the room, looming like an iceberg. *I didn't even think of asking for two beds. Fuck. I'll sleep on the couch. It will be fine. Fuck her. She can sleep on the couch. I'm not risking a backache for her. Seduce me, not by a long shot. Amateur.* She pulled her suit coat off and hung it up in the closet with her overcoat and hat before she removed her boots. Between the wine she'd drunk with lunch and the adrenaline crash from her argument with Lucia, she wanted nothing more than to lie down and nap. Sleet slapped against the window. The cloud cover made the room dim. She pressed the switch and turned on the bedside lamp.

Lucia hadn't spoken since their exchange in the restaurant. Martha looked up at the ceiling and considered her options. *Lie down on the bed and ignore her until tomorrow? Wait for her to speak? Wait for a full apology? Fuck, I'm tired. Tired of this. Tired of trying to figure out why Madame made this request.* Her heart ached when she thought of Madame. *My refuge. The last person I could drop all my responsibilities and be myself with. And she leaves me with a conundrum. A woman I want but can't have. A woman who thinks I don't care who is in my bed. A woman who wants nothing to do with me.*

Martha sat on the edge of the bed. She propped her elbows on her knees and rested her chin in her hands and closed her eyes. The whisper of bare feet on carpet made her glance up. Lucia was standing before her in a red sheer bra and matching underwear. She held Martha's gaze as she came and kneeled at her feet. She took Martha's hands in her own and pressed kisses to their palms. Heat like fire raced inside Martha's belly.

Lucia looked up and met her eyes. "This is real. Not a game. It's not because of Madame. Or lunch. Or anything else but how I feel about you."

Martha inhaled sharply. "And you expect me to believe you? After what you accused me of?"

Lucia held her gaze as she stood up. "Maybe you don't believe my words, but you can believe this." She took Martha's hand and shoved it beneath the waistband of her panties and into the wet heat between her legs.

Martha stood up and thrust her fingers deep. All of the want she had been stifling since Lucia's arrival filled her, and she clasped her arm around Lucia's waist, crushing her body against herself, holding her close. With hard lips she savaged her mouth, taking everything she wanted from her. *Yes. This. Her. Now. Want her.* She withdrew her hand as she turned them and used her body to tumble Lucia onto the bed. Her need burned away every thought, and all she wanted was Lucia. She looked into Lucia's eyes. "Do you have permission from Madame? If you don't want this, say it now."

"Do you see a collar?" Lucia raised her hands and cupped Martha's face, her voice fierce. "This my decision to make. I want this. I want you."

"Why the hell did you get so mad at the restaurant when I suggested we stay?"

"Jealous. Worried I was a rebound choice. Afraid."

"Afraid of me?" Martha whispered. She traced her thumb over Lucia's lip.

"Afraid of what I want from you. Afraid of my desires. Afraid you're only honoring Madame's wishes."

Martha met her gaze. "No one directs my desires." She kissed her soft and slow, taking her time before she broke their kiss to look into her eyes. "Not even Madame."

She lowered her head and kissed Lucia's throat, scattering nips between the kisses. Lucia groaned and shifted her hips under her. Moving her hands lower, she stripped off Lucia's underwear, the thin fabric tearing under the assault of her fingers. She pushed inside, and with steady strokes she fucked her, buried herself in her lush body. She bit and sucked her nipples through the sheer fabric of the bra. Lucia wrapped her arms around Martha and pulled her close, digging her nails into her back. The sharp bite of pain drove Martha on, and she added a finger and thrust hard and deep. Lucia moaned and brought her legs up, wrapping them around Martha's hips and arching to meet her thrusts. She broke beneath Martha, and a surge of wetness poured over her hand. Feeding on Lucia's deep groans and sounds of pleasure, Martha moved up and kissed her way up to Lucia's neck, then the soft spot behind her ear.

Lucia trembled beneath her as she gripped her hard, her legs locked tight around Martha's back, rocking her body under her.

Martha's clit ached, and she slipped her fingers from Lucia's body. She reached under Lucia and unfastened her bra and pulled it off, freeing Lucia's heavy breasts. Gathering them in her hands, she pressed them together and licked the channel between them. She swept her mouth over her skin, nipped at her curves and the tender underside of her breasts, before she moved up to enjoy the sensation of her fat nipples hardening under her tongue. Lucia squirmed under her. She shifted her hips and rolled them so she was on top of Martha. She captured Martha's wrists in one hand and squeezed them hard, forcing them over her head. Lucia held her still as she raised her head and studied Martha's face. She moved her hand down and unbuttoned her fly. Martha gasped and closed her eyes against her need. Lucia eased the zipper down one notch at a time before she worked her hand past the waistband of Martha's briefs and pushed into her. With slow, deep strokes, she fucked her. "Open your eyes."

Martha's eyes fluttered open. *Lust. Want. Need. She needs this. Wants this. I want this.*

"Keep them open. Know it's me fucking you. Me that's making you come." Lucia's eyes were wide, and her breathing shifted as she ground herself against Martha's thigh. Martha sensed she was close to coming again.

Lucia slowed her thrusts and kept her gaze fixed on Martha's eyes. "Give me what I want."

With sure strokes Lucia brought her off, holding her gaze as Martha came, eyes wide open, giving Lucia what she wanted, what Martha had craved since she had met her. She closed her eyes and relaxed as Lucia slid her fingers from her. Rolling to the side, she kissed Lucia's shoulder. Her body was on fire, and all she wanted to do was strip her clothes off and feast on Lucia until dawn.

Lucia mirrored her position and nuzzled Martha's neck along the line of her collar, kissing and licking her way to her ear as she smoothed her hand over her breasts. Her breath tickled Martha's skin and her touch sent a new surge of wetness between her legs and her nipples hardened under Lucia's palm. Lucia plucked at the small white buttons of Martha's shirt. "May I?"

"God yes." Martha lay back.

Lucia unfastened the buttons of Martha's shirt. Martha sat up, and she pulled her shirt off. In one motion she grabbed the hem of her silk tank top and yanked it over her head before tossing it to the floor. Lucia lowered her head and sucked Martha's nipple into her mouth. Martha groaned and rested her hand on top of Lucia's head. She straddled her and continued to suck on Martha's nipple as she tugged at her trousers. Martha lifted her hips, and Lucia drew her pants over them before she kneeled between Martha's legs and lowered her head. She kissed the taut skin over her belly then caught the waistband of her briefs with her thumbs and pulled them down. Martha raised her hips again and then she was naked, Lucia's mouth was on her clit. She groaned as Lucia's tongue caressed her. *Now. Yes. More. Like that. There.* Lucia sucked hard on her clit. Martha pulled the combs from Lucia's hair, freeing it. Soft curls covered her thighs, and she held Lucia in place as she rocked against her. Her body trembled as she curled up, arching off the bed as she came hard with a low groan of satisfaction. Lucia slid two fingers in deep and kept her attention on Martha's clit, driving her up again, finding the spot that made her shake and moan as she came again in a slow rolling wave of pleasure.

Lucia licked gently, waiting for Martha to come down. She kissed her way up her stomach before she curled into Martha's body. Lucia shivered, and Martha reached over and grabbed the edge of the duvet and flipped it over them. The warmth of their bodies and the rhythm of the rain and sleet on the window soothed Martha, and she fell asleep with Lucia tucked beside her.

MARTHA STARTLED AWAKE. Lucia's leg was draped over her, her naked flesh pressed against her. The bedside lamp cast a soft pool of light over the bed. A distinct buzzing sound was coming from her coat pocket. *Phone. My phone.*

Lucia squeezed her tight before she moved her leg. "I'm awake. I know you need to answer it."

Martha scooted off the bed. Her nipples tightened in the chill air. She found her phone and thumbed the button to answer the call.

"You could have called me." Elaine's annoyed tone made Martha wince.

"Sorry. I thought Millie would've called you."

"She did. After the tow truck arrived. Where are you? Do you want me to send someone?"

Martha looked over at the bed. Lucia had propped herself up on the pillows. Her hair was loose, the curls wild over her shoulders. She smiled at Martha and her stomach tightened. *More. I want more with her.*

"No. Ahh. They had a room."

Elaine snorted. "The anniversary suite you reserved last year? For you and Octavia? Well at least it didn't go to waste. How was she?"

"No, we're fine. Send Millie tomorrow. Checkout is noon."

"Can't talk? Got it. You can tell me all about it later. I'll send Millie to pick you up. Enjoy."

Martha ended the call. She turned her phone off and placed it back in her coat pocket.

Lucia stretched, and the comforter pulled away from her body, exposing her breasts. She crooked her finger at Martha. "I'm hungry."

Martha walked back to the bed and stopped next to it. "Are you? After such a spectacular lunch?"

Lucia caught her wrist. Locking her long fingers tight, she tugged hard and Martha tumbled into bed on top of her. "I told you I was greedy." She kissed Martha, her mouth soft and inviting. Martha moved over her and lifted her head, giving her access. Lucia kissed the hollow of her throat.

Her clit was thick and aching, and her desire made her thighs slick.

"I want you." Lucia slipped down to kiss the inside of her thighs, urging Martha into place. She moved over Lucia and lowered her hips. Lucia devoured her, sending waves of pleasure through her. She clasped the headboard to steady herself and gave over to the demands of Lucia's mouth. She groaned as she came, her pleasure spilling over Lucia's face. The soft sound of her licking and sucking was loud in the quiet of the room. She was incredible, hitting all the right spots, building Martha up, making her come again. Unrelenting waves of pleasure filled her. After the third time, Martha lifted her body off Lucia's face. "Enough." She moved to the side, and slid down to capture Lucia's mouth, savoring the honey-salt flavor on her lips.

Lucia wrapped her arms around Martha's neck. "You taste divine. I can't get enough of you." Her sure voice cut through Martha's doubts about Lucia's desires.

She traced a finger over Lucia's cheek. "Your mouth is exquisite."

She rubbed her hand over Lucia's belly, and moved lower, through the tight curls to the slickness between her legs. Lucia's clit was thick and hard. She rolled her fingers over it before jacking it while she kissed her way down her stomach, licking a trail to the apex of her body. With long slow passes of her tongue she licked Lucia's clit. Lucia arched up, trying to push into her mouth. Martha pressed her arms over her thighs, holding her still while she took her time, filling herself with Lucia's essence. She slipped her thumb into her body, stroking her. She pursed her lips and took her clit into her mouth. She sucked hard, goaded on by Lucia's deep groans. "Yes. Just there. So good."

Martha licked on, reveling in Lucia's struggling, the taste of her on her tongue, and the power from controlling her, making her wait.

"Ah. Oh. More."

Martha kept her rhythm, not giving over to her demands. Lucia grew wetter as she struggled to obtain what she needed.

"Yes. Like that. More."

Martha's own clit was hard. She moved from between her legs and lay over Lucia, bracing herself on her arms. "Open yourself."

Lucia held her gaze as she spread her legs and held herself open, exposing her clit. Martha lowered herself and made contact. The slick slide of clit against clit caused her to close her eyes against the pleasure.

"Look at me. Now. Look at me. Let me see you." Lucia's voice was a soft command. She clasped Martha's hips, pulling her tight against her, taking control. "With me. Come with me."

Martha opened her eyes and ground against Lucia with purpose. Rolling her hips, she drove them both toward the peak. Lucia rolled with her, meeting her strokes.

"Now. Together. Now." Martha came as Lucia arched into her and rocked under her. Their groans and sighs filled the room and Martha's heart.

They stayed like that, their gazes fixed on each other, holding on to the moment. *She sees me. Sees all of me.* Martha lowered herself into Lucia's arms. *Safe. Relaxed. I haven't been this way outside of the Onyx. She is perfection.* Martha shifted to her side, and Lucia rolled to face her. "That was exquisite." She brushed her knuckles over Lucia's cheek.

Lucia caught her hand and held it. She pressed kisses to the tops of her knuckles. "You are exquisite." She met Martha' s gaze. "I've wanted you since you touched me your last day at Madame's house.

"Then why so coy?"

"Why were you so *I don't expect anything?* I wasn't sure of you."

Martha cupped the back of her neck. "What changed your mind?"

"When you put my desires before yours, when you asked me to stay instead of telling me we were going to stay, when you told me off."

"So all I needed to do was tell you off?"

Lucia laughed and scooted closer on the bed. "No. Yes. It was the passion in your voice. I knew you were telling me the truth." Her face became serious. "I've not been able to trust many people in my life. I was serious about not wanting to wear anyone's collar after Madame. I want to be equal in my relationships." She clasped the back of Martha's neck and leaned her forehead against hers. "I don't mind giving over in bed every so often, but I don't want anyone to run my life. I was young when I asked Madame for this." She drew Martha's hand to her hip and touched her fingers to a raised mark on her skin. She traced it, realizing it was a script *"G"*.

"You wear her brand." Jealousy ripped through Martha. *What would it be like to love someone enough you wanted to wear their mark forever? To know in your heart you wanted to be owned? To be marked permanently? Madame never asked, and I never offered.*

"I don't regret it. I love Madame deeply. She has always taken care of me." Her eyes became guarded, and she looked down, avoiding Martha's gaze.

The hairs on Martha's neck stood up. *This is where she tells me it was great but it didn't mean anything. This is the 'I'm not looking for anything long-term or to commit' speech. Fuck me, I'm a fool.*

"But when she's gone, I want to make my own decisions. I want to be in control. I don't want—"

"To be owned or involved. You've made it clear." Martha pulled away from Lucia's grip and rolled to her back. She pillowed her hands under her head to stop them from shaking. "I understand." *What is wrong with me? Of course. Why would she want to jump into another commitment? Just a one-off. Fine. Nothing more. Don't press. Take it for what it was—a delightful experience, unscripted, unexpected, and unrepeatable. Get it together.*

Lucia lay next to her and rested her head on her arm. She placed her palm on Martha's chest. The silence between them was thick. *Say something, Lucia. Tell me you want more. Or don't, but say something, please.* Martha waited for Lucia to speak, and the longer the silence stretched out, the more she was sure she had made a huge mistake. Her bladder nagged her, and she left the bed.

Chapter Eight

SHE CLOSED THE bathroom door for privacy, and to give herself some space to think. The lure of Lucia's body made her want to crawl back to the bed and take whatever she would give for the rest of the evening until tomorrow, no matter if it would lead anywhere. *Can't stay in here forever. Bath. Long soak and maybe figure something out.* The large tub with its gold taps appealed, and she turned the water on full before she sorted through the small basket of toiletries and found some bath gel. She opened it and sniffed the soothing lavender scent before adding it to the tub. Martha tested the water and adjusted the taps until it was the perfect temperature, and stepped in. She leaned back and slid deeper into the water and closed her eyes.

Wish I had more wine. What to do? At least she made it clear. Get it together. She doesn't owe you or Madame a damn thing. Madame's brand. Would anyone ever ask me for a permanent mark? Octavia would have agreed. In the beginning. Damn. She should be here. Kneeling beside the tub, her strong hands rubbing my shoulders, begging me to mark her. Instead I've got Miss "I don't want to belong to anyone" in my bed. I'm an idiot. Fuck me.

A knock on the door echoed in the bathroom. "Yes?"

"May I come in?"

"Suit yourself." Martha didn't bother to lift her head when Lucia walked in and closed the door behind her.

"Can we talk?" Lucia leaned a hip against the counter.

"About?"

"About why you stonewalled and then bolted from the bed."

"I needed the toilet. And then I wanted a bath." The lie sounded weak in Martha's ears.

"No." Lucia blew out a breath. "Don't lie to me. Please. I was honest. I've been honest."

"I get it. I understand you're ready to be free. My mistake for wanting more."

Lucia picked up a washcloth and kneeled beside the tub. "Because this is how you want me? On my knees?"

"Not all the time. And I didn't ask for a commitment. I let myself think you might want more. It stung when you said you weren't interested in being involved with anyone."

Lucia held her gaze. "I said I didn't want to be owned. I didn't say I didn't want more with you. Unless the only thing you want is my obedience." She stood up and tossed the washcloth on to the counter.

Martha chewed her lip. "Why would you think that would be all I wanted? I have more than my share of women who only wanted to give me their obedience. To give over to me, to let me control every aspect of their lives. Only one has ever been strong enough I was able to give up my power and let her do for me as I did for everyone else. She let me relax into the peace of serving. I don't know what Madame has meant to you, but she has been my solace for as long as I've worn her collar."

Lucia's eyes grew bright. "And you think you'll never know the joy of submitting again, once she's gone, don't you?"

Martha looked down at the water in the tub, not wanting to expose herself any more than she had. She watched Lucia from under her lashes.

Lucia walked to the tub. She wrapped her fingers in Martha's hair and yanked her head back hard. Thrown off-balance, Martha grabbed for the edge of the tub, her fingers slipping off the wet porcelain. Water splashed over the side from her sudden movement. Lucia's eyes were dark, her mouth pulled into a tight smile. She kissed Martha hard, her lips fierce, her teeth nicking Martha's lip. Martha came unwound in Lucia's fierce hold.

Lucia broke the kiss, leaving Martha panting. "I asked you a question."

Her voice, soft yet unyielding, had the same effect on Martha as when she had watched Lucia with Robin. "Yes"

"Do you want to serve me?" Lucia smoothed her hand down her chest and clasped Martha's nipple. She squeezed it hard and pulled up, the pain focusing Martha's desires like a laser. "Answer me." Her voice was firm and insistent.

Martha shivered in her grip. "Yes."

"Yes what?" Lucia tightened her hold in Martha's hair. She leaned over Martha, her gaze sharp, and brought her mouth a breath away from Martha's lips. "Call me Miss."

"Yes, Miss." Desire blazed through Martha's body.

"Then get your ass out of the bath and draw one for me." Lucia released her grip and stepped back. She rested her hands on her hips and fixed her intense gaze on Martha's face.

MARTHA STEPPED OUT of the tub and dried herself. She sensed Lucia's gaze on her, and she kept her head lowered. She took a deep breath and blew it out slowly. *Breathe. Focus. Obey. Serve.* The water gurgled as it drained from the tub. When it was empty she closed the drain and opened the taps. She kneeled in front of Lucia, the tile cold and hard on her knees. The sensation, bordering on pain, was comforting, and distracted her from thinking about her response to Lucia. Lucia stepped close to her and bent down. She clasped her chin, her fingers hard before she tipped Martha's head back and kissed her. The crash of water in the tub and the sound of her own pulse was loud in her head. She moaned into her mouth as Lucia kissed her with bruising force. She let go of Martha's hair. Martha heard the overflow drain gurgle. She looked to the tub and closed the taps without rising to her feet. Lucia stepped into the tub and lowered herself into the steaming water. She leaned back and closed her eyes. "Wash me."

Martha picked up the washcloth Lucia had dropped on the counter. She wet it and added bath gel, creating a foam. She rubbed the cloth over Lucia's skin. The sensation of being on her knees, caressing Lucia's body, and serving had her clit aching with need. She washed Lucia's breasts, lingering there, rubbing her nipples in slow circles, loving the way they hardened under her attention. She moved to her belly and then lower. She washed her leg, taking her time before moving on to her foot, rubbing the sole of her foot with her thumbs before she massaged each toe. She rinsed the soap off and pressed a quick kiss to the top of Lucia's foot. She did the same with the other leg. She watched Lucia's face from under her eyelashes. "Please, Miss. If you lean forward, I can wash your back."

Lucia didn't respond. She shifted in the tub, giving Martha access to her back. Martha wrung out the cloth and applied more gel to her hands. She smoothed her fingers over her dark skin, pressing into the thick muscles of her shoulders, and was rewarded with deep groans as she worked her hands over the small of her back and lower still to the top of her hips and the muscles there. Lucia sat back, and Martha moved to the front of the tub and rinsed her hands. She sat back on her heels and waited. A calmness settled over her. *I don't have to decide. I can just feel. React. Obey. Serve.*

Lucia stood up, and Martha rose and held out a large white towel. Lucia stepped from the tub, and Martha dried her off. Lucia turned and set her feet shoulder-width apart. "Down." Martha lowered herself to her knees. Lucia placed her hand on the top of Martha's head. "Pleasure me." Martha brought her mouth to Lucia and licked at the sweet heat between her legs. Lucia gripped her head with both hands, holding her in place. Martha sucked on her clit, rolling her tongue over the thickness between her legs. She moaned as Lucia rocked her hips and fucked herself on Martha's face. Holding her in place, marking her, taking what she wanted, what Martha had to give. Soft pants turned into deep groans as she spilled into Martha's mouth, and Martha lapped at her sweetness, taking everything Lucia gave her. Lucia released her, and Martha sat back on her heels. She inhaled the essence of her Miss and savored the taste of her lingering on her lips and tongue. *So sweet. So much. More. I want more of this. Of her.*

She kept her head down, fighting the urge to look into Lucia's eyes, to let her see how much she wanted to serve her. "Would you like a robe, Miss?"

"Yes. And bring the tie from the other robe."

Martha rose and pulled the fluffy white robe from the bathroom shelf. She held it out, and Lucia stepped into it before tugging it around herself and tying it closed. Martha settled the robe on her shoulders. Lucia swayed on her feet, and Martha reached out and took her arm to steady her. "Miss?"

"I'm fine. It's heat from the tub." She swayed again, and Martha picked her up in her arms.

"Put me down. I'm not helpless."

"No, Miss, but if you fall and this ends with us in the local surgery, I wouldn't forgive myself." Martha kicked the bathroom door open and carried Lucia to the bed. She laid Lucia on the bed, avoiding her gaze. She went to the mini fridge and took out a bottle of water. She kneeled next to the bed and offered it to Lucia.

Lucia took the bottle from her. Martha watched as she took two long swallows of the cold water, admiring the way her throat worked as she drank.

She patted Martha's cheek. "You too. My hardheaded one." She handed the bottle to Martha.

She took the water and finished the bottle in one long swallow. "More, Miss?"

"No." She sat up and piled the pillows behind her in the bed.

Martha waited at the side of the bed on her knees.

"Stand up and present yourself. I was in too much of a hurry before."

Martha rose and stood with her feet shoulder-width apart. She clasped her hands at the wrist behind her back. Confident in her body, she held her head high, but kept her gaze on the floor.

"Lovely." Lucia left the bed. She smoothed her hands over Martha's skin and muscles, stopping to squeeze her hips and ass. "Mm, you are built like a large cat. Strong. Lithe. Powerful." She touched her everywhere. Her touch ignited a fire low in Martha's belly, and she trembled as Lucia inspected her. She carded her fingers through Martha's hair. "Like silk. I like your widow's peak with the bit of gray. Sets off your eyes. Beautiful." Lucia pressed her body against her back and brought her lips close to Martha's ear, her voice a whisper. "You disobeyed me in the bathroom." She dug her sharp nails into the tender skin of Martha's ass, making her yelp. "Don't do it again. Close your eyes."

Martha closed her eyes, the lack of vision heightening her other senses. She heard the bed linen rustle and the closet door slide open before Lucia's hands clasped her overlapped wrists. "I don't have my preferred equipment, but I'll make do with what I have."

A whisper of silk passed over Martha's body. *Her scarf. She's going to bind me with her scarf.*

"Open your eyes. On the bed, sit up, feet flat, knees bent, hold your ankles on the outside."

Martha moved to comply. A flush of desire filled her. With her hands clasping the outside of her legs, she was exposed to Lucia's gaze and unable to hide her desire. She was open to her and vulnerable. The longer she held the position, the more her desire flowed, wetting the sheets under her. Her face grew warm and the urge to close her thighs to hide her need filled her, and she flexed her legs.

"No. Wide open, pet. No hiding." Lucia crossed her arms, her gaze focused on Martha's body.

Pet. Madame's name for me. Did Madame share all my secrets? Is this her final gift? To send me what I need? Is she following Madame's command to be this for me? Maybe she's only fulfilling Madame's wishes? Martha swallowed the emotion filling her. *She said it was real.* She rested her chin on her chest.

"Where did you go, pet? Stay with me." The firm tone of Lucia's voice, combined with her exposed position, stoked Martha's desire, and she pushed all her worries from her head. Lucia leaned over, her hands swift, her movements decisive as she passed the tie from the robe around Martha's wrist and her ankle, binding her in the open position.

Once she was bound a calm filled her. *Nothing to do but submit, obey. Give. Serve.* Lucia used her scarf to do the same with the other side. Each movement gave Martha a glimpse of her ripe body as the robe gaped with her movements.

"If I'd known we would be here like this, I would have packed a bag." Lucia went to the closet and opened her purse. She hummed as she rummaged through her handbag. She turned to Martha and flicked out her wrist. The clink of metal sounded with her movements as silver flashed in her hands. She flicked her wrist and exposed the blade of a long knife. In her other hand were two black woven bracelets and a matching collar.

Martha's pulse sped up, and she worked to slow her breathing as she realized the vulnerable position she was in. Bound, naked, and alone in a room with a woman she knew very little about. *Calm down. Madame wouldn't send a violent, dangerous person to you. Breathe. Focus. Obey. Serve.*

She kept her eyes fixed on the blade in Lucia's hand as she walked toward the bed. *Trust. Trust her. Trust Madame.*

Lucia placed the knife on the nightstand. "Safety first." She worked the buckle off the bracelet and unbraided the black cord. Martha watched, mesmerized by the movements of Lucia's hands as she worked swiftly and unraveled the bracelet. She laid the length of cord on the bedside table and repeated the procedure with the other bracelet before she moved to the collar. "Paracord. One foot of rope per knotted length of bracelet or collar. Two eight-inch bracelets, and one twenty-inch collar. Thirty-six feet of rope. Perfect for travel, and those unexpected times you need to bind a beautiful woman. Eyes to me."

Martha brought her gaze to Lucia's face.

Lucia drew the rope through her hand, smoothing it and folding it in equal lengths before she picked up the butterfly knife. She placed the blade next to the lengths of cord. She picked up the longest cord and folded it in half. "I should have asked before we started this, but I was a bit unfocused. Your safe word?"

Martha tilted her head and raised her eyebrow as she held Lucia's gaze. "Will I need it?" She taunted her Miss, and her pulse sped up as she braced for the slap she craved.

Lucia pursed her lips and narrowed her eyes. "Still don't think I'm Domme enough?" She placed another length of cord on the nightstand next to the knife before she leaned close. Her lips brushed Martha's ear as she smoothed her hand over her skin and down to Martha's nipple. She pinched it, her grip fierce. Martha gasped. Lucia released her nipple before she moved lower and grasped her clit. She squeezed once, drawing a moan from Martha. The wetness coated Martha's core and made it easy for Lucia to slip one finger inside. She teased her, skimming her finger over her swollen flesh. "You're wet. You crave my touch, my control, and yet are only giving in superficially. You mock me and challenge me openly. Topping from the bottom is a no go with me." She worked her fingers inside, curling them up and stroking the spot that made Martha pant with her pleasure. Lucia brought Martha to the edge of coming before she removed her hand. "No safe word. No play." She turned her back to Martha. She picked up the thick leather-bound list of the hotel's amenities. "I wonder if they would bring us room service?"

The vulnerability of her position hit Martha. She was bound in the middle of the bed, and although she might be able to move off the bed and onto the floor, she would not be able to cover herself. If she rolled to the floor, her ass would be up, and even if she managed to close her legs, a clear view of her swollen wet center would be on display. She tried the knots. They didn't tighten, nor did they loosen. A deep flush and panic spread through her. *She wouldn't. She might.*

Martha closed her eyes and her mouth, slowing her breath, breathing through her nose, willing herself to let go. *She's trying me. Let her. I won't be the one to blink first.* Her panic in check, she opened her eyes and watched as Lucia ignored her, perusing the menu.

She traced a finger along the page. "I'm a bit peckish. I think the cheese and fruit plate sounds divine. And some wine. Maybe another custard." She picked up the phone.

Wait her out. She's not serious. Martha worked her hands, trying the knots again. She relaxed. *She'll hang up. She's testing me.*

"Hello. Would it be possible to have room service? Wonderful. We'd like the cheese and fruit sampler. And a bottle of wine. No, you choose. Whatever you think would complement the tray. And do you have any of those delightful custards you served at lunch left? That's a pity. How about the chocolate tartlets? Wonderful. Two of those. Yes. That sounds right. Thank you." She hung up the phone.

A drop of sweat tickled the underside of Martha's arm. Lucia ignored her. She picked up a magazine and flipped through it. She tossed it on the table and perused the bookshelf, running her finger along the spines of the books. She pulled one from the shelf. "Henry Rider Haggard. Madame has a bound leather set of first editions of his works. She is fond of *King Solomon's Mines*. But my favorite is *She*." She sat down and opened the book. "There is a delightfully bad B-movie they made of it. I'll show it to you sometime." She leaned against the arm of the sofa and brought her legs up on the cushion and opened the book.

Martha waited for Lucia to untie her, regretting her challenge to her. She knew Lucia's words were true. She had held back, keeping the part of her she only gave over to Madame separate. *She won't expose me like this. Would she? To make a point. Fuck. She might.* She chewed her lip. The only way out was to ask. To give in, to end the scene by revealing her safe word. Or tell her safe word and beg for forgiveness.

The red glowing numbers on the clock on the bedside table changed. Sweat stung Martha's eyes and she blinked, trying to ease the burn. *She won't do it. But then she wouldn't be the one exposed. No one knows her here.* Lucia gave the impression of being absorbed in her book.

The sound of a cart in the hall set Martha on edge. *No. Not this Not like this.* "Untie me. Now."

Lucia looked at her over the edge of her book. "No." She went back to her reading.

"This is not consensual. I demand you release me." Martha struggled against her bonds and only succeeded in losing her balance and falling on her side on the bed. Now her bottom was pointed squarely at the door and would be visible when it opened.

Lucia appeared in her field of vision. "You know what you need to say to end this. You asked to serve me. Your choice." She tucked a lock of hair behind Martha's ear.

A loud knock at the door made Martha startle. Lucia rose and turned away from her and walked toward the door. Martha flushed. "Orange."

"Just a minute," Lucia called out. She turned to Martha and kissed her forehead. "To end the scene, pet? Or do you want to continue now you've given me your safe word?"

"I want to continue, Miss. But cover me before you open the door. Please, Miss. Please cover me." Martha's face burned with her desire and surrender.

"Orange it is." She pulled the duvet over Martha and tucked it in around her, making sure her body was covered. "Close your eyes, pet."

Martha obeyed, silently praying Lucia would keep her dignity intact, trusting her to keep her safe. She heard the door open.

"Where would you like me to set it up?"

"No need, thank you. I'll take it from here." Lucia's firm tone comforted Martha. She zoned out of the rest of their conversation. The click of the latch as the door closed sounded sweet in Martha's ears.

The covers were pulled away, and Lucia stroked her hands down the outside of her thigh. "Such lovely long legs." She pulled Martha to a sitting position. She picked up one of the lengths of cord and began passing it over her thighs and around her knees and under, wrapping her legs binding her legs bent and open, keeping her exposed. "This is open leg crab, *kaikyaku kani.* Simple but effective." She finished binding Martha's legs, and with each pass of the cord Martha's clit grew thicker and her desire seeped from her and wet the sheets under her.

Lucia moved on the bed behind her. "Normally I would have started with this, *mune nawa,* simple breast bondage." She passed the cord around Martha's chest, under her breasts, and around her back before she passed it again over the top. Several more passes and Martha's breasts were bound. The pressure and tightness of the cord heightened the sensitivity of her skin and made her nipples hard as Lucia made quick work of her task.

Lucia traced her fingers over Martha's bound flesh, making her groan. Lucia passed the cord from the breast bondage around her waist and tipped her forward on the bed so Martha's ass was in the air. She threaded the thin smooth rope from the waist tie between Martha's legs, centering a knot over her clit. She moved her back to sitting and finished the tie by fastening the cord to the back of the halter, defining her breasts. "There. I wish you could see how beautiful you look."

Martha shifted on the bed and the knot rubbed gently against her clit. She shuddered with pleasure. "Oh. Miss."

Lucia dug her nails into Martha's shoulder. "Did I tell you to move?"

"No, Miss. I—"

The slap Martha had been waiting for cracked against her cheek. She clenched and unclenched her fingers around her ankles. She wanted to touch her cheek, feel how hot her skin was from Lucia's touch. The heat spread across her body, and she moaned softly, craving more from her hand.

"Don't move unless I tell you. Don't think. Obey."

Lucia moved off the bed, and she clasped the rope harness and tugged. The knot rubbed against Martha's clit again, a whisper of sensation, making Martha groan for more.

"I know what you want, my greedy pet, but first some food." She brought the cart close to the bed. She picked up the wine and studied the label. "What a wonderful cellar. We'll have the wine after. Don't want to dull your senses." She picked up a slice of apple and held it to Martha's mouth. "Eat."

Martha held her gaze as she took the food from Lucia's hand, relaxing into her bonds. She chewed slowly, watching Lucia's face for signs of approval. When she was finished, Lucia ate her own bit of apple. They continued their meal, and with each bite Lucia fed her Martha opened to her, relaxed into her care, and knew she'd made the right decision. *Breathe. Focus. Obey. Serve.* The mantra was the only thought in her head along with her desire to please Lucia and earn the release her body craved.

They worked their way through the plate until only the two chocolate tarts remained. Lucia took the napkin and wiped Martha's mouth. She held her gaze as she folded the other napkin into a wide band and laid it on the bed. She stood and pushed the serving cart to the side. "We'll have those with the wine later." Lucia picked up the napkin she had folded. "Close your eyes."

Martha obeyed, and the folded napkin covered her eyes and was knotted at the back of her head. She waited. Her pulse was loud in her ears, her senses heightened, her vision blocked by the makeshift blindfold. *Breathe. Focus. Obey. Serve.* She heard water splashing in the bathroom, the whisper of fabric and the shift of the bed, and she shivered when Lucia touched her, tracing a line with her fingers over her breasts to Martha's engorged nipples.

"I like this. I wish you could see how beautiful you are, bound for me, total submission on your face. The way your mouth is slightly open as you try to control your breathing." Lucia's tongue licked over her nipple, before her teeth grazed the tip. Martha whimpered, the sensation overwhelming, as Lucia repeated her actions with her other breast. She tightened her fingers around Martha's nipples, and she squeezed and tugged.

Martha fought to keep her balance, and the knotted cord between her legs pulled against her clit. "Oh. Miss. I don't. I can't."

"Shh. Feel." Lucia tugged her nipples again, and the movement set Martha on fire. The sweet sensation as Lucia tortured her made her squirm, and the more she squirmed, the more the knot on her clit drove her closer to coming. Martha's world was reduced to Lucia's hands on her tits and the knot between her legs. In a rhythm now, Lucia's movements edged Martha closer to coming.

"Please, Miss. Please let me. I need to come. Please."

Lucia didn't answer, and her silence was agony as Martha tried to hold on, tried to stop herself, tried to obey the woman who had become her world. "Oh. I can't. Please, Miss."

Lucia stopped and withdrew her hands, and Martha cried out with the loss of her touch. A hand on her shoulder and she was rolled to her back. Her legs wide, still bound, open to her Miss's will. The sensation of Lucia's warm breath on her leg, a kiss on the inside of her thigh, and the soft brush of her fingers as she pushed inside.

"So wet. So sweet. Your clit is so thick." Lucia drew her fingers over her clit and squeezed softly as she pushed another finger in and widened the stretch. She stroked slowly, drawing deep groans from Martha.

She arched her back, trying to get more of her Miss's touch. The movement caused the knot at her clit to rub against her again, and she gasped. "Miss. Oh please, Miss. I don't know if I can stop." She shook with the effort not to come.

Lucia pushed another finger in, the sting and burn driving Martha closer as she fucked her slowly. "What is it you need, my greedy one?"

"Please, Miss, more. Please, all of you." Martha's voice cracked as she spoke.

Lucia pulled back, and when she pushed forward, Martha's body shook as she entered her fully. The sensation of completeness with all her Miss's hand inside her overwhelmed her. With deep thrusts Lucia rocked her. The movement of Martha's body moved the knot over her clit, a sweet torture. She rode the high until the pain and pleasure overtook her. Her body shook and trembled. "Please. Let me come. Miss. I... For you. I can't."

Lucia's silence was loud in the room, as she kept up her rhythm, expert in her motions. Martha grew desperate, needing to come, overwhelmed, burning with desire. *Yes, this. For her. Now. Give her what she wants. What you want. Surrender. Now. Now. Say it.*

"Please let me come. Miss. I... Let me. Please." Martha groaned, biting her lip to keep from screaming.

"Come for me now. Give me what's mine." Lucia increased her speed, and Martha's belly tightened and she clenched around Lucia's hand, bucking up to meet her thrusts and rocking the knot on her clit, the orgasm crashing over her. She shuddered and came, with no thoughts but the sensations filling her and the woman who fucked her into another bone-shaking orgasm, and another until she had no more to give, as Lucia wrung every bit of passion from her. She stilled her motions, letting Martha come down from the high, before she withdrew her hand and eased Martha to her side.

Delirious and boneless from her orgasms, Martha relaxed as Lucia unknotted and unwound her bonds, moving her and rolling her body as she needed to gain access. The removal of the bindings made Martha shiver and regret the loss of Lucia's control. Warm hands rubbed her skin, as Lucia massaged her joints. The blindfold was removed, but she kept her eyes closed, remembering her Miss's directions.

Lucia kissed her in slow and deliberate fashion, her lips soft on Martha's mouth. "Open your eyes, pet."

Martha opened her eyes, blinking them a few times to adjust to the light in the room. A flush filled her face. She gazed into Lucia's eyes a moment before she lowered her chin to her chest, afraid for Lucia to see how much she had loved submitting to her.

Strong fingers clasped her chin, and Lucia raised her head and kissed her again. "Lie down. I'll get you some water."

Martha curled onto her side, trying to process her reaction to Lucia's attentions. Trying to reconcile the way she responded to her, fighting the overwhelming emotions raging in her soul. Guilt filled her as she thought of the way she had betrayed her Madame by her submission to Lucia. She shivered and closed her eyes. Tears squeezed from her eyes, and she pressed the heels of her palms to her eyes to stop them.

Lucia's hand was gentle on her cheek. "Sit up and drink this." Martha pushed herself into a sitting position. She swiped at her cheek, desperate to hide the evidence of her distress. She took the water Lucia offered and drank. Her throat was raw, and the cool water soothed her.

Lucia wiped her thumb over Martha's cheek. She pulled her chin up and gazed in her eyes. Martha handed her back the glass. Lucia placed it on the bedside table and climbed into the bed. She gathered Martha into her arms, and they lay back on the bed. Martha rested her head on Lucia's shoulder.

Lucia carded her fingers through Martha's hair. "Are you okay?"

"I don't know."

"An honest answer." Lucia pressed a kiss to Martha's forehead. "Too much?"

"Just right." Martha moved closer to Lucia, resting in the space of her control. "I haven't..."

"No one but Madame?" Lucia rubbed her hand in slow circles over Martha's back.

"Yes. I feel like I've betrayed her." She held tight to Lucia, feeding on her strength.

"Do you think she'd see it as such?" Lucia tipped Martha's chin up to look in her eyes.

"No. But I don't know how to process this. You."

"Because you didn't like giving over to me?" Lucia drew back, her expression wary.

"Because I did." Martha leaned in and kissed Lucia. "Miss."

Lucia smiled. "Rest, pet. Time for thinking later." She wrapped her arms around Martha and held her tight to her. She draped her leg over Martha's legs, pinning her, keeping her safe in the circle of her body.

THEY SAT ON the bed facing each other. The tray with their plates, holding the remaining bits of the chocolate tartlets, was between them. Lucia poured the wine and passed Martha her glass before taking up her own.

"I love red wine paired with chocolate." Lucia pressed her finger to the remaining crumbs and lifted it to her mouth. Martha was mesmerized, watching her as she licked the chocolate off her finger.

"I like the way you eat. So many women worry over every calorie."

Lucia raised her eyebrow. "There was a time in my life when I never knew when I would eat again. I've been making up for it ever since."

Martha tilted her head and met her gaze. "After your mother?"

"Yes. I was sent to live with my father's family in Northern California. They were farmers. My father had remarried, so I lived with my grandparents who hated me because I looked like my mother. I left as soon as I could. Ran away to LA. Did whatever I could to pay my rent."

Lucia's tone was flat as if she were telling someone else's story instead of her own.

"And then you met Madame?"

"I met a man who convinced me I could make large sums of money and be treated like a princess if I traveled with him to Dubai. Only when I got there, I was one of about fifty other girls he had said the same thing to." Her eyes had a faraway look. She drained the last of her wine and poured herself another glass.

Martha picked up her hand and held it. "You don't have to go on if you don't want to. It doesn't matter to me how you met her."

"You should know." She took another sip of her wine. "I was working in a private club. Madame arrived one afternoon. I don't know how or why, but she picked me out of all the others."

Martha frowned. "It wasn't your choice to go with her?"

"She gave me a choice, offered to give me money so I could go back to the States or go with her. But where would I have gone? Back to the farm? Back to a father who wanted to pretend I didn't exist? Back to a family who treated me like shit because my mom wasn't white?"

Martha sipped her wine before she brought her gaze back to Lucia's eyes. "But you wear Madame's mark. Did you ask for it?" She wasn't sure she wanted to hear the answer.

"I did. Madame sent me to college. Treated me like I was the most precious thing in the world. She trained me. Never denied me anything I asked for. She never made me participate in any of her occasions. I was hers and hers alone. I love her. But I've never known what it is like to be truly free, to be the one who chooses, the one who decides. I owe her my life, and my loyalty until..." Lucia's eyes filled with unshed tears. She looked up and blinked them back. "Until she's gone."

Martha's heart ached for Lucia. Ached for the pain she had experienced and the prejudice she had suffered. She understood so much more about her now. Understood why she would never be owned again. And understood why Martha would never have the most amazing woman she had met in years as hers.

She placed her wineglass on the nightstand before she scooted off the bed. Martha picked up the tray and carried it over to the serving cart.

She turned to study Lucia's profile as she sat with her head lowered, her chin resting on her chest. *So beautiful. So much pain in her life. So much I want to have with her. So much I can't ask of her.* Martha turned Lucia's story over in her head. She would make sure whatever she needed or wanted she had, not because Madame wished it, but because Martha wanted to give her the one thing Madame had not. Her freedom.

"Lucia?"

Lucia startled, spilling a bit of her wine on her robe. Martha crossed the room and sat on the edge of the bed. She avoided Lucia's eyes, knowing if she looked in them she would beg Lucia for something she couldn't give. "I meant what I said. I don't expect anything of you. You're free. I'm so grateful for what we had today, but I don't expect this will be more than what it was."

"Is." Lucia's voice was warm.

"Is?"

"What it is, pet. I'm not giving you up so easy." She patted the bed next to her hips. "Come sit with me. We have to discuss how this will be. I'm not an autocrat other than in the bedroom, most of the time. Outside I want to be equal. What goes on behind closed doors is between us. I expect you're not anxious to have your staff know you are a switch."

Martha slid across the bed next to Lucia. "It would make it difficult. I don't see myself as a submissive. I'm not. I haven't been..." She looked down at her hands. "With anyone except Madame. And now you."

With a shrug of her shoulders Lucia shed her robe. She shifted on the bed so she was centered in front of Martha. "Put those big hands of yours to work."

Martha started at the top of her back, working her fingers into the tight muscles across Lucia's shoulders.

"Marvelous. I like it hard. Mmm, just so."

Martha rubbed her back, pushing her thumbs into the knots of muscles on either side of Lucia's spine.

Lucia groaned under her hands. "When we go back to Rowan House, I want us to be as we were before. Two Mistresses. Equal. No one but ourselves needs to know about how we are with each other."

Martha paused in her massage. "Elaine will know we were together here. She'll ask me. I can't lie to her."

"I'm not asking you to lie. I'm asking you to not share details."

"All right. And there is Millie. She will know we spent the night together, but she won't say anything to the others. Most of them are on holiday right now." *Myfanwy. Myfanwy will know.* Martha chewed her lip. "Have you met Myfanwy?"

"No. Why?"

"She and I... We've been... She's not committed to me, but she knows me. She knows about Madame. She'll sense how it is with us."

"Do you love her?" Lucia moved to sit facing Martha. She held her gaze. "Do you want her to commit to you?"

Martha held Lucia's hand. "I love her. She doesn't want my collar. She's said as much."

"A collar and commitment are two different things."

"She says she'd have to quit Rowan House if she committed to me, she'd feel she was cheating if she was with anyone else. That she'd want me to be only with her."

Lucia frowned at her. "And you think she means she doesn't want to commit to you? What the hell is wrong with you?"

Martha huffed out a breath. "I've asked her. Why would she lie to me?"

"I'm not saying she's lying. Maybe she wants to be more, have more than to work and serve you? Did that occur to you?"

Martha met Lucia's hard expression with one of her own. "She said she knew she'd not be able to be all I needed. What I had with Madame. And she didn't want me to be unhappy."

Lucia cocked an eyebrow. "She loves you, doesn't she?"

"More than I deserve."

Firm fingers gripped her chin, and Lucia pulled her head up. She pinned Martha in place with a demanding expression. "No. Don't say that about yourself, Martha MacLeod, ever. You deserve to be loved." She kissed her then, her lips soft and gentle, a contrast to the harsh tone of her voice. "And by someone who is woman enough to give you what you need."

THEY HAD SPENT the night finding more ways to explore each other's bodies. Martha had slept better than she had in the months since Octavia had left. Even the breakfast with each other had been magical. She wished they had a few more days, just the two of them. Even the stares of the other diners at breakfast as they took in their rumpled, out-of-place outfits couldn't dampen Martha's joy. Lucia's spell over Martha was complete, and she had to sit on her hands to keep from touching her. How she was going to manage when they got back to Rowan House, she didn't know.

"This is divine. Thank you." Lucia tucked into her breakfast.

"The company would make soggy toast divine." Martha stared at her over the rim of her coffee cup. "And I seem to have an amazing appetite this morning."

Lucia smiled at her. "We'll need to do this again."

Martha smiled at her. "I'll check my calendar to see if I'm free in six months."

Lucia wiped her mouth and smiled. "I will as well."

They lingered over the breakfast. "Well, with no luggage it sure makes it easy. If you had better shoes I'd suggest a walk to see the Minch. Millie won't be here until noon."

"I should split this with you." Lucia sipped her tea.

Martha touched her arm. "No. Please. Let me. It was only supposed to be lunch."

Lucia held Martha's gaze. "I will pay half. And you are going to let me. Or we can't do this."

Martha back stiffened. "I thought we cleared this up. I didn't plan for this, but it is my responsibility."

Lucia set her mouth in a thin line. "And I want you to understand you need to let me pay my share of this expense."

"Or what?"

"Or we won't be doing any more of this. I won't argue with you about this. I'm not yours to take care of. Or broke. I don't need you to pay my way."

Martha huffed out a breath. "Why can't you accept this from me? Why is it a problem?"

"Because I don't like feeling like I've been bought. I don't ever want to feel that way again." Lucia stood up and picked up her purse. "Let's go."

Martha raised her eyebrow. "I want to finish my coffee."

Lucia leaned close to her and whispered, "Unless you want the people in this dining room to know who is the Mistress in this adventure, you will stand up now and follow me."

Lucia's eyes had the same fierce stare she'd had when she pulled Martha from the bathtub and asked if she wanted to serve her. Martha's body responded, and she pressed her legs together to stem the flow of wetness between her thighs. She held Lucia's gaze and placed her cup gently in the saucer and whispered, "Yes, Miss."

The small flare of Lucia's nostrils and the slight smile on her lips told Martha all she needed to know about how they would be spending their last hours in their room.

They left the dining room with Martha trailing after Lucia. They arrived at the door, and Martha opened it, stepping to the side to let Lucia in first.

She tossed her coat and bag on the bed. Martha slipped her coat off and placed it on the chair. Lucia stepped close her and stopped an inch from Martha's face. She reached up and clasped the back of her neck and pulled her into a hard kiss, before she pushed her back against the wall. Surprising Martha with her strength, she gripped her shoulders. She held her there, kissing her way along Martha's neck, scattering nips among the kisses. "Kneel." She pushed down on Martha's shoulders, and she sank to her knees. Lucia pulled her dress up and leaned into Martha, dropping the hem over her head. With strong hands she held Martha in place while she pushed herself against her. "Pleasure me."

Martha grabbed her thighs and lapped at the sweat-salt heat between her legs. The sensation of her skirt over her head and being held in place by Lucia's strong hands made her wild with a yearning to please her Mistress. Nothing existed for her but Lucia. She had no desire but to please her, to feel her release on her tongue. She closed her eyes against the pleasure of having her mouth on her Miss.

Lucia rocked harder on her face and her voice was rough. "Fuck me. Now."

Martha pushed three fingers in and obeyed her Mistress. Using hard thrusts in rhythm with attention to Lucia's clit, she worked to bring her to the edge. Lucia stilled and emptied her pleasure in Martha's mouth, the soft sound of her release sweet in Martha's ears. She slowed her strokes and dared to take her Mistress up again, making her shudder and quake with another orgasm. "Enough."

Lucia pushed Martha away and down and drew her dress from over Martha's head. She leaned down and kissed her, taking her time. Martha let herself get lost in the kiss, wanting nothing more than to be given the gift of her Mistress's pleasure.

"On the bed, pet. Take those trousers off. Briefs too." Lucia watched as Martha complied. With trembling fingers, she stripped off her pants and briefs. She sat on the end of the bed, her feet on the floor. Lucia came and stood between her legs. "Lie back, pet, hands over your head. Keep them there." Martha raised her arms and clasped her hands in the required position.

Lucia swept her hand over her belly and pinched the skin there, making Martha gasp. She moved her hand lower and touched Martha's thick clit with one finger before she brought her finger to her mouth and licked it. "So wet. Do you want me to touch you?"

Martha flushed. "Please, Miss. Please touch me."

Lucia traced her finger down through the soft curls above Martha's clit and dragged the tip of her finger over her clit. She used her other hand to hold her open. Martha shivered as the air hit her exposed clit. "I'll give you ten strokes. If you come before then or don't come by the tenth stroke, I'll have to punish you."

Martha's breath was loud in the room. Lucia touched her again, the press of her finger directly on her clit so intense it boarded on pain. She ached, wanting more, fearing she would disappoint her Miss. She forced herself to focus. Another stroke, and she gasped, her body shuddering under Lucia's deliberate attention. By the fifth she was sure she would not make it, sure she would come with the next slow, deliberate stroke of her finger. She panted, holding on to her pleasure, a gift for her Miss. Her body responded with fear and desire to Lucia's threat. *How could I ever have thought she was not Domme enough to be my Mistress?* Her gut clenched and her hips bucked, trying to get more of what she needed to come.

"Two more. Unless you want me to stop."

"Oh. No. Please no, Miss. Please touch me. Make me come. Let me come."

Lucia drew her finger down her clit again. Martha's orgasm was so close.

"Now we see how well trained you are. Come now." The menace in her voice and the final touch of her finger on Martha's clit sent her over. And she arched up, her body responding and shaking as she bit her lip to keep from screaming as she came.

Lucia smoothed her hand over her thigh before she leaned down and placed a kiss on Martha's stomach. "Well done, pet."

Tears burned in Martha's eye, and she blinked them back and closed her eyes. *When? When will we have this again? Not at the house. Too risky.*

Lucia touched her cheek. "Are you all right, pet?"

Martha turned her face and kissed Lucia's palm, pushing into her touch. "Yes."

Lucia leaned down and cupped her face. "Liar." She kissed her. "I know. We'll find a way. Where you feel safe, and we can be like this again."

Chapter Nine

"YOU LOOK LIKE hell. Up all night?" Elaine's smirk made Martha wince.

"No. And thank you, sister dearest." Martha turned her back to her and bent to slip her boots off, not wanting to discuss what had happened.

"She turned you down? I knew she was a bitch. Why'd you waste your time?"

Martha turned back to face Elaine and quirked her mouth at her. "This is not open for discussion. Please don't ask."

Elaine's taunting expression morphed into sisterly concern. "I won't. It had to be hard to be there without Octavia."

"I wanted to have lunch there. And I didn't expect to have to stay." *Change the subject. Get her talking about something else.* "How bad is the car?"

Elaine snorted. "At least seven thousand. They've given us a loaner."

"At least Millie wasn't hurt."

"I don't know what we'd do without her. We'll be fine. We only have two more guests scheduled before the winter break."

"The couple from Brazil? They came around this time last year?" Martha pulled off her trousers and shirt and tossed them on the chair.

Elaine pulled a small notebook from her pocket. "Yes. They requested Myfanwy and Roxy again. I've got Robin and Gale preparing their room now." Elaine flipped the cover shut and stuffed it back in her apron.

Damn it. I wanted Myfanwy this afternoon. Martha stretched and stifled her disappointment. "I need to bathe and then nap. Do you need me for anything else?"

Elaine frowned. "I'm concerned about Rachel."

"Is she not working out? Or is Roxy angry?"

Elaine flushed. "No. Roxy is fine. But Rachel is obsessed with Robin. I'm worried it will be Bridget and Octavia all over again. I think we should..." She stopped herself as if suddenly remembering the pain Octavia leaving had caused Martha. "Sorry."

Martha chewed her lip and looked away from Elaine. "I can't think about it now. Let's discuss it at dinner."

"Yes. Is it just us? Or will Her Highness be joining us?" Elaine had one hand on her hip and the other on the doorknob.

"I don't know. Ask her." Martha walked into her bathroom. "And be nice." She closed the door and leaned her head against it and blew out a breath. *Damn. So hard. At least she dropped it when I asked her to. I hate not telling her, but she already doesn't trust her. Do I? She changed her mind so fast. The rope in her purse. Who on earth carries a knife like that? How the hell did she get it past customs?* Back at Rowan House, the time she had spent with Lucia seemed like a dream. A wonderful dream. *So what if she was wet? She could be into the physical part of it. It could all be part of who she is. Doesn't mean she cares. The problem with professionals. Not like I haven't been accused of it. More than once.*

She turned the taps on, ready to soak in a long bath. She added her favorite bath salts, the mossy evergreen scent soothing. She lowered herself into the steaming water. *What to do? How to do this? How do I pretend I'm not hooked on Lucia's dominance? I want her over me as much as I want Myfanwy under me.* She lay back in the tub and her body relaxed, her mind refusing to follow. *How do I work out both sides of myself here? Things with Madame were clear-cut, my life there separate. I refused Octavia's desires, denied her what I crave myself. And she left me.* Melancholy settled in her soul. *Lucia won't change her mind about being committed. She'll leave in the end. She's honoring Madame's request. She'll leave Rowan House, leave me. She wants as far away from the life as she can get. With her history I can't blame her.* Martha smoothed her hands over her nipples, sore from Lucia's attentions, and closed her eyes, letting her memories of Lucia's hands on her body soothe her anxiety. The water cooled, and she got out and dried herself. The pleasant ache between her legs made from her time with Lucia warmed her, and as tired as she was, a steady hum of desire filled her body. She brushed her teeth before she tugged on her pajamas. Sleep. It would be better after she slept. Or wouldn't. Right now, she didn't care.

HOW DID I survive only going to the Onyx a few times a year? She and Elaine had argued for an hour over what to do about Rachel. Martha pointed out her excellent care of horses and the way she kept the barn. She had her own issues with Robin but there had been no complaints, and she had gotten several large tips from guests. Her head ached with the stress of trying to make the decision. Elaine was ready to axe both of them, not worried about the expense of buying out their contracts and interviewing and hiring new staff. Martha wanted to let things play out. They had agreed to wait until after the winter break to make a decision. Elaine wasn't happy, but they had left it as such. Now all Martha wanted to do was lie down and let someone else make the decisions. She had always been the one in charge ever since they were girls. As the oldest she had fallen into the role naturally, often feeling like Elaine's mother rather than her sister.

She had not seen Lucia since their overnight stay at The Stone Hearth. Caught up with making arrangements to repair the car, her financial management obligations, and the running of the house, she had not attempted to engage with Lucia. She was glad Lucia had not joined them for meals, worried she would not be able to hide her emotions from Elaine. She had spent more than one evening staring down the hall at Lucia's door, struggling with her desire to see her and her need to keep herself safe.

This morning she was desperate for her counsel. She needed a neutral party to discuss her problems with, and she trusted Lucia. Elaine's hotheadedness had cost them plenty of money in the past. Rowan House was more than solvent, but Martha had the burden of keeping the books balanced. She tapped on the door.

Lucia opened the door, a neutral expression on her face, and raised her eyebrow at Martha. "A pleasant surprise. I was beginning to think you'd forgotten about me."

Martha gripped the edges of the doorframe to keep herself from grabbing Lucia and kissing her like she wanted to. "Would you like to go for a ride? It's going to be gorgeous. We won't have many more days like this."

Lucia tilted her head to the side and studied Martha's face. "Anyone else going with us?"

Martha smiled at her and held her gaze. "Just us. Unless you'd like one of the others to join us?"

Lucia shook her head and looked away. "Not anyone I had in mind."

"Dress warm. Meet me at the stable in half an hour."

"See you then." Lucia closed the door.

Martha kept herself from skipping down the hall, but it was close.

RACHEL HAD THE horses saddled when Martha arrived. Bruno was tacked out for her and Clyde for Lucia. Unsure of Lucia's riding ability, Martha had asked Rachel to choose one of their more sedate trail horses. Clyde was a perfect choice, and Martha checked the condition of the barn while she waited for Lucia. It was immaculate. *She keeps the barn as clean and tidy as Octavia ever did. Don't want to find another barn manager.* Robin was there helping Rachel, holding on to Bruno's halter. *Why is she here?*

Robin cocked a hip at Martha. "Good afternoon, Mistress. You're looking well today." She held Martha's gaze, openly ignoring the jealous glare she got from Rachel. "Pleasure ride?" She nodded at the bottle of wine Martha held in her hand.

Martha summoned her icy Mistress voice. "Afternoon." She turned away from Robin, ignoring her question. "Rachel, did you get the picnic I asked Cook for?"

"I brought it, Mistress, and two plastic glasses like you asked. I added some water bottles for you. The front saddlebags are packed. It might be a tight fit with the wine." She eyed the bottle in Martha's hand.

Robin inserted herself in their conversation. "Do you need anything else? Company? I would be so happy to serve you." The eagerness in Robin's voice and the vitriol on Rachel's face, directed at Robin, was unsettling.

Martha kept her tone cool. "No." Normally polite, she would have said thank you, but she didn't want to encourage her. Rachel blew out a breath, and Martha now understood what Elaine was worried about. Robin was oblivious to Rachel's reactions.

"What time will you return, Mistress? I want to be here to cool the horses out and brush them before I put them up." Rachel passed Bruno's reins to Martha.

"We should be back by half four at the latest."

"Very good, Ma'am."

The crunch of boots on gravel announced Lucia's arrival. She wore tight black riding pants, with knee-high burgundy boots. A dark-gray thick cable-knit sweater over a black turtleneck completed her outfit. It fitted her perfectly, hugging her curves, and Martha looked down to keep from staring. She busied herself packing the bottle of wine into Bruno's front saddlebag. Martha took a breath to steady herself before she glanced at Lucia again. "Right on time."

"I am nothing if not punctual." Lucia looked the two horses over. Rachel inclined her head at Clyde and patted him on the neck. "This is Clyde. He's a charm on the trail, Ma'am. Solid and calm."

Martha waited while Rachel led Clyde over to the mounting block. Lucia climbed on his back, and Rachel helped her fasten her stirrups at the proper length.

Martha led Bruno to the block and mounted him. Rachel had learned her stirrup length, and the meticulously clean tack gleamed in the sunlight. She watched as Rachel interacted with Lucia in a respectful way, offering her advice on handling Clyde. *It will be so hard to replace her if we have to.* A touch on her thigh startled her. "I've missed you, Mistress." Robin's voice was a whisper, and she pressed a quick kiss to the calf of Martha's boot. "So much."

Martha stiffened and looked down into her face. "Do not put your hands on any Mistress of this house unless you are asked." She did not modulate her voice but spoke loud enough for Rachel to hear. "In the future such an egregious error in conduct will result in whatever punishment I see fit." She leaned down and pinned Robin in place with her gaze. "And it will not be one you enjoy."

Martha urged Bruno forward with her legs, away from Robin. Lucia considered Martha with a raised eyebrow before she raked her dismissive gaze over Robin. Rachel made a disgusted noise and stormed from the stable yard. Robin followed her into the barn. Their raised voices were audible in the yard. Martha toyed with the idea of following them into the barn to sort things.

Lucia rode up next to her, concern on her face. She inclined her head toward the barn. "Do you need to attend to them?"

Martha shifted in her saddle. "Not sure if now is the time. And it was one of the things I wanted to discuss with you. But not here."

"Lead on."

They rode through the stable yard and out into the fields. The trail was wide enough for them to ride side by side. They rode together, not speaking, Martha wanting to put some distance between Rowan House and them before she discussed her worries.

The day was crisp, the sun warm in contrast to the gusty cold wind blowing from the mountains.

When they were on the other side of the field, Martha broke the silence. "Elaine thinks we need to fire both of them. She's worried their behavior will get worse. I'm okay with buying Robin out of her contract, but I hate the idea of losing Rachel. She is so good with the horses. The cost of buying both of them out, and then hiring new people to replace them, is not something I want to take on right now. We're closed for the winter break at the end of this month, and our income decreases. We've not had the best year this year. And then there are the repairs to the car. If we do have to let them go, I want to wait until their contracts are up. But it means six more months with Rachel and eight more for Robin."

Lucia listened, letting Martha get all her concerns out before she spoke. "Is Elaine annoyed her relationship with Rachel did not turn out as she wanted? Is it why she wants to get rid of her?"

"You're observant. I don't know. Roxy is still the love of her life, even if Elaine won't commit to her."

"Robin did well for the demonstration. Rope play is intense and she handled it well." Lucia pursed her lips. "I don't know her history, but she's here because it's safe, not because she wants to be in the life. Rachel is a puzzle. She was very much into Elaine when she left the demonstration but clearly has some possession issues with Robin. I don't envy you your decision."

Martha reined Bruno to a stop. "I appreciate your observation skills. What would you do?"

Lucia brought Clyde up next to her. "I'm inclined to let things play out. Unless it impacts your guests, or other staff, negatively. If that were the case then I would be swift in dismissing both of them. Her aggression toward seeking your attention and touching you without your permission would certainly earn her a pay docking, if it were the Onyx. The second offense would be a firing."

Martha shifted in her saddle. "Thank you. I think that is best too. It might even work out on its own with one of them choosing to leave." They had reached the place where the trail split. Martha raised her arm and pointed to the east and the woods. "There is a fire pit and turnout for the horses if we want a fireside picnic. If you prefer an open field in the sunshine, we can ride a bit more, and there is a glen. It is secluded as well but rougher." She turned to look into Lucia's eyes.

Lucia met her gaze. "I take it both are private?" A tight smile played over her mouth.

"Yes." Martha smiled back at Lucia. "Very private. Miss."

Lucia's face took on a cool expression and she sat up straighter in her saddle. "How presumptuous of you to call me Miss. Let alone think I might want to be in a private place alone with you. You've all but ignored me since we returned from The Stone Hearth. You haven't even asked me to dinner. And now you assume I want more than lunch with you." Her voice was snow and ice. "I don't mind eating alone every night, but I don't like feeling like one of your employees, someone you can pick up and put down as you will."

"I...I'm sorry." Martha flushed, angry with herself. *What was I thinking? And I'm an ass. I should have asked her to dinner.* "Why have you asked for meals in your room? I thought you didn't want to see me. Elaine said you asked to be served in your room. I thought you had found one of the others you wanted to be with."

"I don't think blaming your sister is reasonable. If you were concerned at all you would have walked the twenty-five feet to my door and knocked on it. Or is it too much for the Mistress of Rowan House? Afraid to ask an equal to dinner? Afraid of what others will think? Or maybe you only want women you can control with your money and position?" Lucia's eyes were dark, the blue gone the color of the sea before a storm.

Elaine. Meddling again. Martha leaned away from Lucia's uncaged anger and lowered her gaze. "I'm sorry." *It's true. I did act like she would be there. If I wanted. She's not mine. She's free.* She had so many things she wanted to tell Lucia, none of which she could say now she knew how angry Lucia was with her. "Please forgive me. This wasn't a good idea. I was wrong to assume. We can ride back." She turned her horse back in the direction of Rowan House, keeping her head down. Wanting to avoid Lucia's eyes, wanting to hide her shame.

"Stop." Lucia's voice was harsh.

Martha reined Bruno to a halt.

"I didn't ride all this way to not eat lunch."

Martha's stomach clenched and she turned her horse back toward Lucia. "The wood? Or the glen?"

"The wood." Lucia pursed her lips. "Pet."

Martha's heart squeezed in her chest. *She forgives me. Maybe she'll punish me. Please let her punish me.*

EVEN WITH THE sun the wood was cold, and Martha wondered about their choice. The turnout shed would offer shelter to the horses, and if she built a good fire at least the front of them would be warm. Lucia's silence on the ride made Martha anxious and wet and ache for her. *Pet. She called me pet. Maybe it will be more than lunch. Maybe she'll let me touch her, serve her, pleasure her.* Saliva pooled in her mouth as she thought about Lucia's body.

When they reached the fire circle, Martha dismounted. She held Bruno's reins and held Clyde while Lucia dismounted. She walked away from Martha, surveying the fire ring and the surrounding area. Martha led Bruno and Clyde into the shed. She left them tacked up but loosened their girths and slipped their bits so they could enjoy some hay. She didn't expect them to be there long enough to make it worth her while to pull off their saddles. She unstrapped the saddlebag and carried it to where Lucia sat. She had picked one of the wooden seats spread around the ring. Lucia didn't acknowledge her, so she busied herself with setting out the lunch. She bent over and stacked some wood in the fire ring. "Would you like me to build a fire?"

Lucia quirked her mouth. "Are we going to be here long enough to enjoy it? Or do you have other appointments?" She pulled her gloves off slowly, one finger at a time.

Martha stood up and met Lucia's gaze. "I've apologized. I can't do more than I have."

"Oh, I think you can do a lot more." She pointed to the ground in front of her. "And don't stand over me."

Martha clenched her jaw and bent her knees. She lowered herself to the ground.

"Much better." Lucia reached out and clasped Martha's jaw. "Don't like it when it's my idea?" She reached down and pushed her hand inside Martha's jacket. She cupped her breast and squeezed Martha's nipple through her shirt. "Too bad." She leaned forward and kissed her hard, holding Martha still as she savaged her mouth and rolled her nipple with hard fingers. Martha kept hold of the seam of her pants to stop herself from grabbing Lucia. She made a small noise of need in her throat, wanting her Mistress to give her permission to touch her. Lucia pulled back and Martha panted, trying to get herself under control.

Lucia patted her cheek. "Set the lunch, pet." Her voice was cool and commanding.

Martha went to one knee to stand up. Lucia's hand on her shoulder stopped her. "Did I tell you to stand up?"

"No." Martha deliberately left off the "Miss," needing to connect to Lucia, needing her punishment, as much as she needed air. She ached physically, her clit hard from the rough kiss and the command in Lucia's voice.

Lucia's hand snaked out fast, and she slapped Martha's cheek. "No what?"

Martha swallowed hard as the heat from Lucia's slap spread to her body. "No, Miss."

Lucia favored her with a small smile. "I like the way that sounds on your lips." She pressed a kiss to the spot on Martha's cheek where it was still warm from her slap. "Go on now, set the lunch. I'm famished."

Martha stayed on her knees. She spread out the small oilcloth over the seat next to Lucia's, taking her time arranging the slices of fruit and bread, crackers, spreads and cheeses Elaine had packed. "Would you like wine, Miss?"

"Water to start."

Martha poured them water, thankful Rachel had remembered to add it to the saddlebag.

"Very nice, pet. Come, kneel here by me." Martha crawled over to Lucia's side. Lucia picked up the wet cloth scented with lemon and cleaned her hands. "How delightful. Elaine thinks of everything. Or was it you?" She picked up the dry towel next to it and dried her hands.

"It was Elaine. She packs all the lunches with wipes as she's worried about germs."

Lucia spread a cracker with soft herbed cheese and took a bite. Martha watched her eat, loving the way her mouth worked, the way her muscles contracted in her throat as she swallowed. She wanted to kiss her neck, to lick the soft skin over the taut muscles, to sink her teeth into the tender skin until Lucia cried out.

Lucia finished her bite of cracker. "Why does she want to keep me away from you?"

Martha held her Mistress's gaze. "Jealous."

"Of me? She doesn't seem to have a problem with any of the others showing you attention. Not even Myfanwy." She took another bite of her cracker and finished it.

"She's protective. She worries I'll get hurt."

"Are you worried?"

Martha shifted her gaze and avoided her Mistress's eyes. "It makes no sense to worry about pain, Miss. It wouldn't be life if there wasn't pain."

Lucia reached down and touched Martha's chin. She lifted it and looked into her eyes. She rubbed her thumb over Martha's cheek, her gaze soft. "No, pet, it wouldn't be." She clasped her chin for a long moment and then released her.

Lucia held out a cracker topped with cheese for Martha. "Here, pet." Martha opened her mouth and accepted the food from Lucia's hand, keeping her eyes on her Mistress's face as she took the bite she offered. She chewed slowly, savoring the food as much as Lucia's attention. "Thank you, Miss."

They ate lunch with Lucia picking and choosing their fare, eating first then feeding Martha. It was peaceful, and Martha relaxed under her attention, knowing she didn't even have to choose what she ate. All she had to do was eat. Her Miss handled it all, stopping to give her water from her own glass. Martha's legs ached from the packed earth beneath her knees, and the dull pain complimented the sweet attention Lucia gave her.

When they had finished their lunch, the wood was cooler, and Martha glanced at the sky. Lucia touched her face, drawing her gaze. "I know, pet. We've run out of time and good weather." She leaned forward and touched her forehead to Martha's brow. "Thank you for a lovely lunch, pet." She stood up. "Clean it up and let's get back. I'm freezing. You may stand."

Martha stifled her disappointment and bit back the begging that wanted to spill from her mouth. She pressed her lips together. Lucia was right. They needed to go. They should have left earlier in the day. She'd been too busy with paperwork and nonurgent decisions. *How to do this? How am I going to go back and act normal? How many times have I left a submissive like this?* Aching with want, desperate for her Mistress's touch, she chewed her lip as she cleaned up their lunch. Martha bent at the waist to collect the saddlebag.

Lucia placed her hand in the middle of her back. "Stay like that, pet. I like the view. Put your hands on the seat to steady yourself." She ground her hips against Martha's ass as she reached around and cupped her through her breeches. Martha groaned as Lucia unbuttoned her pants and unzipped her fly. She pushed the pants down over Martha's hips, leaving them bunched at the knees. Martha was wet, her clit thick with desire. The cold air on her ass made her shiver. Lucia pushed her fingers into Martha from behind, the slick slide making Martha moan. She tried to widen her stance to open herself to Lucia. Restricted by her pants around her knees, she growled in frustration.

Leaning against her hips, Lucia draped herself over her back and fingered Martha's clit while she fucked her, taking what she wanted. Martha's exposed position and the rough way Lucia took her had her fighting to keep control. Lucia's deep sigh as she finished against Martha's ass had Martha panting to hold back her own pleasure. "Please, Miss. Please let me come for you. Please."

Lucia curled her fingers over Martha's sweet spot. "Come for me, pet. Give me what's mine."

Martha broke, spilling her pleasure over Lucia's hand. She locked her knees to stay upright. Lucia lay over her back. She pressed a quick kiss to the back of Martha's neck before she straightened up. "Stand for me, pet. We need to get back." Martha shivered, and Lucia pulled her pants up, tucking her shirt in before she refastened her breeches. She reached up and pushed her fingers into Martha's mouth. She sucked them hard, hoping her Mistress would allow her a taste of her before they returned to Rowan House.

Lucia pulled her fingers from Martha's mouth and kissed her. Her mouth set Martha on fire. A fresh surge of wetness soaked her pants. Martha dared to reach up and grab her Mistress's hips, pulling them hard against her. Lucia leaned into her and gripped the back of her neck.

Martha brought her lips close to her Mistress's ear. "Please, Miss. Let me serve you. Let me taste you."

Lucia placed her fingers over Martha's lips. "Another time, pet. We need to get back before they come looking for us."

Martha fought her desire to disregard her Mistress's command. The side of her pleading with her to strip Lucia naked and feast on her until she screamed Martha's name as she came. Lucia held her gaze and Martha slowed her breathing. *Breathe. Focus. Obey. Serve. She's right. We need to go. Another time. But when?*

She relaxed her grip on Lucia, and they walked to the turnout shed together. Martha tightened the girths on the horses and set their bridles to rights. She led Clyde out and helped Lucia mount him. When she was secure in the saddle, Martha mounted Bruno, and they rode back to Rowan House.

Chapter Ten

THE DAY AFTER the picnic Martha sat at her desk and ran the figures again. Elaine had been upset with her decision to wait until Robin and Rachel's contracts were up before making a decision about their continued work at Rowan House. Martha won the argument after showing Elaine the spreadsheets tallying the expenses of repairing the car, and what the projected costs of rehiring for their positions would be. She didn't confront Elaine about her attempts to sabotage her relationship with Lucia.

The house would last another year. They had been successful, marketing themselves to a certain clientele, but Martha worried their business was starting to lag. They would pick up some clients when the Onyx closed, but the appeal of the Onyx was Madame. And Martha was not her. Try as she might she would never be able to manage the iron Mistress, the hard-ass appeal of Madame.

Lucia could pull it off, but she doesn't want to. Martha had eased away from the physical side of the business, only taking those clients who had been hers for years. She left anyone new to Elaine. She had been deprived of a major player with the loss of Octavia. *I need to replace her with another Domme, or a strong switch. I need to talk with Elaine. I could ask Lucia, offer her a position. She'd never agree. Doesn't want that kind of life anymore. I don't want her to have clients. Truth. I want her all to myself. My secret pleasure. I'm so fucked. She doesn't want me that way.* As far as she knew, other than the demonstration with Robin, Lucia had not asked for any of the women of the house to serve her.

A soft knock on the door made her start. She didn't have any appointments, but she told her staff they could knock on the door any time they needed to talk. "Enter."

The door opened, and Myfanwy walked in. She closed the door behind her. Her jaw was rigid and she twisted her skirt in her hands. Martha's stomach clenched. "What is it?"

Myfanwy met Martha's gaze. "Mistress Lucia asked for me." She pressed her lips in a thin line. "I've prided myself on not refusing anyone, Mistress, but..."

Martha kept her expression smooth even if her stomach churned. *She wants her. Done with me.* "I see." She twisted her fingers together. "No one is required to serve anyone. You know you can say no." *Please say no.*

"That's just it, Mistress. She asked you attend as well."

"What?" Martha worked to keep her voice even.

Myfanwy fisted her hands in her skirt. "She asked for me to come to her and asked me to bring you as well."

Martha flushed. "I see." She gripped the arms of her chair as white-hot anger filled her. *So much for secrets. Fuck. Why did I trust her?*

"I told her I didn't think it was proper." Myfanwy pursed her lips. "She's a puzzle, Mistress."

"Indeed." Martha held her gaze. "What do you want, Myfanwy?"

Myfanwy straightened her shoulders. "Whatever pleases you, Mistress."

Martha's thoughts spun as she turned over the possibilities in her head. *What is Lucia thinking? Does she want to test my relationship with Myfanwy?* She remembered Myfanwy's words about rope play. "Did

Mistress Lucia give a time she wanted us to attend her? Or did she expect I could be summoned at any time?"

Myfanwy met Martha's gaze. "She asked for us at eight, after dinner, Mistress."

"Were you to return to give her an answer?"

"She didn't command me to, Mistress."

Martha stood up and walked to Myfanwy. She cupped her face in her hands and kissed her. Her soft surrender soothed the turmoil in Martha's body. She broke their kiss and met her gaze. "Are you afraid of her? I need to know your true wishes, Myfanwy, not what you think I want to hear."

"I can't read her, Mistress. She's enticing but she scares me."

"Would you fear her if I was with you? If we were with her together?" Martha rubbed her thumb over Myfanwy's cheek. The change in Myfanwy's face as she realized what Martha was asking made Martha's heart crack wide open.

"Do you need me to be there, Mistress? I would do anything for you." She rested her hands on Martha's hips.

"I want her to use the ropes."

Myfanwy frowned. "I love you, Mistress, but it's a hard limit for me."

"I don't want her to use them on you." Martha held her gaze, letting her see the truth of what she wanted from Lucia.

Myfanwy studied her face a long moment before she hugged Martha close. "Should I meet you there, Mistress, or do you want to bring me to her?" She looked up into Martha's face. "Maybe I could have a bit of time with you before?"

Martha kissed her, taking her time. *What did I ever do to deserve her love?* "Yes. Come to my room at six. Then we'll go to Mistress Lucia."

Chapter Eleven

A KNOCK AT the door announced Myfanwy's arrival, and Martha checked herself in the mirror one last time. She waited a few minutes, letting the tension build before she answered the door. She and Myfanwy had been together many times, yet desire raged in Martha's body as strong as it had been the first time she touched Myfanwy. She opened the door to find her standing there in a simple red corset over a tight black skirt. She walked into the room and lowered herself to her knees. Martha's mouth watered as she took in the sight of her submission. She walked to her and trailed her fingers over her shoulders, and Myfanwy shivered under her touch. Martha had planned their time together to get herself in the proper headspace. Exercising her power and causing pain were at the top of her list. "Rise. Sit on the stool."

Myfanwy rose gracefully and settled herself on the low stool Martha had placed in the middle of the room. She placed her hands on the side and lifted her shoulders, displaying herself for her Mistress. Martha stood in front of her and traced a finger over her cleavage. She bent and unbuttoned the tiny buttons of the busk, opening the corset to expose her breasts and thick nipples. She bent her head and sucked hard, drawing her nipple deep into her mouth before grazing it with her teeth. Myfanwy shifted in the chair, arching her back to push more of herself into her Mistress's mouth. Martha raised her hand and pinched

Myfanwy's other nipple. The needy noises Myfanwy made as Martha tormented her made her clit hard. She pulled back and lavished her attention on her other nipple, forcing more soft moans from Myfanwy.

She picked up a low melt candle from the side table before she pulled her lighter from her pocket and rolled the flint. The flame jumped, and she lit the candle. She placed the lighter back in her pocket. "Hold your breasts up for me."

Myfanwy lifted her heavy breasts in her hands and held them out like an offering. She pushed them together, creating a compelling cleavage. Martha tilted the candle, and the hot wax splashed over Myfanwy's skin. The sharp intake of her breath made desire pool between Martha's legs.

She waited until the wax cooled before she tilted the candle again. Pouring a thin line of liquid wax over Myfanwy's breasts, she drew a longer squeal from Myfanwy. She pressed her legs together and shifted on the stool. Her nipples were thick and hard. Martha tilted the candle again, pouring the wax in a pattern as she moved the candle back and forth over Myfanwy's skin. No scream this time, a soft whimper of desire, and panting as Myfanwy gave over to the pain her Mistress gave. Martha set the candle aside. She bent over and leaned down and flicked away a spot of candle wax with her nail. The skin beneath the wax a bright red. Myfanwy groaned as Martha worked slowly, removing the wax.

When she had finished, she pressed her lips to the red spots and over the pattern she had made on her skin. "Lower your hands. Hold the sides of the stool." Myfanwy obeyed, and Martha tongued Myfanwy's nipple before she lifted her head and pulled a nipple clamp from her pocket. The custom-made clamps were thick silver filigree with a weighted medallion bearing Martha's initials. She placed one on Myfanwy's nipple and tightened the clamp so it would not slip. She did the same with the other. Myfanwy panted. Her knuckles were white where she gripped the stool. Martha tipped the weight with her finger, and it swung freely. Myfanwy pressed her legs together, and Martha pushed her hand under her skirt and shoved her thighs apart. Her thighs were slick, and her lack of panties made it easy for Martha to tease her clit.

Myfanwy shifted and spread her legs for her Mistress. Martha rubbed her clit with the pad of her thumb, two fingers just inside Myfanwy's velvet center.

A deep groan shook her body as Martha tapped the other weight, setting them both swinging. The light in the room reflected off the medallions as they swung from the clamps. Myfanwy's nipples were a claret color, the tips swollen from the clamps. Martha pushed deeper, slipping another finger inside.

Myfanwy panted, her breath ragged. "Please, Mistress. Let me come for you. Please." Her arms were trembling as she shook with the effort not to come. Martha was ruthless as she fucked her, urging her toward the pinnacle of pleasure, knowing her body like her own. She pushed Myfanwy to the edge and then over, her own need driving her. "Come for me, sweet girl. Give me what's mine."

Myfanwy came, with sharp cries and deep groans as she lifted her hips to meet Martha's thrusts. "Oh yes, Mistress. Please fuck me. More."

"Greedy girl." Martha rocked forward, gripping the back of the stool for leverage, and thrust another finger inside and sped up her stokes. She fucked her deep, curling her fingers up to draw profound sighs and moans from

Myfanwy. The motion set the weights swinging, and Myfanwy came again, her body clenching around Martha's fingers. With her other hand Martha clasped one of the clamps and snatched it free. Myfanwy screamed and clenched harder around Martha's fingers. She panted, and when Martha freed her other nipple she came again silently, her mouth a perfect O. Martha watched and waited until her body had relaxed. She pulled her fingers free.

Martha tugged Myfanwy's head back and kissed her throat and mouth. She opened her pants and let them fall to her knees and straddled Myfanwy on the stool. She brought Myfanwy's mouth to her hard clit. Myfanwy pressed her tongue deep and licked and sucked. She rolled her tongue over her clit, making Martha buck her hips. She came with a shout and held her in place, taking what she needed, what Myfanwy was desperate to give.

THEY ARRIVED AT Lucia's room exactly at eight o'clock. Martha held Myfanwy's hand, rubbing her thumb over the back of her knuckles in an attempt to soothe her, sensing her nervousness. Their time together beforehand had been the connection they both needed to embark on whatever Lucia had planned for them. Martha knocked on the door.

Lucia opened the door and raked her gaze over them both. The small hairs on the back of Martha's neck tickled as they stood up. Myfanwy gripped Martha's hand tighter.

Lucia favored them with a half smile. "I suppose this where I should say enter freely and of your own will."

Martha laughed at the horror movie reference, grateful for Lucia's attempt to break the tension. Myfanwy relaxed her grip on Martha's hand. Lucia lifted her hand, palm open, and Martha took it and followed her as Lucia led them both inside. Myfanwy followed close on Martha's heels. Lucia led them to the middle of the room before she dropped Martha's hand. She went back to the door and locked it. The click of the lock as it settled in place made Martha's heart race. She licked her lower lip.

Lucia was dressed in a lavender gown. The satin shimmered as she moved, and the long slit in the front skirt showed off glimpses of her elegant thighs. Black pumps completed her outfit and gave her a height advantage, forcing Martha to look up to meet her gaze. A straight-backed leather armchair was set close to the fireplace. A small braided rug covered the floor next to the chair. A fire blazed in the room's gas hearth and the room was warm.

Martha had dressed in black trousers and a white tailored shirt for the short walk to Lucia's room. Myfanwy's corset was splattered with the remnants of their wax play. A battered trunk was open near the closet. Large skeins of creamy white and light-brown rope filled one side. Smaller bundles of thinner, brightly colored rope were stored in neat rows on the other end. Desire, thick and heavy, wove its way through Martha as she studied the thick coils of white cotton rope arranged on the side table next to a large pair of bandage scissors. Martha missed the edge the open butterfly knife had added to their encounter at The Stone Hearth. She pressed her thighs together against the flow of want soaking her briefs.

Lucia pursed her lips. "Myfanwy, are you here of your own choosing?"

Myfanwy raised her chin and met Lucia's gaze. "Yes, Mistress, and with my Mistress's approval." Her posture and her tone were respectful but left no doubt about her loyalty. Martha had to work to suppress her smile at her words. *My Myfanwy. Mine. Always.*

Lucia held her gaze. "Understood." She ignored Martha, focusing on Myfanwy's eyes. "What are your hard limits?"

Myfanwy tilted her head. "No breath play. No extreme humiliation, name-calling and such, no race play, no scat, no water sports, Mistress."

Lucia narrowed her eyes. "Pain? Edge play?"

Myfanwy smiled, for the first time since they had entered the room. Her voice was strong with an underlying challenge. "No limits, Mistress."

Lucia's eyes glinted, and her mouth pulled into a feral smile. "Call me Miss. Safe word?"

Myfanwy lowered her head and focused her gaze on the floor. "Yes, Miss. Cake, Miss."

Martha wiped her damp palms on the front of her trousers. A trickle of sweat ran between her shoulder blades as she watched their exchange.

Lucia pointed to the small rug next to the armchair. "Kneel there, Myfanwy."

Myfanwy walked to the rug and lowered herself to her knees before she sat back on her heels, her hands resting on the top of her thighs palms up in the pose of the House. Martha heart ached with pride at her submissive's performance. *Perfect. She is perfect. And mine. Even if she doesn't wear my collar.*

Lucia turned her attention to Martha. "I understand certain conventions need to be maintained outside of my suite. But in the future when you come to my rooms, you will come dressed for play, not business." Lucia grasped Martha's shirt with both hands and ripped it open, her movement fast. Buttons flew and skittered across the room. Martha shivered as Lucia dragged the edge of her fingernail along the swell of her breasts. "Strip."

Lucia sat down in the chair to watch as Martha took off her clothes. Her fingers trembled as she folded her torn shirt neatly before she toed off her shoes. She sensed Lucia's gaze on her and her impatience. She took off her trousers and briefs and added her tank top to the pile. She stood naked before Lucia and clasped her hands behind her back.

Lucia crossed her legs, and the split in the gown fell open to reveal the sensuous shape of her thighs. "I'll ask you the same. What are your hard limits?"

Lucia's movement had given Martha a glimpse of her body and the dark curls between her legs, and she struggled to focus on her words. *Breathe. Focus. Obey. Serve.* Martha met her gaze. "No scat, or water sports. No race play. No extreme humiliation, Miss."

"And your safe word hasn't changed, has it? Not since last week?"

Martha flushed. "No, Miss."

Martha heard the small gasp Myfanwy was unable to suppress. She watched from under her lashes as Lucia rested her hand on Myfanwy's shoulder. "Shh. My protective one. This is a safe space. You are under my care. I'll keep you both safe." She saw Myfanwy's chest rise as she took a deep breath and settled under Lucia's touch.

"Come to me, properly." Lucia sat back in the armchair as regal as a queen.

Martha lowered her gaze and bent her knees and crawled to her Miss, desire pooling in her gut and wetting her thighs. She lowered her head to the floor, barely stopping herself from kissing the toe of the black pumps she wore. *Not without permission.*

Lucia touched the toe of her shoe to Martha's shoulder. "Eyes to me. Both of you."

Martha sat back on her heels. She risked a quick glance at Myfanwy's face before she met Lucia's gaze.

"What we do here is for us. No one else. It is between us and us alone. Do we all agree?"

"Yes, Miss," Myfanwy answered first, her voice strong.

"Yes, Miss," Martha answered, her gaze fixed on Lucia's eyes and the strength and promise she saw there.

"Good." She stood up. "Martha in the chair. Myfanwy with me."

She led Myfanwy to the table set out with the ropes. Martha sat as she was directed, the leather warm on her skin.

She watched as Myfanwy listened to Lucia, her voice so low Martha only saw her lips move. Myfanwy's back was to her and she admired her figure, how the corset ties highlighted her broad back and the way it nipped in her waist to set off her wide hips and thick shoulders. They turned to her. Lucia carried a large skein of white rope, and Myfanwy held a matching one. Lucia placed her skein on the small rug. Myfanwy unwound the rope and dropped the bulk of it to the floor. She fixed her gaze on Martha's eyes. Lucia stood next to her as Myfanwy ran the rope through her hands. She gathered it in loose coils as she passed it through her fingers and over her palm. Martha glanced at Lucia. She stood with her arms folded, observing Myfanwy. She looked at Martha and raised a brow, a warning in her eyes. Martha quickly shifted her attention back to Myfanwy's face as she focused on completing her task. She finished gathering the rope in her hand and looked to Lucia.

"Very good. Go stand on the right side of Martha. Face me." She turned and walked to the side of the room and rolled a wood-framed round mirror in front of Martha. The mirror was large enough to allow Martha to see herself and Myfanwy.

Lucia began the same process with the rope in her hand. Martha shifted her gaze to the mirror and watched as Lucia's hands passed over the rope. The slow, deliberate way she touched the coils made her squirm. She panted, anxious to feel the rope on her skin. She trembled and pressed her legs together, her desire flowing freely.

Lucia finished and came to stand next to Martha. She held her gaze in the mirror. "Mirrors are funny things. We see what we want to see in them, no matter how things are in life." She slid her hand down and pinched Martha's nipple. The pain focused her. The effect of watching her Mistress touch her, the vision of her own vulnerability, gave her the sense of being stripped to her soul. She glanced at Myfanwy's face in the mirror. Her eyes were dark, worry and concern showing on her features. Martha watched in the glass as Lucia reached over and touched Myfanwy's chin, drawing her gaze.

"Look at her face. Is she distressed?" Lucia directed Myfanwy with a soft voice, commanding yet kind.

Myfanwy's eyes locked on Martha's reflection in the mirror, and Martha opened her eyes wide, showing her beloved she was okay with the scene.

Myfanwy answered Lucia but kept her gaze fixed on Martha's face. "No, Miss."

Lucia rested her hand on Myfanwy's shoulder. "Imagine us spinning a cocoon around her, and when we're done, her spirit will emerge. She'll be free. Free to be as she wants to be, free to be herself. She'll be safe with us." She held the end of the rope in one hand. "Follow me on the opposite side. Keep the coils smooth, the tension the same." Lucia lowered herself to her knees. She looked up and met Martha's gaze in the mirror. "Spread your legs."

Martha flushed and opened her legs, the mirror showing her glistening center. Lucia smiled and tilted her head. "So wet for me already." She reached between Martha's legs and touched a finger to her clit while she held her gaze. "My greedy pet."

Martha moaned and lifted her hips toward Lucia's hand, anxious for more of her touch. A sharp pinch on the inside of her thigh made her gasp, and she settled. *Breathe. Focus. Obey. Serve.*

Lucia tied the end of the rope to the leg of the chair on her side. Myfanwy did the same, the concern on her face replaced by concentration. Martha watched as they worked. Myfanwy copied Lucia's movements. The sensation of the rope encasing her as they wrapped her legs and bound her to the chair ramped up her excitement. *Contained. Safe. Controlled.*

"Stop below her knee, make it even with my side."

Myfanwy obeyed and sat back on her heels. She held the rope in her hand, keeping tension on it. Martha watched her face as she shifted her gaze to the space between Martha's legs. Her tongue slid over her lower lip, and the open desire in her expression made Martha's gut clench.

Lucia traced a finger over the slick skin on the inside of Martha's thigh, stopping short of the wet heat between her legs. Martha groaned but held back, not moving. Her legs were spread wide. The pressure from the evenly spaced coils of rope added to her feeling of being confined. The sensation comforted her and excited her in a swirling mix of emotions. Each coil was an extension of Lucia, her touch, her control, her care. Lucia finished her side and tied the length of rope off. She moved to Myfanwy's side of the chair and checked her work. She pulled and tugged in a few spots and straightened a coil before she tied it off the line.

"Eyes on the mirror, pet. Keep your hands on the arms of the chair." Lucia's face was severe in the mirror, her eyes dark with desire.

"Yes, Miss."

Lucia stood up and wrapped her hand in Myfanwy' s hair and forced her to rise to her feet. Releasing her hair, she cupped the back of Myfanwy's neck and pulled her close. Martha watched them in the mirror. Myfanwy reacted to Lucia's strong grip, her breath shifting, and Lucia kissed the side of her neck and brought her lips close to her ear. "A very good first job, my reluctant one. But we're not finished yet." She unbuttoned the top two buttons of the busk, exposing the fullness of Myfanwy's breasts. The edge of her nipples was visible. Martha stared, entranced by their interaction.

Lucia lowered her head and licked a trail down Myfanwy's chest before she sank her teeth into the soft flesh there, drawing a deep moan from Myfanwy. "I think you need a bit of an attitude adjustment. Martha, eyes on the mirror. Do not turn around or close your eyes." Her voice was full of calculated menace as she closed her hand on the back of Myfanwy's neck to guide her away from Martha. They moved out of Martha's line of sight, and she was left with her own reflection. The sounds of soft murmuring, the whisper of kisses, the harsh slap of a hard hand on bare skin, mixed with Myfanwy's soft groans and cry of release, sent a sharp wave of want through Martha as she imagined what Lucia was doing to Myfanwy. She kept her gaze fixed on the mirror as she had been ordered, fighting the urge to turn and watch them. Her clit ached with need, and the temptation to touch herself was overwhelming. She gripped the chair arms, her knuckles white with effort. Sweat stung her eyes, and she lost all sense of time as she struggled to obey Lucia's orders.

When they returned, Lucia stroked her shoulder before she pressed a kiss to her temple, rewarding her and letting her know she was pleased with her. Myfanwy's face was flushed, her eyes bright. She avoided Martha's gaze. *Look at me, please. Let me see you, Myfanwy. Let me see you are okay with this.* Martha wouldn't say her safe word for herself, but she would say it in a minute if she thought Myfanwy was distressed, knowing she would not use it if she thought Martha wanted her to continue. Her mind was consumed with fear for Myfanwy. She shifted in the chair and chewed her lip, uncertain and afraid.

Lucia returned and handed Myfanwy another skein of rope. "As before. I ran this before you arrived, so I know the rope is safe. This time we'll do her arms. Keep the tension firm but not too tight." She tied off her skein to the arm of the chair before she began wrapping the coils of soft white rope around Martha's arms. Myfanwy did as she was directed. She kept her eyes on her work, avoiding Martha's gaze. A flare of panic lit in Martha's chest as she realized she would be even more vulnerable, completely at Lucia's mercy. Her hands clutched the smooth wood of the chair, her fingers wet with sweat. She closed her eyes and worked to control her breathing.

"Stop." Lucia's sharp tone startled Martha. "Keep your eyes open, pet." Her tone was soft and commanding, warm but firm. "What do you need?"

Martha met Lucia's gaze. "I need to know Myfanwy's okay with this."

Lucia pressed her lips together. "She's my responsibility right now."

"Yes, Miss." Martha lowered her gaze and bit her lower lip to stop it from trembling. A soft touch on her shoulder and the strong squeeze of Myfanwy's grip made her look up.

Myfanwy met her gaze in the mirror. Her eyes were serious, questioning. Martha tilted her head and studied her face. *She's worried she's betrayed me because I witnessed how she responded to Lucia.*

Martha turned her head and pressed a kiss to her knuckles, lifting her shoulder to lean her cheek against Myfanwy's hand. Her expression changed to one of love and desire, and she gave Martha's shoulder another squeeze before she went back to her task. Lucia tapped her on the shoulder. Martha met her gaze in the mirror. The set of her mouth and depth of her expression told her all she needed to know to relax into the scene.

Lucia and Myfanwy worked together, their motions synced, and the sensation of watching them work as they restrained her increased Martha's excitement. She clenched and unclenched her hands on the arms of the chair. They stopped short of her elbows and, as before, Lucia finished her side then came and checked Myfanwy's work. She tied it off and straightened. Lucia pulled Myfanwy in and kissed her, before unbuttoning several more buttons of her corset. She teased her nipples, pinching and rolling them, drawing small gasps and squeals from Myfanwy. Martha groaned as she watched them, her clit thick and needy, her desire pooling beneath her. She squirmed as much as she could within her bonds. Her mouth was dry, and she licked her lower lip.

Lucia stepped away from Myfanwy to pass her hands over Martha's joints. Everywhere she touched Martha's skin burned. "Myfanwy, check her feet, make sure they are pink and warm." Lucia gripped Martha's chin and turned her face. She held Martha's gaze and kissed her, taking her time, the touch of her lips making Martha ache for more. Lucia broke their kiss and Martha panted. "Myfanwy, while you're down there, attend to her. Mouth and tongue only, she doesn't come until I say."

"Yes, Miss." The eagerness in Myfanwy's voice made Martha's heart ache. The first touch of her tongue threatened to make her come, but Myfanwy knew her body, knew how to keep her on the edge.

Lucia pulled coils of the final skein of rope through her hands as she watched Martha's face in the mirror. Martha was torn between watching Myfanwy as she kneeled, her thick hips and excitement on display in the mirror as her short skirt pulled over her hips, her face between Martha's thighs and Lucia's face as she drew the coils of rope through her hands. Lucia stepped behind the chair and began wrapping the thick coils of rope over Martha's ribs, and under her breasts. She crossed them and wrapped another layer of coils. The thick white rope framing Martha's breasts, the pressure and pleasure of being bound by Lucia mixed with the attention to her clit made her pant to keep from coming.

"Please, Miss. I can't. I'm going to... Oh. Please. Ahh."

Lucia paused in her work. "Stop, Myfanwy." Myfanwy groaned but complied with Lucia's direction and sat back on her heels. And Martha cried out at the loss of sensation. Lucia brushed her knuckles over Martha's face. "Shh, pet. Trust me."

She finished wrapping the coils of rope around Martha. Now she was bound completely to the chair. Her legs were spread wide, arms fixed in place, her upper body completely encased with thick coils of rope. *Open. Exposed. Safe. Loved.* Her mind stuttered over the last bit. *Love. Is this love? Or just a whim? Myfanwy loves me. Does Lucia feel anything for me? Is this relief? Entertainment?* Her thoughts folded back on themselves, and Martha cursed herself for thinking. She closed her eyes and worked to get her head back in the scene.

Lucia leaned over the back of the chair and brought her lips close to Martha's ear. "Where did you go, pet? Am I boring you?" She reached down and flicked Martha's nipple. The sharp sting made Martha flinch. "Let's see what we can do to keep your attention. Myfanwy, as you were." Myfanwy's warm breath on her thigh and the softness of her lips as she sucked Martha's clit sent her senses reeling.

Lucia kept her mouth busy as she kissed and nipped Martha's neck. With both hands she rolled and pinched her sensitized nipples. "Look at yourself, my beautiful pet. Bound for me. I love the way your nipples are so swollen and hard, the way your chest heaves as you struggle to hold on for me."

Martha was lost, lost in the sensations flooding her body. She was floating, the only ties to herself the mouth between her legs and the hands sending sweet spikes of pain rocketing through her body. Lucia moved a hand up to her neck, a loose collar of sinew and bone. Martha's body shook as she tried to hold off, to go on, waiting on her Mistress's pleasure.

"Oh please, Miss. Please let me. I can't..." Martha struggled against her bonds, her breath ragged. "Please, Miss. Let me come for you. Please." The last was a shout.

Lucia held her gaze in the mirror, pure triumph in her eyes. She flexed her fingers on Martha's throat. The threat sent her tumbling into an abyss of pleasure. "Come for me, pet. Myfanwy, fuck her. Now."

Myfanwy sucked hard and thrust her fingers deep, and Martha screamed as she came undone. A surge of wetness poured from her. The sounds and sensations of Myfanwy as she thrust deep while she sucked and lapped at her drew out her pleasure. She closed her eyes, riding the high of sensations, and came again, enveloped by a floating feeling. Her body shook with aftershocks as she came once more with a long low groan.

Warm hands stroked her as the ropes were unwrapped. *No. Leave them. Let me stay wrapped in you. Yours.* She shivered and fought back tears. She wanted to stay swathed in her bonds, cozy in her cocoon of sensation, the center of Lucia's attentions. Cherished.

Myfanwy's strong hand squeezed her shoulder. "Drink, love." She held the glass for Martha as she drank. Lucia's firm voice whispered in her ear. "Stand up slowly."

Myfanwy supported her on the left and Lucia on the right. Martha concentrated on moving her feet. She trembled, and Myfanwy pulled her closer against her warm body. Her legs bumped against the edge of the bed, and she sat down. Lucia's arm was around her shoulders as she lowered her on to the mattress. Myfanwy lifted Martha's legs and climbed in the bed next to her. She curled her body around Martha, settling her head on her breast, grounding her. The duvet was pulled up over them, and Martha closed her eyes. Myfanwy rubbed her body, her hands soothing and warm. *Where is Lucia? Is she leaving aftercare to Myfanwy? Was it why she asked for both of us, so she didn't have to be bothered with aftercare? Bothered with me.*

Martha leaned her head against Myfanwy's soft breasts, cozying into the comfort of her familiar body and her love. She pushed away her disappointment over Lucia's lack of presence. The ache in her body was delicious, the ache in her heart torture.

"Can you sit up, pet?" Lucia's rested her hand on Martha's head.

Myfanwy released Martha and pushed herself up in the bed. She arranged the pillows for Martha and helped her sit up.

Martha kept her head down, avoiding Lucia's gaze, fearful of what she would see, or not see in her eyes, afraid for Lucia to know the extent of her need and want.

Lucia reached over, and with firm fingers she lifted Martha's chin. She stared into Martha's eyes as she spoke. "Well done, pet." She leaned in and kissed her.

Martha pressed into the kiss and wrapped her arms around Lucia, pulling her down into her embrace. She held the kiss, taking her time. Lucia opened to her, her mouth echoing the passion of Martha's kiss. She broke the kiss and saw in Lucia's unguarded expression the truth. *She cares for me. And doesn't know what to do about it.*

"Let me go, pet. You'll wrinkle my gown." Lucia patted Martha's face. "You need to eat."

She left and disappeared behind the changing screen in her room. She rolled out a serving cart with covered dishes, a water pitcher, wineglasses, and a bottle of red wine.

Where the hell did the food come from? Did one of the others deliver it? Oh hell. I can hear the rumors now. Fuck. The staff will know. They won't respect me. Fuck me, why did I do this?

Lucia pursed her lips. "You're thinking again. What is it, pet?" She poured a glass of water and held it out for Myfanwy.

"Thank you, Miss." Myfanwy took the glass from Lucia's hand.

"The food. Who delivered it?" Martha twisted the sheets in her hands, working hard to keep the edge out of her voice, knowing from Lucia's raised eyebrows she had failed.

"Worried your staff will know you're keeping company with me?" Lucia's voice was like ice water down Martha's back.

"No. I…"

Lucia pressed her mouth together in a thin line. "I had it delivered prior to your arrival. If you're worried about your reputation, you should go." She spun her on her heel and walked to where Martha had left her clothes. She bent and gathered them up in her arms. Lucia's heels made a sharp sound on the floor as she stalked back to the side of the bed carrying Martha's clothes. "Go." She tossed Martha's clothes to the floor next to the bed. "Now you've got what you came for."

Myfanwy dug her fingers into Martha's thigh. "We can go, Mistress, if it pleases you." She shot a hard look at Lucia.

Martha looked down, avoiding Lucia's gaze again, fearful of what she would see in her eyes. *I've hurt her. I'm an ass. I want to stay. I can't leave. Not like this. Please let me stay. Feed me. Care for me. Let me know I didn't imagine what I saw in your eyes.*

Lucia turned away from Martha and Myfanwy and walked over to the fireplace. Her back to the bed, her shoulders set square, hands clasped behind her back. Martha raised Myfanwy's hand to her mouth. She kissed her fingertips as she looked into her eyes. Martha placed her hand on the covers, giving it a squeeze before she left the bed and lowered herself to her knees. She crawled to her Mistress's side and waited.

She's done. Ask. Beg. Apologize for not trusting her. Beg. Martha crept forward and kissed the top of Lucia's shoe. She pressed her forehead to the floor. "Forgive me, Miss. Please forgive me."

Lucia reached down and wound her hand in Martha's hair and yanked hard, arching her back, half lifting her off the floor. "This is the last time. If you don't trust me enough to protect you, then we can't do this. I won't be questioned. I demand complete trust and expect complete obedience." Her eyes were hard, the blue gone dark. "Or you can find someone else to get you off like you want." She released Martha, who sank to the floor.

The only sound in the room was the soft tick of the mantel clock. Lucia walked away from her, and Martha stayed in place, weighing her options. *I could beg. Agree to her demands. Grovel at her feet. Or say my safe word and stand up, take Myfanwy, and leave. Walk away from her and try to gather the ragged parts of my soul back together. Why did I think I could do this here? Why did I think I could have more?*

The sharp rattle of a cover being removed from a dish shook her from her thoughts. "Get off the floor and into this bed, pet. And don't test my patience again."

Martha snapped her head up and crawled as fast as she could to her Mistress's bed.

Chapter Twelve

"YOU'VE BEEN SPENDING a lot of time with her." Elaine plopped a scoop of scrambled eggs on her plate.

Martha sat back in her chair. "Is it a problem? I wasn't aware I had to clear with you who I spent my time with."

Elaine forked a bite of egg into her mouth, avoiding Martha's gaze.

Martha sighed. It was easier when Elaine was angry than when she pulled in and remained silent. She drank her tea and waited.

"I'm only thinking of you." Elaine finished half of her eggs before she spoke. "She's trouble. I can sense it."

Martha pursed her lips. "What do you base your assessment on other than your jealousy? Afraid she'll give you a run for your money in the Cruel Mistress of the Year award?"

Elaine narrowed her eyes. "How would you know what she's like as a Mistress?"

Martha shifted in her seat. "I've observed her." She took a sip of tea, willing herself to be calm and not give Elaine any information to use against her. "If she is going to work here after the Onyx closes, then we need to know how she is, how to market her services to guests."

"Work here? When was I consulted about this? I own half of this business after all." Elaine pushed her plate away, spilling what was left of her eggs.

Martha twisted her napkin, her anger rising. "I spoke to you about it when I returned from the Onyx, not that you listened to me. It is part of my obligation to Madame. I promised to provide a place for Lucia to live and work if she chooses to stay. She inherits most of Madame's estate. She won't have to work if she doesn't want to, but if she chooses she will have a place to live and work here."

Elaine pressed her lips together in a thin line. "I suppose my wishes don't matter? It's all about you. And your obligation." She snorted. "I don't understand you, and why you ever committed yourself to her."

Martha threw her napkin down on the table. "I don't care what you think. And we are not having this discussion again." She stood up, rage and sorrow numbing her. "She'll be dead soon, and then you won't have to worry about it anymore."

Martha walked away, ignoring Elaine's voice as she called her. *What do normal families argue over? What am I going to do? I can't keep it a secret forever.*

MARTHA OPENED HER email. She clicked through the messages quickly, answering those that only took a few minutes and filing others that required a more delicate response and guest inquiries into the respective folders. On the walk to her office she had calmed down. She knew she would have to address the issue of Lucia with Elaine, but at this point she didn't believe Lucia would stay. She sensed the way Lucia always had one foot out of the door. *No commitments. She's been clear.* Martha chewed her lip. *She won't change her mind. No matter what happens. She'll leave to go back to the Onyx when Madame needs her and not come back.* She opened the email folder with guest inquiries. She sent her standard response with the guest application paperwork to the first two emails.

She opened the next email and was startled to see a full screen shot of Robin and another person in the middle of a scene. Robin was bound to a Saint Andrew's cross, facing out. The other person was holding a flogger and had her fingers buried between Robin's legs. Along with the picture was a demand for money. The body and face were blurred in the photograph. A cold sweat trickled down Martha's back. *How the hell did this happen?*

Each guest's luggage was searched on arrival, and the intake bathing experience provided the opportunity to search the guests for hidden recording devices. No one should have been able to smuggle a camera into the playrooms. She scrolled down, studying the shot. *Maybe this wasn't taken at Rowan House. Maybe this was her game all along. But why wait four months into her contract?* The email continued with screen shots of two other scenes. Robin's face was clear in both of them. Martha studied the sender's address. *Who? Time. I need time. And help.*

She wrote back: *These photos are very generic and could have been taken anywhere, why do you expect me to believe they were taken at Rowan House? Let alone pay you not to send them to the police? Provide proof these were taken at Rowan House.*

She hit send and sat back in her chair. She pulled up a spreadsheet with the guest list and worker assignments since Robin had arrived. *Millie. I need to talk to Millie. And Elaine. Fuck, I wish I had left it better with her.* She pulled out a legal pad. She isolated Robin's assignments and made a list of the clients she had been with since she had started. She studied the list of guests. All were long-time clients, none of whom would need money. *Robin? Maybe she set this up. She is the common denominator in all the photos. But why? She makes good money. She's earned some large tips, seems happy. Is it all an act? Lucia. I need to talk to Lucia. Not Elaine yet. She'll go crazy and fire her and then we won't be able to figure who is doing this.*

She turned away from her computer. *All these years and we've never had any trouble like this. What would Madame do?* She pulled out her phone and scrolled to Madame's private number. She pushed the button and waited for the call to connect.

An unfamiliar voice answered. "Madame's line."

"This is Martha MacLeod. May I speak to Madame?"

"Yes, Martha. This is Gia. Madame is resting. Is it urgent? Should I wake her?"

"No. I'll try later. Please give her my…" *Regards? Love? What the hell to say?*

Gina's voice was warm. "Your love, Miss?"

Martha wanted to climb through the phone and hug Gia. "Yes. Gia. My love."

"Very good, Miss."

Martha hung up, trying not to think about the time when she wouldn't be able to call Madame for advice. She placed her phone on her desk and went to the window and looked out at the mountains in the distance, and the land surrounding her house.

Her email alert sounded. She sat down and opened the email from the blackmailer.

Will this do? This time the photo featured Robin and Rachel, with Elaine's face clearly visible.

Martha did not respond to the email. She closed her laptop and drummed her fingers on the desk. She looked at the portraits covering the walls of her office. Rowan House had been their family home for more generations than Martha could count. *Like hell. Like bloody hell I'm going to give one penny to a blackmailer.* She clenched her jaw. *I don't know who you are, but you are about to find out why you should not mess with a MacLeod.* Martha searched her guest list. *Jaya Pomroy. Maybe she can help.* She quickly composed her message. Her hand shook as she pressed Send. She picked up her phone, stuffed it in her pocket, and went to find Lucia.

Chapter Thirteen

MARTHA KNOCKED ON Lucia's door. She held her coat over her arm, her gray fedora in her hand.

Lucia answered the door, an e-reader cradled in her palm. She raked her gaze over Martha and raised her eyebrow. "Going out?"

"Would you like to go for a walk?" Martha met her gaze. "If you're not busy?"

Lucia pursed her lips. "Well, I was about to find out who the killer is in this book, but I can wait." She stepped back into the room. "Do you mind if I bring my camera?"

"Not at all." Martha waited while Lucia gathered her gear and coat. *It will look like we went for a walk to take photos. Clever. And taking care of my reputation. Of me.*

The house was quiet. Most of the staff were occupied with their daily duties. They had almost made it out of the house when they encountered Elaine. She shifted her gaze between them, quirked her mouth, and turned away from them. Martha expected her to comment, but her silence spoke volumes. If she cared about Elaine's behavior, Lucia's face betrayed nothing. They exited the side door, skirted the stable, and walked along the trail edging the field. Martha kept their conversation to pleasantries until they were far from the house and anyone who might overhear. Martha stopped on a small rise and turned to look back in the direction they had come. Lucia held the camera up to her face and pointed the lens at Rowan House.

"I've always liked this view of the house." Martha studied the way Lucia steadied the camera before she pressed the shutter and took a few pictures.

She pulled the camera away from her face and looked at the screen on the back. "I imagine you did not whimsically decide to take me for a walk so I could photograph Rowan House from its best side." She kept her head down, studying the screen on the back of her camera. "And your eyes tell me you're worried." She pointed the camera at Martha and pressed the shutter button. "Are you going to tell me what the problem is? Or do I need to persuade you?" Lucia lowered the camera and gave Martha a half smile.

Martha met her gaze. "I received an email with some photographs and a demand for cash so they would not be sent to the police."

"Blackmail? Do people even care enough about their reputations to worry about blackmail anymore?" She held up her camera to her face and pressed the shutter again. "How positively old-school."

"The guests of Rowan House expect the utmost discretion. Even if the person who was exposed in the photographs didn't care about their reputation, it would ruin the business. And expose all of us to criminal charges." Martha chewed her lower lip.

"Would it be a bad thing?" Lucia lowered her camera and looked into Martha's eyes.

Martha opened her mouth to speak and closed it again as words failed her. She jammed her hands in her coat pocket and looked up at the sky, trying to get her anger under control before she responded to Lucia.

"What? Yes of course. I don't fancy spending time in jail or having any of my workers end up in jail either. I don't think the service we provide our clients is unnecessary, or criminal, but we do operate in an area gray enough to make us liable for prosecution."

Lucia tilted her head to the side. "I wasn't referring to the criminal charges. I was referring to Rowan House. Would it be so bad for you to not have to stress over running the house? To give up worrying 24/7 about everyone and everything? Would it be so bad to be free of your responsibilities?"

Martha focused her gaze on Lucia's face. "Rowan House is my life. My sister and I built this business, and I'm not ready to retire. I'm sorry I involved you in my problems. Forget we had this conversation. I'm sure you can find your way back to the house." She turned away from Lucia and stormed down the path toward the wood. The wind was chill, and she flipped the collar of her coat up around her neck. *Why did I think she'd care? Or help? Close Rowan House. Like hell. Fuck me. I'll call Madame later. She'll know what to do. Myfanwy. No. Don't want to worry her. Or give her a reason to attack Robin.* She kept her head down and focused on the path in front of her. The trees were bare now, and their twisted shapes cast complicated shadows ahead of her. *Alone. I am alone. And I need to get used to it. Stop feeling sorry for yourself. You're strong. You've done more with less. Always. Hold fast. That's what I have to do. No matter who is for or against me. Could she be behind this? Maybe. Maybe she wants to open her own house after the Onyx? Maybe it's her. We let her keep her photography equipment. Fuck me.*

She followed the trail to the fire ring. The long walk gave her time to sort her thoughts. Rachel had moved the firewood under the turnout shed roof in preparation for winter. The fire ring was raked and clean. *That's it. We need to clear the house. Examine every room and area.* Martha took a deep breath and squared her shoulders. "I will do what I need to do. I will fight this. Find this bastard. Hold fast. No matter what." She spoke out loud, drawing strength from the sound of her voice echoing in the empty wood.

MARTHA SAT AT her desk and went over her plans again. She wanted to have everything organized before she talked to Elaine. When she had cooled off, she realized suspecting Lucia was rude and ridiculous. She had no need for money and seemed to be impatient for the Onyx to be closed. Martha had not received a response from her would-be blackmailer. The reply from Jaya was encouraging. She believed the email originated from somewhere in the house and had even offered to come and take care of the problem herself. *Seventy-two hours since the email. Maybe Robin's working with someone on the outside. But how? How did she take the photos? Maybe Lucia's working with Robin. They seemed to have something the first night, when Lucia gave the shibari demonstration.* Martha's head ached almost as much as her heart. She'd avoided all contact with Lucia since the day she tried to talk with her about the blackmail situation. She still had not talked to Madame. Especially now she wondered about Lucia working with Robin. *No need to worry Madame.* But why? It was the why of it making her crazy.

She tossed her pen down when a sharp rap sounded at her office door. She opened her top drawer and slipped her file and notes inside. "Enter."

Lucia opened the door. She stepped into the office and closed the door behind her. "Am I disturbing you?"

"Not at the moment." Martha chewed her lip. "Did you need something?"

"I wanted to talk to you about—" she frowned at Martha "—the matter you spoke to me about the other day."

Martha sat up straighter in her chair. "It's no concern of yours."

Lucia looked down at the floor before she brought her gaze back to Martha's face. "If it affects you, it concerns me."

Martha snorted. "Since when? You've made yourself clear. Several times. You're only here out of respect for Madame. I appreciate the personal time you've graciously shared with me. But I'm clear on where you stand. Even if I could give you what you require of me, you don't want it." *Want me. Want what I want to give you.*

A flash of anger crossed Lucia's face. "You are not Rowan House. It is a business."

"It is my business. And I know the difference. Thank you." Martha stood up and walked to where Lucia stood. She was a bit taller in her boots, and she leaned close to Lucia, stopping a breath away. "No matter how I feel about you, I will not let anyone destroy what I've built." She looked into Lucia's eyes. "I will do whatever I need to do to eliminate any threat to my business." Martha touched her cheek and softened her gaze. "I'm sorry. I let myself believe you were a final gift from Madame to me. I was foolish. Forgive me." She walked away from Lucia and sat at her desk. "I've made arrangements for you to return to Lake Como. I'm sure Madame will be glad to see you. Here is your itinerary." She pushed a sheet of paper across the desk toward Lucia.

Lucia picked up the paper and tore it in half. She let the pieces fall on the desk. "I'm not one of your employees. You have no say in where I go, or what I do."

"You're right. Absolutely right. You are a guest. And your visit is over. Go wherever you like after you leave here. It is no longer my concern."

Lucia's eyes were dark as she crossed the floor and rounded Martha's desk. "Is this your idea to test me?"

"This is my idea to put my house in order. I don't know who took those photos. I am clearing the house of nonessential personnel until we get this sorted." Martha turned in her chair to face her.

"I don't work for you." Lucia's voice was harsh, her eyes full of fire.

"If I have to carry you, you are leaving this house." Martha stood up. Lucia shoved her back with both hands on her chest, catching her off-balance, and Martha sat down hard. Lucia grabbed the front of her shirt and pulled her to a fierce kiss. Martha moved her hands to Lucia's waist and gripped her hips, her anger melting into passion.

Lucia broke their kiss and leaned back. "You're wrong about Madame." She cupped Martha's face with both hands and met her gaze. "You're her gift to me." Martha gazed into Lucia's eyes. *Truth. She cares for me.*

Lucia kissed her again, softer this time. She leaned her forehead against Martha's brow. "I protect what is mine. And I'm not letting you go no matter how hard you push me away." She kissed her neck and straddled her in the chair. Martha relaxed under her touch and the comfort of her kisses. Lucia brought her mouth close to Martha's ear. "Trust me. Trust what you feel for me. Trust in us. I'm not leaving you."

"I KNOW THIS is a bit different than how we usually operate, but we are closing the house four weeks early this year. There is some extensive repair work we need to have done to the house and the dorms. Since this is normally a slow time for the house, we're having the work done now so we can start fresh in the spring."

A low murmur swelled from the group of women gathered around Martha in the ballroom. She lifted her chin and spoke loudly over the whispers of the women. "For those of you worried about your leave, we are covering your pay so instead of the usual twelve weeks of paid leave, everyone will get sixteen weeks in all. Most of the house and the dorms will be closed during the repairs and renovations, so you will need to find accommodations away from the house." The assembled group grew quiet. Martha looked around the room, studying the body language and faces of her employees. "Any questions?"

"Will we need to clean out our rooms, Ma'am?"

"No need. Make sure you take any valuables with you. We will have outside people working, and they won't be supervised. I am happy to store any items in the house safe if there is something you want to leave behind. Are there any other questions? Anything anyone is worried about?"

"What if we don't have anywhere to go?" Robin's voice sounded from the back, and the group parted as she stepped forward.

Roxy snorted. "I bet Rachel can find a place. Right between her legs." The rest of the women chuckled. Robin rolled her eyes at Roxy before she brought her gaze back to Martha's face.

Martha ignored Roxy. She tilted her head and met Robin's gaze. "Please see me in my office later and we will discuss it. Anyone else have an issue with sixteen weeks paid vacation?"

"Hell no, Ma'am." Raucous laughter filled the room, lifting Martha's spirits.

"If there are no more questions, see Millie to make arrangements for your transportation. As always please leave us a copy of your itinerary and call the main number if you have any difficulties."

The women filed out quickly in groups of two and three. Robin hung back. Myfanwy lifted her hand and waved at Martha before she shifted her gaze to Robin then to the door leading to the viewing gallery. Martha inclined her head in confirmation, and Myfanwy left her alone with Robin.

Robin walked over to Martha. "Could we talk now? I don't have anywhere to go." She frowned at Martha. "I don't want to stay in a hotel by myself for four months." She crossed her arms and wrapped them around herself.

Martha studied her face, looking for signs of subterfuge. Lucia's words about Robin liking the house because it was safe came back to her. Gone was the brassy woman she had bedded. In front of her stood a frightened, unsure woman.

"A few others are staying. Mistress Lucia will be staying. Myfanwy is staying to help Mistress Elaine in the kitchen. Rachel will be here to care for the horses." A flash of fear traveled over Robin's eyes before she smoothed her features, and Martha noted it. "I'm sure Mistress Elaine would be happy for more help in the kitchen."

"Thank you, Ma'am."

"We'll have to move you to the main house."

Robin's eyes went wide. "Why can't I stay in my room?" Her knuckles were white where she gripped her arms.

Martha kept her tone neutral. "We need to have the dorms vacant while the work is being done."

"Very good, Ma'am." Robin pressed her lips together in a thin line. "Can I ask a favor, Ma'am? If it's not too much. Do you have an interior room? One without windows?"

Martha raised her eyebrows. "I'm sure we can find something to meet your needs."

Robin's smile did not reach her eyes. "Thank you, Ma'am. Excuse me, Ma'am.

"Certainly." She watched as Robin left the room, her steps quick, her hands clenched by her side.

Angry? Scared? Acting? Martha waited until she was sure Robin had disappeared from the hallway.

"She's gone. What do you think?"

Myfanwy looked down from the viewing gallery above the ballroom. "She's frightened and angry, Mistress. A puzzle. She's odd about her room. She asked for a room without windows when she first arrived. She's not let anyone in to clean, or for other activities since she's been here. Says she likes to do her own cleaning. She was furious when she left, even if she tried to pull it off that she wasn't."

"My thoughts too."

"Do you think it's her?"

"I don't know, but we're going to find out. Come down, let's go talk to Elaine."

Chapter Fourteen

ELAINE TURNED THE oven on before she paced the small kitchen. "I don't see why I can't make her talk."

Martha raised her eyebrow. "Because information gained through torture and intimidation might not be true. And it's illegal."

Elaine tilted her head and smirked at Martha. "Hello. We run a brothel. Now you're worried about legality?"

Martha snorted. "We run an exclusive all-inclusive private resort."

Myfanwy placed a cup of tea in front of Martha and set a tin of biscuits on the table. "Tea, Cook?"

Elaine sat down. "Yes. Please." She pulled the tin near to her and opened it. The papers crackled as she fished around in the box and selected a biscuit. "We should have let her go when I wanted to." She bit into her biscuit.

"We don't know if it is her." Martha took a sip of her tea. "Or if she's acting alone."

"She's in all the photos." Color rose in Elaine's cheeks. "All these years and we've never had anything like this happen."

"Technology has changed since we opened. Ten years ago, all we had to do was to not allow phones. Now we're not safe even with the rules we have."

Elaine finished her biscuit and started on another one.

Myfanwy bought Elaine her tea and sat down. She sniffed the air a few times. "Is there something in the oven, Cook?"

Elaine shook her head. "No. I'm preheating it to roast tonight's veg."

Myfanwy frowned. "It smells like something's burning."

Elaine tossed the last bit of her biscuit on to the table. She glared at Myfanwy. "I don't smell anything."

Martha raised her eyebrow and inclined her head toward Myfanwy.

"I'll check the temperature." Myfanwy pushed back her chair.

Elaine stood up. "I'll check it if it will make you shut up about it."

She stalked over to the oven and snatched the door open. A wall of flame shot out. Martha shoved away from the table. Elaine's jacket caught fire. Martha tackled her and rolled Elaine around on the floor. She beat at the flames with her hands until they were out. Myfanwy stepped over Martha's splayed legs. She gripped a small fire extinguisher. After yanking the pin and tossing it aside, she aimed the stream of foam at the base of the fire. The flames died back, and she advanced, spraying the blaze, sweeping the bottle from side to side.

"The gas. Martha. Turn off the gas." Elaine's hand trembled as she pointed at the valve on the wall opposite the stove. Martha pushed herself up off the floor and ran to it. She pushed the lever to shut it off. Myfanwy kicked the oven door closed with her foot.

Elaine sat up. Her eyes were glassy. The sleeve of her coat was charred. Martha dialed the number for the fire department and an ambulance.

Myfanwy knelt next to Elaine with her arm around her. Martha could hear the soft soothing tone of her voice. The flames were extinguished, but the oven was still smoking. "We need to get out of here."

Elaine turned her head and looked up into Martha's face. "I can walk."

Myfanwy helped Elaine to her feet. "We'll go out the side door. Let's take her out front to meet the ambulance." She nodded at Martha's hands. "And get you checked out as well."

"I'm fine."

Myfanwy raised an eyebrow, and Martha fell in behind them. *Not an accident. The smoke detectors didn't sound an alarm. Elaine keeps her ovens pristine. No way it was a spontaneous grease fire.*

"IF IT'S NOT the two of them, who is it? Open your eyes." Elaine scowled at Martha. "If you and Myfanwy hadn't been there, who knows what would have happened." She looked down, avoiding Martha's eyes. "I can't smell anything anymore." Her chin was on her chest. "The whole damn thing could have gone up, and I wouldn't have known it."

Martha's heart ached as she heard the pain in her sister's voice. "The smoke alarms would have gone off if they hadn't been tampered with."

Elaine barked out a bitter laugh. "Smoke alarms should not be used as cooking timers."

"And you are changing the subject. We're the only people in the house. You didn't do it. Myfanwy didn't do it. And I sure as hell didn't do it. It only leaves Robin and Lucia."

"And Millie and Rachel, and everyone else. The staff has only been gone for two days. You said you hadn't used the oven for over a week. Disabling the smoke alarms and leaving a pan of grease could have been done before anyone left." Martha tapped her finger on the table top, punctuating her point.

"General sabotage? To what end? It was directed at me." Elaine took a sip of her water.

"Or one of your staff. Why does it have to be about you?" Martha stood up and stretched.

Elaine shifted in her seat. The loose gauze covering the burns on her arm was discolored. "I need to change this dressing. Can you help me?"

"Of course. Do you have the antibiotic ointment?"

"I think Myfanwy left it in the bathroom. She helped me this morning. How's she doing in the kitchen?"

Martha found the ointment in the bathroom next to a box of bandaging supplies. "What else do I need to bring?"

"Bring the whole box. And a towel. Bring the pain medicine too."

Martha placed the box and bottle of pills on the table and spread the towel out. "She and Robin are going down your list. The new oven should be here next week. I'm having sprinklers installed as well. I should have done it after the fire with Bridget."

Elaine pursed her lips. "That one." She placed her arm in the center of the towel.

Martha waited for the gut clench, a regular occurrence whenever Elaine brought up Bridget and she would automatically think of Octavia, but for the first time since Octavia had left she didn't. No pang of regret or moment of sadness. Peace. At last. Or at least what passed for it.

She picked up the bandage scissors and cut the tape holding the gauze. She unwound the dressing slowly, stopping every time Elaine flinched, and sucked in her breath when a bit of the gauze stuck.

"For fuck's sake, we will be here all day if you stop every time I make a little noise." Elaine frowned at Martha. "Get it over with."

"No wonder the nurses were so happy when I came to collect you." She finished unwrapping the burn. Her stomach roiled when she looked at the wound covering the lower half of Elaine's arm. Martha swallowed hard and blew out a breath. "Thank God your jacket took the worst of it."

"How's your hand?" Elaine glanced at the reddened area on the back of Martha's hand.

"Healing. It's annoying more than anything else." Martha changed the dressing, following Elaine's instructions, and took her time as she applied the fresh bandage. "Are you sure you don't want me to call Roxy? I'm sure she'd come back to help you."

"No. She was excited to have the extra time with her niece and the new baby. I'm fine." The color had gone from Elaine's face. Her hand shook as she picked up her water glass to take her pills. She grimaced as she moved her arm off the table.

"You need to rest." Martha expected a fight, but Elaine nodded. Martha helped her to her bed and arranged a pillow to rest her arm on before she tucked Elaine in. She placed Elaine's phone on the table. "I've got to do some work. Call me if you need me."

"Thank you." Elaine caught Martha's hand as she turned to go. "For everything. It would have been worse if you hadn't put the fire out as quick as you did."

Martha smiled at her. "It's what big sisters are supposed to do." She squeezed her hand and let go of it before she turned off the bedside light.

Elaine closed her eyes, and Martha waited a few minutes to make sure she was asleep before she left.

"I KNOW ELAINE is in pain right now, but I will not be spoken to the way she has been talking to me. She all but accused me of trying to kill her." Lucia shoved her arm in her jacket sleeve.

"I'm sorry, I'll speak to her." Martha rolled the brim of her fedora in her hand. "I know it wasn't you."

Lucia opened the door and stepped out, and Martha followed her. They didn't speak as they crossed the yard to pass by the stables.

Rachel passed by them, rolling a barrow of muck. "Morning, ladies," she called.

"Good morning," Martha answered.

Rachel dumped her load and rested the barrow. "You feeling better, Ma'am? Is Cook okay? It was lucky you were there."

"I'm fine. And Elaine is getting better every day." Martha adjusted the brim of her fedora and turned to go.

"Ma'am?"

Martha turned back to Rachel.

Rachel glanced at the barn. "I reviewed the fire plan for the barn. If you have time later, would you go over it?"

"Certainly, Rachel. I'll do it this afternoon. Come to my office at three."

"I'll be there, Ma'am." She took up the wheelbarrow and started whistling on her way back to the barn.

Lucia kept her hands in her jacket pockets. Martha did not miss the angry set of her shoulders. They walked in silence. The wind picked up as they rounded the pond, and Martha pushed her fist deep in her pocket, wincing when the tender spot on her hand brushed against her coat.

"It's sore still?" Lucia's voice broke through Martha's thoughts.

"A bit. Nothing like what Elaine is going through."

Lucia looped her arm through Martha's and held on to her. "Do you think the blackmail and the fire are connected?"

"Don't you?" Martha leaned into Lucia's body as they walked side by side, hips touching occasionally. "It seems like someone wants to destroy Rowan House one way or another." They arrived at the trailhead, the rise providing a stunning view of Rowan House.

"Sex work and employing sex workers is tricky. Some believe it's never voluntary, that it always begs the question, are the workers truly free or are they being exploited? It's never simple to run a house." Lucia squeezed her fingers around Martha's arm.

"I'm not a pimp." Martha pulled her arm free from Lucia's grasp. "I've never forced anyone to work here."

"I didn't say you did. But you do offer bonus pay for them compromising their physical and emotional safety. And you control their access to communication and transportation." Lucia's tone was neutral. She met Martha's gaze. "I've been on both sides. I don't regret what I've been and done, but I don't want to do it anymore."

Martha flushed. Lucia's words stung. "I've tried to be fair."

"I know you have." Lucia's gaze was steady, her voice kind. "I know you model your house after the Onyx, and the option of play without a safe word makes your house unique. But I can't condone it, nor work anywhere the workers don't have a say in how the house is run."

A flash of anger and overwhelming sadness filled Martha. *She's going to leave. She won't return after she leaves to attend Madame. She said I was a gift. But she doesn't have to accept a gift. She doesn't want what she could have here. Doesn't want me.* "How would you propose to run a house?" *Maybe Elaine was right. Maybe she wants to run her own house and wants to shut down the competition.* Martha met Lucia's gaze. "Is it what you'll do? After Madame..." She hated saying it, saying Madame would die, hated thinking about it.

Lucia frowned at Martha. "No. I don't know what I'm going to do. I'm uncertain. I've never been free to make my own plans. The time I've spent here is the closest I've been to being free since I committed to Madame."

"If you hate it so much, why haven't asked to be free? Asked her for your freedom?"

Lucia pressed her lips in a thin line. A wave of sadness crossed her face. "I don't think I can explain to you why it would be wrong for me to ask." Unshed tears filled her eyes. "I know she would say yes, and that would be worse than her saying no. I don't want to not belong to her. I wanted us to be equal. For her to respect the part of me that wanted to have her. I wanted her to give me what I gave her. She loves me. But not all of me."

Memories of screaming fights with Octavia, the hurt in her eyes, the silences, were worse than her begging Martha not go to the Onyx, to give to Octavia what she grew to need and wanted from Martha. She looked down and away from Lucia's face, convicted in her heart by Lucia's speech. At a loss for words she kept her focus fixed on the tops of her boots.

Lucia broke the silence. "I got a letter from Madame. She wants me to return by the end of next week."

Martha looked up and met Lucia's gaze. She tried to hide her sadness, the tender expression on Lucia's face letting her know she had failed.

Lucia reached out and touched her cheek. Martha grabbed her hand and brought her fingers to her lips and kissed them. She swallowed hard, struggling to keep her voice even. "Tell Millie what you need; she's at your disposal." She let go of Lucia's hand and straightened her shoulders. *Get it together. You knew it was coming. Keep it together.*

"Don't." Lucia gripped Martha's shoulders.

"What?"

"Don't shut me out. Don't act like I've already left." She pulled Martha close and pressed a kiss to her mouth. "Please."

She's been leaving since she got here. Had one foot out the door. I am a fool. Get it together. Madame needs her. She must be ready. Ask to go with her. You can't leave the house now. Don't ask. She needs this time with Madame. They need to make their peace. "I'm fine. I knew what I was getting into from the first time we were together." Martha moved out of her embrace. "Have I shown you the glen? You should see it before you go."

Lucia smoothed her features. "I'd like to see it with you."

She took Lucia's hand, and they walked toward the glen, each lost in their own thoughts, the silence between them heavy and thick with unspoken dreams and desires.

MARTHA STOMACH'S CLENCHED when she saw the email from the blackmailer come up in her feed. She clicked it open.

I'm growing impatient. I don't think you know who you are dealing with. This will be sent to the authorities in forty-eight hours if you don't transfer the funds. Because you've tested my patience I'm doubling my demand. I thought you might enjoy this. I must say the new addition is marvelous. Ta.

Martha tapped the video attachment, and it started to play. Lucia's voice was clear, and Martha's face came into focus. She shut it off. The video was of the first night she and Myfanwy were with Lucia. Bile filled her mouth. She rushed to the bathroom and vomited her breakfast.

What the hell am I going to do? It has to be Lucia. Who else had access to recording equipment and would be in her room? Fuck. Why? Why? Maybe she's crazy. She wiped the back of her mouth with her hand and closed the lid and flushed. The stench of her vomit set her stomach off again, and she swallowed the bitter taste in her mouth. She opened the bathroom window, the icy fresh air welcome on her face. Martha leaned her head on the sill until her stomach settled. She rinsed her mouth and brushed her teeth. Her head ached. *Fuck. Elaine was right. How to catch her? Do I want to? Why would she do this? Got to talk to Elaine.*

She changed her shirt and paced her room. *Why does she want money? Maybe she doesn't know Madame is leaving her most of her estate. Maybe she's afraid she'll be broke again. Or maybe she hates everyone who does sex work. No, hates pimps. She sees me as a pimp. Am I? Maybe she's right about the safe word. Elaine. I need to talk to Elaine. And Myfanwy.*

ELAINE DID NOT suppress the smug look on her face. "Now you're not dazzled by her body, you've come to your senses. I knew she was trouble."

Martha rested her head in her hands. "Spare me the lecture. We need to have our shit together when we confront her."

Elaine drummed her fingers on the table. "If my arm was better, I know how I would want to handle it."

Martha snorted. "Flogging is not the answer to everything. I just want to know why. I have put a call in to the security specialist who stayed here a few years ago. I need to know how she did it. I was in the room. I would have noticed video equipment."

"Where's Myfanwy? She was there too. Does she know about this video?"

Martha flushed. "No. I hadn't told her yet."

Elaine pursed her lips. "I told her to come to us after she finished cleaning the kitchen. She's so paranoid now she checks behind everyone. It makes Robin crazy. Or should I say crazier."

Martha frowned. "Crazier?"

"She insisted on the room under the stairs. The one we used for seclusion before we got the pit outfitted."

"Myfanwy said she had a thing about windows."

Elaine raised her eyebrows. "And she won't eat anything she hasn't fixed herself."

"Has she always been so odd?" Martha frowned.

"No. I don't know. She could have hidden it before. I don't pay attention to who eats what at staff dinner, or if people even show up."

A tap and the door opened. Myfanwy entered, a frown on her face. "Sorry I'm late, Ma'am, Cook. I went to check on Mistress Lucia."

Martha sat up straighter in her chair.

"She didn't call for breakfast or lunch. I knocked on her door and she didn't answer." Myfanwy rested her hand on the doorframe.

Elaine looked at Martha. "She wasn't at dinner last night. Do you think she's left?"

"Millie would have told us if she had requested to use the car." Martha stood up and dug her passkey from her pocket. "Let's go see if she's gone."

Myfanwy bustled out the door ahead of them. Martha nibbled her lip. "Why wouldn't she answer the door?"

"Maybe she knows you've figured it out." Elaine walked close to Martha in the hall.

"Figured what out, Ma'am, if it is okay for me to ask?" Myfanwy stopped and turned to stare at Martha and Elaine.

"She's behind the blackmail." Elaine's voice rose in pitch.

Myfanwy frowned and shifted her gaze to Martha. "Is it true, Ma'am?"

"We don't have proof. Something my sister likes to forget."

"Who else could have made the video?"

"Video?" Myfanwy met Martha's gaze.

"Of the night. The night we were all together."

Myfanwy moved her hand to cover her mouth. "It's my fault. I bought you to her."

Martha reached out and clasped Myfanwy's hand. "It's not your fault. Don't blame yourself." Martha leaned in and kissed Myfanwy's cheek.

"I hate to interrupt a tender moment, but we have a criminal to apprehend." Elaine quirked her mouth at them.

Martha held on to Myfanwy's hand, and they crossed the center stairs to Martha's side of the house. They stopped outside Lucia's door.

Before Martha could stop her, Elaine pounded on the door with her good arm. "Come out of there. No use hiding from us."

Martha stepped in front of Martha and held up the passkey. "So much for surprising her." She used the key and opened the door. The room was empty.

Myfanwy stepped around Martha. She opened the bathroom door. "She's not in here."

Elaine opened the drawers of the dresser. "Her clothes are here."

Martha opened the closet. She picked up her handbag and looked through it. "She might have left without her clothes, but she wouldn't have left this behind. Her passport and wallet are still here."

Myfanwy came and stood next to Martha. "Her personal things are in the bathroom, Ma'am." She crossed her arms. "She wouldn't have left with nothing. Her glasses are by the bed."

Elaine pressed lips in a thin line. "Maybe she's not working alone. Maybe whoever she's working with wanted her gone."

Martha's pulse sped up. "Call the others. We need to find her. Myfanwy, have Robin and Rachel check the grounds outside. You and Millie check the lower house. Elaine and I will check all of the rooms on both sides of the upper level of the house." She handed Myfanwy her phone. "Call if you find her. Meet us in the ballroom in an hour."

Myfanwy left to carry out her instructions.

Elaine waited until she was gone. "Let's search the room while she's gone. Maybe I was wrong."

THEY SEARCHED EVERYWHERE in Lucia's room for a hidden camera and came up empty. They moved down the hall, checking each room and locking them after they left. Anxiety rose in Martha with each room they cleared. They finished their search and went to the ballroom to meet the others. They arrived before the rest of the group.

Martha noticed how drawn Elaine looked. "You need to rest."

"I'm fine. We need to check the playrooms and the dungeon." Elaine met Martha's gaze. "I know I've been hard on her, but if she's in danger, or hurt, we need to find her."

Martha pulled a folding chair over. "Sit down while we wait for the others."

"We need to check the lower-level playrooms and the dungeon."

"Why? You and I are the only one with keys to the dungeon." Elaine patted her pocket.

"With what has gone on, I'm not taking anything for granted." Elaine's face was pale.

Martha rested her hand on her shoulder. "Why don't you wait for the others? I'll go check the playrooms and the dungeon. If I find her, I'll bring her back here."

"Okay." Elaine leaned back in the chair. "Be careful."

Martha hurried down the stairs to the lower level. She checked the playrooms. They were empty. She opened the door to the dungeon and turned on the lights. Everything was in place. *The video monitors.* She pressed the button, and the tapestry moved to reveal the video screens. She turned them on. The pit was empty. She leaned her head against the wall. *Where are you, Lucia? Where did you go? And why? Did you plan this? Are you hiding?*

She turned off the monitors and pressed the button, and the tapestry slid back into place. She returned to Elaine. She could hear Myfanwy's voice and the rest of the group talking excitedly as she approached. Hope filled her chest.

She entered and the room fell silent. "Out with it. You are as subtle as a red dress."

Elaine held out a pile of clothes. "They found these by the pond."

Martha frowned. "And?"

Myfanwy looked at her. "Footprints, Ma'am."

Martha took the pile of clothes from Elaine. The blue shirt Lucia had worn on their last walk was on top of the pile and a pair of trousers she recognized as Lucia's. *No shoes? She wouldn't have walked out barefoot. Not willingly.*

"We walked by the pond the day before yesterday. It doesn't mean anything." Martha refused to let herself think of what else it could mean.

"We've searched everywhere, Ma'am." Robin's voice was soft. She looked up and met Martha's gaze. "Maybe we should call the police."

Martha tilted her head at Robin. "Maybe. Thank you all. Return to your work."

The others filed out of the room. Myfanwy gave Martha a glance over her shoulder as she left. Martha clutched the clothes to her chest and inhaled. The faint smell of Lucia's perfume clung to them, and she closed her eyes against the fear welling up inside her.

Elaine tapped her shoulder. "It doesn't mean she's at the bottom of the pond. Check out these clothes." She turned the edge of the waistband of the pants. A dry cleaning label was pinned inside. "Who wears clothes with the dry cleaning tabs in them? No coat. No shoes. It's freezing cold outside. Whoever took her wants us to think she's at the bottom of the pond."

"I thought the same about the shoes. But she could have been forced out, and then..." Martha swallowed on a dry throat.

Elaine fished her phone out of her pocket. She thumbed it on. "Didn't you let her keep her phone?"

"Yes."

"I didn't see it in her room, did you?"

"No. I didn't." Excitement built in Martha's chest.

"Did you add her to the tracking app?

"Yes. Just like everyone else."

Elaine turned the phone so Martha could see it. A green dot flashed on the screen. "Let's go."

Martha had to stop herself from running down the hall. She dropped the key to the dungeon twice before she got it in the lock.

Elaine held the phone out in front of her and stared at the screen. "She's here. Or at least her phone is." She climbed the dais and sat down.

"I checked everywhere when I was here." Martha bustled around the room, moving the furniture and looking for Lucia's phone.

"The pit?"

"I checked the cameras. It was empty."

Elaine narrowed her eyes. "Someone is tech savvy enough to film you without you knowing it, and send you untraceable emails, most likely from inside this house. Who says they can't fuck with the observation cameras?"

Martha pushed back the rug over the door to the pit. Elaine pressed the button, and the trap slid back. Elaine activated the second button that lit it up, and the ladder emerged from the wall.

"Lucia!" Martha rushed down the ladder, sliding the last few feet. Lucia lay on her side, her hands and feet bound. Large, noise-canceling headphones covered her ears, a ball gag distended her mouth, and a thick black blindfold covered her eyes. Bile rose in Martha's throat as she took in the stillness of Lucia's body. She touched the side of her neck, feeling for a pulse. Lucia thrashed and screamed around the ball gag in her mouth. Relief flooded Martha, and she snatched the headphones off her ears.

"It's me. Lucia. You're safe. It's me." Martha tore off the blindfold and helped Lucia sit up. She looked into her eyes. The fear and pain etched on her face made her want to cry.

She pulled her handkerchief from her pocket and unfastened the ball gag. She wiped the drool off Lucia's face.

Lucia sobbed quietly while Martha tugged at the ropes around her wrists. "I can't get these untied." Another sob shook Lucia's shoulders. Elaine had come down from the dais and looked down at them over the edge of the pit.

Martha glanced up at her sister. "Find something to cut the ropes."

Elaine disappeared from view.

Lucia's sobs had slowed. Martha held her and rubbed her shoulders. Elaine's head appeared at the edge of the pit. "I can't climb down. I'm going to drop it."

Martha sheltered Lucia with her body. Elaine dropped a knife into the pit. It clattered on the stone, landing well away from them. Martha cut through the ropes holding Lucia's hands and feet.

Martha checked Lucia's skin and rubbed her wrists where the ropes had pressed. "Do you think you can climb?"

Lucia wrapped her arms around Martha, her embrace fierce. "I thought I was going to die. I'd climb a mountain to get out of here." Martha helped her to her feet and steadied her. "How did you find me?"

"Your phone. I added you to the surveillance program we use for all the staff phones."

Lucia leaned her forehead against Martha's chin. "We can't let them know I survived. Can you get me to my room without anyone seeing me?"

"Are you two moving in down there? I'd tell you to get a room, but you have one." Elaine's caustic voice echoed in the pit.

Martha lifted her face and yelled, "Not helpful," at Elaine using a singsong voice. She touched Lucia's shoulder. "Let's figure out details once we're out of here. You climb up first, and I'll climb behind you."

Lucia clenched her jaw and clasped the bottom rung of the ladder. She stopped and reached back to cup Martha's face with one hand. "Don't let me fall." Her arms and legs trembled, but she made steady progress. Martha stayed close, her arms framing her as Lucia climbed the rungs, making sure she was safe.

When she reached the top, Elaine assisted as much as she could with her one good arm. Lucia lay down on the rug next to the pit. She was breathing heavily.

"Who did this to you?" Elaine's face was contorted with rage. "I'll make them wish they'd never existed."

Lucia shook her head. "I don't know. I was in my room. I don't remember anything after lunch."

"Did you take lunch in your room? Who brought it to you?" Elaine narrowed her eyes.

Lucia shook her head. "I don't know. There was a knock at the door, and when I opened it, the cart was there with my lunch. I know we're short-staffed, so I didn't think anything of it."

"If they wanted you dead, why not just poison you?" Martha chewed her lip.

"Then they would have had a body to get rid of and couldn't frame you for an accidental death." Lucia closed her eyes. "I need some water."

Martha opened a cabinet behind the dais and took out a bottle of water. She opened it for Lucia and held it out to her. Lucia took a long drink.

"Go easy or you'll vomit." Elaine tugged on Lucia's sleeve.

Lucia stopped drinking. "We can't let them know I'm alive."

Martha rubbed her chin. "It will be easy to hide you from Rachel and Millie. Myfanwy and Robin have rooms in the house."

"What about your suite?" Lucia tilted her head.

"Myfanwy would wonder, but I could pass it off as concern for you and the house."

Elaine stood up. "I'll go occupy Myfanwy and Robin. I'll text you when I get to the kitchen and it's safe for you to go to your room. I'll bring up food as soon as I can."

"Get my phone back from Myfanwy."

Elaine left them. Lucia sat up.

Martha kneeled next to her and wrapped an arm around her shoulders, holding fast to what she had almost lost.

Chapter Fifteen

THEY WAITED FOR the text from Elaine before they exited the dungeon. Martha locked the door behind her. She kept her arm around Lucia's waist. *She could've died.* She hugged Lucia closer to her body. *I could've lost her. A murder arranged to look like a BDSM accident, charges, and the end of Rowan House.* When they arrived at her door, she ushered Lucia inside and locked it behind them before she flipped the bar lock, securing the room against all entry. Lucia went into the bathroom and closed the door behind her.

Martha waited until she heard the bath running. She opened the door a crack. "May I come in?"

"Yes."

Martha pushed the door open. Lucia was in the bath. Her eyes were closed, her head resting on the edge of the tub.

"May I help you?"

"If you'd like." Lucia's voice was quiet, and Martha had to strain to hear her.

Martha picked up a washcloth and soap. She kneeled beside the tub and studied Lucia's face. She dipped the cloth and soap in the water. Lucia sat up in the tub, her face a mask, devoid of emotion. Martha lathered her hands and began washing Lucia's back. Lucia flinched when she touched her.

"I'm sorry. Do you want to do it yourself?"

Lucia shook her head no. "It's okay. I'm okay."

"You are many things right now. Okay is not one of them." She rubbed Lucia's back. She set the cloth over the edge of the tub and lathered her hands. She massaged Lucia's shoulders, working to loosen the tense knots of muscles under her fingers.

Lucia wet the washcloth and wiped her face with it. "When I woke up in the pit, I was right back where Madame found me. Drugged and forced into a scene. I thought I was going to die. You know what made me the saddest about the whole thing?"

"No."

"That someone was going to use my death to hurt you. And that I wouldn't get to help Madame with her exit. I promised her. I hate to break a promise." Lucia cupped the water in her hands and let it dribble out. "Before Madame bought me—and there is no doubt in my mind that is what transpired. The men who held me wouldn't have released me unless she paid them back for their investment—I thought my life would end that way. With a client who lost control, in a scene gone wrong, or I would be sold for death porno."

Martha rubbed the nape of her neck gently. She didn't speak, waiting for Lucia to go on, knowing she needed to process what had happened to her.

"I thought I was over it once I was with Madame. I only submitted to her. I went to Japan to study *shibari* so I could have complete control of a scene. I was Madame's most in-demand Mistress." She reached back and clutched Martha's arm and pressed the side of her face to her forearm. "Right now, I want two things. Food, and you. I want you around me, next to me. I want to feel safe."

Martha pressed a kiss to the top of Lucia's head. "Let's get you out of the bath. I'm sure Elaine will be here soon with the food. She'll prepare it and bring it herself."

Lucia raised her chin. "I want to burn those clothes."

"I'll do it myself." Martha rinsed her hands in the water.

"We need to keep them until after this is over." Lucia stood up, the water rolling off her body, and stepped from the tub. The faraway look in her eye had been replaced by storms of anger. "When we catch the person or persons who did this to me, I will not be merciful."

Martha draped her in a towel and wrapped her arms around her. "I think you'll have to get in line for vengeance. Whoever is doing these things has threatened my livelihood, my family, and—" She looked into Lucia's eyes. "—and my love."

Martha gave Lucia a pair of her pajamas and her dressing gown. She turned the gas fire on, and Lucia sat in front of it to dry her hair.

A sharp rap at the door made them both startle. Lucia got up and went into the bathroom and closed the door.

Martha opened the door a crack with the bar lock in place. Elaine was there with a serving cart. Martha closed the door and opened it for her. As soon as she could, she closed the door and flipped the bar lock back in place.

"Why the bar lock?" Elaine rolled the cart to the center of the room,

"It occurred to me whoever did this has a set of keys. They had to unlock Lucia's door after they drugged her. They had to unlock the dungeon and have enough time to alter the surveillance camera feed."

Elaine pressed her lips in a thin line and handed Martha back her phone. "So it had to be someone who has had access to our keys." She pulled her key-ring from her pocket. "I don't let this out of my sight."

Martha retrieved her own key fob. "Even Millie doesn't have a key to the dungeon, and she has most of the other keys."

Lucia came out from the bathroom. She picked up a glass and poured herself some water before she lifted the lid from the covered dish and inhaled. "So someone would have needed time to take your keys and make copies of all of them?"

"No, only my passkey."

"And the dungeon key. The lock was keyed after the others." Elaine sat down.

Martha chewed her lips. "But when? And how? It's not as if we live close to any hardware stores, or key-cutting shops."

Lucia tilted her head to the side. "When Elaine was in the hospital in Portree, who was in charge of her keys?"

"I don't know. They were in the pocket of my chef jacket." She glanced at her arm. "I don't remember what happened after they pulled it off me outside."

Martha frowned. "Myfanwy and I pulled your coat off. Rachel brought cool water to pour on your arm while we waited for the ambulance. I don't know what happened to the jacket. I assumed Myfanwy took care of it."

Lucia picked up an apple and took a bite. She chewed slowly, and when she finished, she met Martha's gaze. "So the only people who would have had access to Martha's keys were Myfanwy and Rachel."

"And Robin. She was here alone with Rachel. Elaine and I rode in the ambulance. Millie followed in the car with Myfanwy."

"No one would have had time, means, or access to have keys made." Elaine drummed her fingers on the table.

"Maybe they're able to pick locks." Lucia took another bite of her apple.

"Don't you need special tools?" Martha sat down next to Lucia.

"Which you can acquire on the internet for cheap." Elaine passed a plate piled high with bread to Lucia who took a slice and bit into it while she put two more slices on her plate. "We installed the hotel bar locks because the locks are so easy to open. They're decorative rather than functional and don't offer much in the way of security."

"We've never worried about it because we screen our guests and our workers thoroughly." Martha paced the room. "Not thoroughly enough this time."

Lucia sat back in her seat. She looked at the food in front of her and to Elaine. "You were the only one who prepared this?"

Elaine met Lucia's gaze. "Yes. Except for the bread. Myfanwy made it this morning."

Lucia blew out a breath. "I'm freaking out. I can't remember what I ordered. It was most likely something they added to my food or wine when they delivered it." She moved a slice of cheese to her plate and took another apple.

Martha touched her hand. "I know I've asked you before, but do you remember anything?"

"Nothing coherent. I have disjointed visions. Nothing clear. No faces. I don't even know if it was more than one person." She folded her hands in her lap.

"It would take a very strong person to carry you down the ladder to the pit. Or you were so compromised you went willingly."

Elaine frowned. "The only people physically strong enough to go down the ladder with her over their shoulder would be Millie or Rachel. Robin is too slight, and Myfanwy's back would not allow her to lift Lucia."

Martha sat down at the table. "Millie was out most of the day yesterday running errands, and Myfanwy was in the kitchen in the morning." She took a sip of water. "And with me in the afternoon. Which leaves us Rachel and Robin unaccounted for."

"I don't know how long I was in the pit. I could have been left in my room until night. If I went willingly, you would have heard me as I passed by your room." Lucia pushed her plate away. "I was so hungry, and now I don't feel like eating."

Martha frowned. "Myfanwy and I were in my office after lunch."

Elaine sat up. "It has to be Rachel or Robin—or both of them." She pulled Martha's phone from her pocket and pushed it toward her. "How do we catch them?"

Lucia leaned closer to the table. "We keep it a secret I'm alive. We wait. My guess is they want us to call the police. They want to involve the authorities so the place will be shut down. They want to ruin Rowan House and the two of you. They will wait, figuring without food and water it will take me a few days to expire. They might even want to check to make sure before they call the police. When they were sure I was dead, they would call the police."

Martha steeple her fingers. "What do we do when the police arrive and want to search the house?"

Lucia raised her eyebrow. "I appear. And we wait for the person who reported it to freak out. Meanwhile, we are going to set up a camera in the dungeon and wait for them to check and make sure I'm dead. Since otherwise it could be explained as private play between consenting adults."

Elaine drummed her fingers on the table. "I hate waiting."

"Me too. But I think the plan is workable. As long as we keep Lucia out of sight." Martha picked up a slice of bread and buttered it.

"This has to only be between the three of us." Lucia pressed her lips in a thin line. "Not even Myfanwy or Millie can know. I know you both believe them above suspicion, but I don't trust anyone but you two."

Elaine snorted. "Well, at least you don't think I did it."

Lucia arched an eyebrow. "I'm certain if you wanted to get rid of me, you would have chosen a more direct method."

Martha looked at the fine lines at the corner of Lucia's eyes and the worn expression on her face. "No one will know but us. Elaine will prepare and bring us all our meals. We will keep up our usual routine."

Elaine tilted her head. "What if we act like we are trying to cover it up? What if we tell everyone we found her, but she is ill, and she will need to rest in her room for a few days?"

Lucia frowned. "You think they would be worried I might remember something. And we knew who was behind it."

"And they might try to kill her to keep her quiet." Martha chewed her lip. "No. I don't like your plan."

"We would set up the camera in her room. And one in the dungeon. Set a trap in both places. She would still be here with you."

Lucia spread her hands out on the table. "It would avoid involving the police. Something we all would like. It would be easy to set up cameras in my room."

Martha shifted in her seat. "I'm all for not involving the police." She reached out and clasped Lucia's hand. "I'll not leave you alone. I can set the feed for the camera for the pit to show on the computer in my office."

Lucia squeezed her hand. "Thank you. Let's wait to tell the others until we set things up in my room. And I want to get a few things."

ELAINE MADE SURE the hallway was clear, and Martha and Lucia went to her room. Martha locked the door after them. Lucia went the closet and pulled out a small carry-on, her camera bag, and her purse. She handed the purse and camera bag to Martha. Quietly she moved around the room gathering clothes. She took a few minutes in the bathroom and collected her toiletries.

Martha watched her pack. She'd wanted to ask Lucia to stay with her in her rooms since their time at The Stone Hearth and had been too afraid of rejection to ask. And now she was staying with her because someone had tried to kill Lucia. *Under my roof.* Anger burned through her for not keeping Lucia safe. For not keeping Elaine safe.

Lucia finished packing. She handed her bag and her tablet to Lucia. She turned the phone on and tapped an app. She opened it. "Watch the screen."

She moved to the desk and arranged some books and propped her phone up and turned on the camera. "Can you see the door clearly?"

The screen in front of Martha mirrored the screen on the phone. "It's dark, but you can see it."

Lucia moved to the bed and turned on the lamp. "How about now?"

"Better."

Lucia plugged the charger into the phone and left it in position. She came over and stood next to Martha and looked at the screen. "Good. Let's go."

Martha cracked the door open and checked the hall to make sure it was clear. They made it back to Martha's room. Martha placed the camera bag on the floor.

Lucia placed her overnight bag on the floor. "We should plug the tablet in too. It takes a lot to run the connection and the camera."

Martha pulled the cable up for her phone and plugged Lucia's tablet in to charge it. "Done."

Lucia fished in her purse. She brought out her butterfly knife and placed it on the nightstand. She looked up and Martha met her gaze. "Safety first."

Martha laughed. "Yes. And I feel safe with you and your shiny sharp toy. Wherever did you learn to handle it?"

Lucia smiled. "We spent a few years in the Philippines when I was a girl. It was the thing to learn to do when I was in middle school. My mother almost killed me when we traveled to Japan and they found it in my luggage." She sat on the end of the bed. "Do you ever wonder what your life would have been like if your parents were still alive? I know mine would have been so very different."

The wistful quality in her voice made Martha's heart ache for her. "We'd all put in for a different past with parents if we could, I think. But I've met enough women who are happy to be where their family couldn't find them I know it can go either way. Our parents were good to us, but they would have had strokes if they learned I was queer let alone both of us. They would have insisted we marry and carry on the name."

"You don't have to be married to have children."

Martha laughed. "True enough, but neither Elaine nor I have any desire to carry a child."

Lucia met her gaze "Or be a parent?"

"Is this a test?"

"No. I'm curious. I've often thought about it. But haven't ever been in a secure enough position to have a child. Madame was so heartbroken over her losses I never brought it up."

Martha tilted her head. "Is it what you'll do? Once she's gone?"

Lucia pursed her lips and blew out a breath. "I'm not sure. I don't want to be a single mother. It was so hard on my mom. My birth was the result of a one-night stand. She referred to him as 'the sperm donor,' never as my father."

"I don't know what they pay foreign service members, but you'll be in a much better place financially than your mother was."

"It's not the money. What if something happened to me? I wouldn't want my child to be left alone like I was."

"Having two parents is no guarantee." Martha walked over and sat next to Lucia on the bed. She picked up her hand and rubbed her thumb over her knuckles. "I promise you if you ever do decide to have a child, I'd be willing to take care of him or her if anything ever happened to you."

"I wouldn't want my child to grow up in a brothel."

Martha nodded. "I wouldn't, either. I would do whatever I needed to do to make sure your child was safe."

"And loved?" Lucia met Martha's gaze.

Martha picked up Lucia's hand and kissed her knuckles. "As I love you I would love your child."

Lucia's eyes were bright. She looked up at the ceiling before she looked to Martha's face. "You do love me, don't you?"

Martha kissed her cheek. "Yes. And you don't have to say it back."

Lucia placed her hand on Martha's chest. "Why do you think you don't deserve to hear it?"

"Because I don't want you to feel obligated. I didn't say what I said to push you. I know you aren't ready to settle down. I'll be here. If, or when you decide you want what I'm offering you."

Lucia leaned over and pressed a fierce kiss to Martha's lips. Martha gathered her in her arms and pulled her close. Her body responded to Lucia's touch, and she moaned into her kiss. Lucia shifted on the bed, and Martha lay back and pulled her over on top of her. Lucia pulled at Martha's clothes and slipped her hand under her shirt. She smoothed her palm over Martha's stomach and pushed her leg between Martha's legs. The press and rocking of her body made Martha's clit hard. Lucia shoved her hands higher and cupped Martha's breasts. The dressing gown she wore gaped open at the top. Martha brought her hands up and tugged at the tie. The robe opened, and she pushed her hands under her pajama top.

Lucia sat up, straddling her. "I want to feel you." Martha unbuttoned her shirt, and Lucia helped her get it off. She tugged at Martha's belt buckle and unfastened it. She stood next to the bed and Martha lifted her hips, and Lucia stripped off her pants and briefs. She shrugged out of the robe, letting it fall to the floor. She unbuttoned the top few buttons of the pajama top and pulled it off over her head. She shoved the bottoms down and stepped out of them. Martha scooted up in the bed. Lucia planted a kiss on the top of her foot and the inside of her calf, the top of her thigh, the curve of her breast, the hollow at the base of her throat as she made her way up Martha's body. She stretched out over Martha.

Warm skin on warm skin, the weight of Lucia pressing her down into the bed. Martha brought her hands up and cupped Lucia's ass and squeezed. The soft moan from

Lucia's throat made her ache. Lucia kissed the side of her neck and nipped her earlobe, the sharp sweet sting causing Martha to moan. Lucia rocked into her, the pressure on her clit delicious, and Martha arched into her, seeking more contact. Lucia brought her hand down between them and rubbed the pad of her finger over Martha's clit. Martha trembled at the sensation. She kissed Lucia's neck, before running her tongue over the taut muscles of her shoulder. Lucia pushed her fingers in deep and stilled her motion. Her voice in Martha's ear was soft. "What do you want, pet?" She bit down on her earlobe.

"Please, Miss. Let me taste you. Come in my mouth, Miss. Please."

Lucia kissed her, lips soft and gentle, before she nipped Martha's lip and curled her fingers over her sweet spot. Martha rocked her hips up, and a deep groan rattled her chest. The pressure of Lucia's hand on her clit and the motion of her fingers had her panting. "Oh please, Miss. I'm going to come." Martha struggled to hold back.

"You are." Lucia kept up her motions. "Now, pet, now. Give me what's mine."

And Martha broke, her body shaking, her hips rocking into Lucia's touch. Lucia drew out her pleasure, not relenting until Martha came again. She slowed her strokes and kissed Martha's eyelids, her cheek, and her mouth. Slow and sweet, the heat built between them again.

Lucia shifted her weight and rolled to the side. She cupped the back of Martha's neck and squeezed. "Now, pet, you can have what you asked for. Pleasure me." She moved her hand to the front of Martha's throat. Her fingers circled her neck, and for a moment Martha let herself imagine what it would be like to wear her collar. She looked into Lucia's eyes, holding her gaze and letting Lucia see the depth of her desire, the unfettered want, the unwavering truth of how much she wanted to belong to her. Lucia squeezed her fingers lightly before she released Martha and lay back on the bed. She spread her legs and put a hand on Martha's shoulder and pushed her into place.

Martha kneeled between her Mistress's legs. She kissed her way up Lucia's thighs, slick with desire, the salt-honey taste of her skin and scent of her want made saliva pool in Martha's mouth. She lay down and pushed her hands under Lucia's hips and brought her lips down and over the thickness of her clit. The soft groan from Lucia's mouth sent a rill of desire through her, and she needed to hear more, to have her Mistress come for her, to know she pleased her. She pushed her tongue deep.

"Fill me, pet. I need to feel you." Martha pressed her legs together, Lucia's words sending a cascade of wet heat pouring from her. She lifted her hand and thrust three fingers deep, sucking her clit and rolling her tongue up and over it. Lucia arched her hips, and Martha rocked her, her strokes even and measured. Liquid silk coated her hand, and she added another finger, pushing down, going slowly. Lucia shook and trembled under her, and she stilled her thrusts, keeping her rhythm on her clit. "Don't stop. Let me feel you. Fuck me, pet."

She pulled back and pushed deep again, and Lucia opened to her, her body welcoming Martha as she wrapped her legs around Martha's shoulders. She locked her heels over Martha's back, the weight comforting as she held her in place. Martha slow fucked her, taking her time and enjoying each soft groan and sigh as Lucia gave herself to Martha, letting her gorge herself on the sweetness between her legs. Delicate salt honey flowed from Lucia and wet her chin. Lucia's breathing shifted, and Martha focused herself, waiting until her Mistress was ready to come, edging her, her only thought the pleasure of her Mistress.

"Now, pet. Now." Lucia lifted her hips and met Martha's thrusts as she gripped Martha's head and held her in place while she came, taking all Martha had to offer. Lucia rocked on Martha's face with soft cries as she came again. She lay back and released Martha's head.

Martha eased her fingers from Lucia, and kissed and suckled her clit, before she rested her head on Lucia's thigh. *Mine. How can I want her so much? This. Her. Us.*

"Come here, pet." Lucia touched the top of Martha's head.

Martha moved up in the bed, and Lucia raised her arm and Martha curled up under her arm, resting her head on her breast. Lucia carded her fingers through Martha's hair. She stopped when her fingertips brushed over the raised scar on her scalp, a physical reminder of Martha's childhood, the accident that took her parents, a recurring nightmare. Martha's hair covered it most of the time, and unless she dreamed, she would forget it was there.

"What's this, pet?"

"A bad memory, Miss."

Lucia didn't ask, just pulled Martha tighter into her embrace.

Chapter Sixteen

MARTHA GROOMED BRUNO, sweeping the brush over the horse's flanks. The mindless motion and the quiet of the barn was soothing. The large doors were closed against the cold. A gust of wind blew in under the door and scattered a bit of sawdust in a tiny whirlwind down the center aisle. The horse's breath puffed out in a steamy cloud. Martha had managed to put the blackmailer off for another twenty-four hours. She finished brushing the horse out and patted his shoulder. She placed the saddle pad on his back then the saddle and fastened the girth. She turned around and realized she had forgotten his bridle. She smoothed her hand over his shoulder. "Behave. I'll be back."

Martha left him in the crossties and went to the tack room. One of the barn cats raised his head and looked at her from his perch atop a folded stack of horse blankets. Bruno's bridle hung on the peg was where she had left it. "I'd forget my head if it wasn't tacked on." The cat yawned and stretched and curled up to sleep.

Martha stepped out and closed the door to the tack room. The sound of boots scuffing on the floor made her glance up.

"Oh, it's you, Mistress." Rachel's tone was annoyed. She held a pitchfork in front of her, the sharp tines pointed directly at Martha's midsection.

The small hairs on the back of Martha's neck stood up. "Were you expecting someone else?" She kept her tone even and firm. "And lower the pitchfork, please, before someone gets hurt."

Rachel lowered the tool. "Sorry, Ma'am. It's just…I'm skittish. With everyone gone. I'm out here alone so much."

Bruno blew out his breath and tossed his head. Martha lifted the bridle. "I'm going out for a ride."

Rachel stepped aside to let Martha pass. "Going out alone? Is Mistress Lucia feeling better? Should I get her horse ready?"

"Some. No need." Martha buckled the bridle in place. She unfastened the halter and crossties and led Bruno out into the stable yard and to the mounting block.

"You forgot your helmet, Ma'am." Rachel held up Martha's hard hat as she walked toward her.

Martha took her helmet from Rachel. She met her gaze. "Thank you."

She tugged on her gloves, and after buckling her helmet in place she mounted Bruno. "I'll be back before lunch." She lifted her hand and waved at Rachel as Bruno trotted out of the yard.

The air was biting cold in spite of the bright sun. She kept Bruno at a fast walk along the trail through the wood. She stopped at the rise and turned him to watch Rowan House. She pulled a pair of binoculars from her pocket. The glass fogged a moment and cleared. With the advantage of Bruno's height, she had a clear overview of the house from the rise. She watched and waited. The sun on her back was warm. Bruno was impatient and shifted under her making her bobble the field glasses. "Damn it, Bruno. We'll go in a minute."

She kept her binoculars trained on the stable yard and the path leading from the house. *Maybe this is a waste of time.* After fifteen minutes she was ready to give up. She lowered the glasses and patted Bruno's withers. A flash of brightness in her peripheral vision made her raise her binoculars. Robin crossed the stable yard. She had wrapped a pashmina around her shoulders and covered her face, but Martha could tell it was her by her slight build. Robin looked around the courtyard, before she stepped onto the covered porch and the stairs leading to Rachel's bedsit over the barn. *So what? What does it prove? Nothing other than her fear of Rachel is an act. Or is it? Rachel looked ready to use the pitchfork when she saw me. Why? For Robin? Maybe Robin wants to destroy the house and is using Rachel's love for her to help her?*

Martha waited and watched until Robin left Rachel's room. Her movements across the yard were furtive. They had told the staff about Lucia in the morning. Martha had shared the news, Elaine standing behind her to watch everyone's reaction. Millie and Myfanwy had been full of questions. Robin and Rachel had kept poker faces and acted appropriately concerned. "If it is you two, heaven help both of you when I'm certain."

Martha tucked the binoculars back in her jacket. She turned Bruno's head and rode toward the wood. She chewed her lip as she went over the details of their plan. She hated leaving Lucia alone. She had woken up to Lucia sitting in the chair by the fire, her feet drawn up under her. The glow of the fire backlit her face, leaving her features in shadow. She was flipping her knife, opening and closing it, the clink and rattle of metal rhythmic. Martha had watched and waited for her to come to bed, not wanting to disturb her and only guessing at what dark thoughts passed through her mind.

Her own thoughts of vengeance scared her enough. She knew Elaine would be hard to contain; her fury was epic on a good day. The wood was quiet as she entered. The sun through the bare trees cast scattered shadows on the path in front of her. She rode past the fire circle, her mind filled with memories of Lucia and their lunch. She loved her. Not as she loved Myfanwy, not as she loved Octavia, and if she were honest, not as she loved Madame. She loved Lucia for herself. *A gift? A legacy? I promised to raise a child if something happened to her. She'll never want to live here. Another one I'll have to let go. And Myfanwy. I'm a fool for not asking her to wear my collar. Now if I ask it just looks like I'm desperate.*

She came to the edge of the wood and turned to the left, circling the wood and back toward Rowan House. Bruno tossed his head. "Too much time in your stall?"

On the verge of the field between the wood and Rowan House, she turned him home, urging him into a trot. When they got to the grassy flat, she gave him his head. "Let's go, boy."

He took off at a canter, and she pushed him to a gallop and leaned low over his neck. Lifting her hips, she moved with him, the bunch and flow of his muscles under her exhilarating. They closed the distance, and she slowed him to a trot as they neared the path. She sat and eased him into a fast walk. *Time. Time to spring this trap.*

You try my patience. I'm done waiting. If I don't have the funds in my account by noon tomorrow I will contact the authorities. Don't put me off again. I don't think you'd like jail. Then again, after watching the video maybe you would.

Ta

Martha sat back in her chair and unlocked the bottom drawer of her desk. She took out a bottle of Edradour and a glass, suppressing a twinge of guilt it was not Talisker. She poured herself two fingers of the single malt and placed the bottle on the desk. She stared down at the pistol in her drawer. Her great-grandfather's Webley, a souvenir of his time during the war. They had found it hidden in a storage room when they were renovating the house. Martha had a gunsmith restore it and had practiced with it enough she was confident in her skills.

The whiskey was warm on her tongue, the smooth burn as it went down a reminder of why she kept this particular bottle for herself.

She pulled the pistol out and placed it on her blotter before she took another sip of her drink. Martha had to get out of her chair to reach the box of ammunition tucked in the back of the drawer. Once she had retrieved it, she took out six cartridges. Her fingers trembled as she lined them up on the desk. *Will it come to this? Who is it? Will the game play out? Will I spend the rest of my life in prison or on the run?*

She sat down and loaded the pistol. She spun the cylinder slowly, making sure she had seated each cartridge before she closed it and placed it on the desk.

"Are you in there?" Elaine pushed the door open. Her gaze settled on the pistol and the glass on Martha's desk.

She closed the door behind her and turned the lock.

"You better have enough left in the bottle for me." Elaine pulled a chair closer to the desk.

Martha slid the bottle toward Elaine. "We'll have to share the glass."

"Wouldn't be the first time." Elaine refilled the glass. She lifted it in a salute to Martha before she took a long drink. "Do we have more of this?"

Martha raised her eyebrow. "Aren't you in charge of supplies?"

Elaine smirked at her. "Yes. But the last time I checked you were in charge of spirits."

Martha leaned back in her chair and looked up at the ceiling. "When this is over, I am going to take a trip to the distillery and buy as many cases as they let me have."

"I'll go with you. We'll leave Lucia in charge and take off, just us."

Martha brought her gaze back to her sister. "She's leaving. Madame needs her."

"I was just getting used to her." Elaine pursed her lips. "Will she come back?"

Martha poured herself another drink. "I don't know. Who knows if she'll have a house to come back to."

Elaine rested her fingers on the pistol. "I don't think this is the solution."

"I wasn't planning on murdering anyone. I wanted it for protection." Martha's face flushed with the whiskey.

"Is it loaded?" Elaine frowned.

"Yes." Martha leaned forward in her chair. "I think they'll try something tonight. I don't want to be caught without a weapon. What if they are desperate?"

Elaine tilted her head to the side. "I'm usually the impulsive one, but for once I'm going to be the voice of reason." She picked up the pistol and thumbed the tab to open it. She took each shell out and placed them neatly in a row on the desk before she pressed up on the barrel and closed it. "Put it away. We don't need this."

"When did you get to be so wise?" Martha opened the drawer. She tucked the pistol back in its place. She slid open the box of shells and replaced the cartridges one by one before she placed it next to the pistol. She reached for the bottle of scotch.

Elaine caught her arm. "Don't get carried away." She pried Martha's fingers off the bottle. "You're one up on me."

Martha laughed, grateful for Elaine's ability to make her laugh even as her world seemed to be on the brink of destruction.

Elaine raised the glass and finished her whiskey before pouring herself another. "When I finish this, we're going rat hunting. I have an idea. Who searched the dorms?"

"Myfanwy and Millie."

"Do you think they searched Robin's room? Or Rachel's bedsit over the stable?"

Martha frowned. "I don't know. I didn't think to ask them."

"I think I need some things. And I think Robin and Rachel are going on an errand."

"They pretend to barely stand each other. What makes you think they'll agree to go?"

Elaine smiled a sick smile. "I'm not accustomed to being refused. They'll go."

Chapter Seventeen

"MILLIE CONVINCED THEM to go?" Martha raised her eyebrows.

"They agreed before they knew what they were getting into." Elaine smoothed her hand down the front of her skirt. "Are you ready?"

Martha held up her phone and a screwdriver. "Yes."

"Did you tell Lucia what we're doing?"

"Yes. That's what the phone is for. She'll join us virtually."

Elaine led the way, and they started with Robin's room. Martha turned her passkey and they entered. The room was spotless, the overwhelming smell of bleach distinct. Martha called Lucia and set up FaceTime. Lucia's face filled the screen.

"Too bad it's not smell-a-vision." Elaine grimaced. "Let's make this quick."

They flipped the mattress, opened drawers, the small chest, and searched the shelves.

"Nothing."

Martha opened one of the books on the bookshelf and shook it. Two scraps of paper fell to the floor. A bank deposit slip and a bit of paper with drawings on it. She stuck the deposit slip in her pocket and handed the drawing to Elaine. "Do you know what this is?"

"Martha, show me what you have. I had to look away; it was like the *Blair Witch Project* when you were searching."

Elaine held the paper in front of the phone.

"It's a schematic, and I'm guessing a direction on how to rewire the cameras in the dungeon. Have you found anything else?"

"A deposit slip. Nothing else." Elaine blew out a breath. "This paper doesn't prove anything."

"I'll call you when I get to Rachel's room." Martha thumbed off the phone. "One down."

Elaine wrinkled her nose. "Let's hope Rachel does not have a similar thing for bleach."

They hurried across the yard and took the back stairs up to Rachel's room over the stable. Martha's gut churned as she thought of the times she'd walked up the stairs to Octavia's room. *So many memories. Good and bad.* She missed a step and barked her shin. "Fuck."

Elaine turned around on the stairs. "So much for stealth mode."

Martha rubbed her shin. "It's why we sent them away."

"Is it bad?"

"I've had worse." She scooted past Elaine on the landing. The door swung open on well-oiled hinges.

"How the hell did she do this?" Three notebook computers and several routers were arranged around the room.

"Seems a bit much for a hobby." Elaine pursed her lips. "The day you went for a ride I wanted to come up here and she put me off."

Martha put her finger to her lips and motioned to the door. Elaine backed out and Martha followed her. They crept down the stairs, not talking until they were outside the barn.

"What was that about?" Elaine frowned at her.

"What if she had the room set up like we have Lucia's room?"

Elaine pressed her lips in a thin line. "This is ridiculous. And we need to end it."

Martha looped her arm through Elaine's. "I think you're right. Let's go talk to Lucia."

"I WAS WAITING for you to call me." Lucia had her hands planted on her hips.

"Rachel's room was like some crazy hacker's den. At least three computers." Martha handed Lucia the paper they had found. "I was worried they had the room rigged for surveillance." She sat down in the chair.

"They? Are you sure?"

Lucia examined the paper Martha had given her. "Why wouldn't Rachel have done this herself? Why have Robin do it if she's the expert?"

"It would have been suspicious. And who knows when they did it. The dungeon has not been used in six months." Elaine poured a glass of water and took a sip.

Martha drummed her fingers on the table. "So it could have been anyone, and they choose Lucia? Gods, it would have ended us if it had been an outside guest."

Lucia blew out a breath. "And possibly the end of the guest."

"So what do we do now? Jump them when they get home?" Elaine placed both hands on top of the table.

"Easy, killer." Lucia cocked an eyebrow at Elaine. "Homicide is a hard limit for me."

Martha gnawed on her lip. "We confront them."

"With what evidence?" Elaine tapped her finger on the table. "We still don't know how they managed to get Lucia into the pit."

"They may think we're bluffing. It's been three days. Maybe they just wanted to have the cops find her in bad shape to expose us, or maybe they think we'll pay and then they'll just take off." Martha leaned back in her chair and looked up at the ceiling.

Lucia came and stood with her hands on Martha's shoulders. "Let's spring the trap. Tell them the two of you are leaving for an overnight trip and I'm in charge."

"You think they'll think we're leaving the country? Running away?" Elaine frowned. "Not even Robin and Rachel would believe we ran away."

"What if we have a big row and let them hear it? Have it be so it seems we are arguing about how long we can keep it quiet about Lucia's disappearance?" Martha rested her hand on top of Lucia's.

Elaine laughed. "Everyone would believe we disagreed. But we need to have the argument where at least Robin will hear it, or Rachel. Other than this car trip they avoid each other."

Lucia pursed her lips. "I think her hate and fear is real. I think maybe Rachel has forced Robin into this."

A smidgen of jealousy bubbled up in Martha's soul. She forced herself to keep her voice even. "Are you protecting her? Do you have feelings for her?"

Lucia squeezed her shoulder hard. "I have feelings for anyone who has been unsafe in their work. She's been abused. She's here because she thought she was safe. Which one did you hire first?"

"Rachel."

"Did she apply, or was she recommended?" Lucia sat down next to Martha and held her gaze.

"She was recommended."

"By who?" Elaine sat forward her lips in a thin line.

"The woman we met at the Hartpury Festival."

Lucia sat up straighter in her chair. "Who had she worked for before?"

Martha turned her palms up. "I don't have her application memorized."

"Lucia, what are you thinking?" Elaine took another sip of her water.

"Maybe this was longer in the making than we think." Lucia touched Martha's arm. "Can you find their employment applications?"

"Give me fifteen minutes." She left Lucia and Elaine together, heads almost touching as they talked rapidly with each other.

Chapter Eighteen

MARTHA PLACED THE tabbed file folders with Robin and Rachel's applications on the table.

Lucia touched the top file. "May I?"

"Please. And tell me what you are looking for?"

Lucia passed her finger over the application as she scanned it. "Where are the references listed?"

"Third page. Halfway down."

Lucia opened the papers and flipped so the list showed. She opened Robin's and did the same thing. "Did you notice this when you hired Robin? They have the exact same references listed."

Martha felt the heat rise in her face. "No. I was..."

"Feeling sorry for herself and not paying attention to fuck all." Elaine spoke over Martha.

"Fuck you, Elaine, you didn't notice either." Martha glared at her sister.

A half smile crossed Lucia's face. "Under the circumstances—" she shifted her gaze to each of their faces in turn "—there is no time for sibling squabbles."

Martha pursed her lips. "So I let them in. It's my fault."

Elaine reached out and touched her sister's hand. "I didn't notice either. Not your fault we missed it.

"Their background checks?" Lucia continued to sort through their files methodically, removing pages out and laying them next to each other.

"Last tab."

Lucia's face grew somber. "There you are. Rat bastard." She bought her gaze to Lucia's face. "How long have you used this company?'

"We just started this year. The other company we used closed." Martha's stomach churned. "Why?"

"Two years ago, Madame had a similar issue on a smaller scale. Not physical threats like the fire, or what happened to me."

Elaine raised an eyebrow. "What has that go to do with this background check company?"

Lucia tilted her head at Elaine. "Have you ever met Madame?"

"No. I have not had the pleasure." Elaine met Lucia's gaze.

"She's ruthless when it comes to eliminating threats. I didn't ask for details. What she was able to find out was the background company she used sets up blackmail operations as it vets workers. They offer them money to be their agents. The workers get the images and do the work on the ground."

"And take all the risk. So they planned this? They sent Rachel and Robin?" Martha chewed her lip.

"No. I think they tried to recruit Robin, and when she said no, they moved on to Rachel." Lucia took a sip of her water.

"But she works in the stable. How would she get images in the house?" Elaine pursed her lips. "She has to have someone inside."

"And the reason she needs Robin. I'm guessing the company gave her some information to hold over Robin's head. When you sent everyone but your driver, Myfanwy, and Robin away, it forced her hand." Lucia's gaze settled on Martha's face. "They are desperate. We need to end this."

"Tonight." Martha stood up, her anger building. "When they come back we are going to confront them, meet them as they get out of the car. I told Millie not to get back until four."

Elaine looked at the clock on the mantel. "We have just about forty-five minutes."

Lucia stood up. "Where?"

"Millie will pull into the drive by the back door. We'll wait for them in the stable yard." Martha had her hand on the doorknob. "I'm going to find Myfanwy and let her know the plan. Elaine, will you bring our friend from my office?"

Elaine frowned. "I don't like your idea."

"Friend?" Lucia raised both brows.

"She's watched *Reds* way too many times, and thinks we need to bring our pistol with us." Elaine huffed out a breath.

Lucia reached into her robe pocket and brought out her knife. She flipped it open, the soft clink and click making Martha smile as Elaine's eyes widened. "I don't know if I agree either. I prefer more personal weapons."

"Me too." Elaine smiled. "I'll tell Myfanwy to bring the large rolling pins."

Martha rolled her eyes. "If you two are finished. I need to go. Let's all meet in the kitchen at 3:45."

Chapter Nineteen

"MISTRESS, LET ME practice with the video again. I want to be sure." Myfanwy's voice was strong, but her hand trembled when she held up Lucia's phone. "I want to make sure I get every word the little bitch says."

Martha cupped her cheek and looked into her eyes. "You're going to do fine. And yes, we can practice until we have to meet them." She brushed Myfanwy's mouth with her lips and leaned her forehead against her brow. "*Cariad,* when this is over I'm going to spend an entire day showing you how much I love you."

Myfanwy gripped Martha's arm. "I going to hold you to it, Mistress." She moved her head so her lips were against Martha's ears, her words just for her, her voice a whisper fierce. "*Dw I'n care ti.*"

Martha heart squeezed hard in her chest. In all their time together, they had never said those words to each other. She hugged Myfanwy close. "*I love you too.*" They walked to the yard side by side, and Martha prepared to do what she had to protect her loves and her house.

"MYFANWY, YOU STAND here. The hedge will block them from seeing you." Lucia held Myfanwy's gaze. "They can't know they're being recorded until we want them to know."

"I understand, Miss." Myfanwy gripped the phone. "I'll keep recording from the time you raise your hand and tug your ear, until you call me, or cross your arms."

Lucia smiled at her. "Perfect."

Martha shifted on the balls of her feet and pulled her phone out to check the time. "Any minute."

Elaine stood with her hands behind her back, a ridiculously large rolling pin in one hand. Martha tried to ignore the slightly gleeful look on her face.

"You're enjoying this?" Martha suppressed her own smile.

"I'm ready to end this. And you know I love a good fight."

"We are not going to fight them. We are going to talk like civilized people," Martha reminded her.

"Unless one of them starts anything."

"Look to Rachel to start something." Lucia was off to the side of Martha where she would be out of line of vision of the car until she stepped out. "Animals are never more dangerous than when cornered."

"Where the hell are they? Millie's never late."

"Probably another damn sheep," Elaine muttered.

"Shh." Martha held her finger to her lips. The crunch of tires on gravel sent a shiver of excitement through her.

THE CAR ENTERED the drive with Millie behind the wheel. Robin was in the front seat and Rachel sat in the back. After the car stopped Robin was the first to exit, her door opening before Millie turned the engine off.

She eyed Elaine and Martha. "Hello, Cook, Ma'am." She nodded her head at them, a frown on her face.

Rachel opened the car door and exited. "Evening, Ma'am, Cook." She started for the barn, and Elaine moved to the left and cut off her exit. "I need to feed the horses, Cook." Her voice had an edge.

"They won't starve. We want to talk to you." Martha kept her tone even as she fought her own desire to grab Rachel and shake her like a rag doll. "Both of you."

Rachel shifted her feet and glanced at Robin before she looked down at her boots.

Lucia stepped out from behind the hedge. She tugged on her earlobe as if in thought. "Yes, I'd like to know how the hell you two got me down the pit."

Rachel's eyes went wide, and she clenched her hands into fists.

Robin turned and pointed at Rachel. "It was her. I didn't want to. She threatened me."

Rachel spun and lunged at Robin, grabbing her by the hair. She wrapped her thick forearm around her neck in a chokehold. "Shut up, you stupid cunt."

Robin squirmed and fought, twisting her body. Rachel pressed her arm tighter, the muscles bulging. Robin gasped and stopped fighting.

Elaine took a step toward them. "I want to know how you got all of your equipment set up in your room without us knowing.

"Raintree will expose you if you don't pay him." Spit flecked Rachel's lips. "Back off. I'll snap her neck." Martha could see the sweat on her forehead, and the fear and doubt in Rachel's eyes.

"Go ahead." Martha kept her voice calm. She took three steps toward Rachel, closing the distance between them. "It will save us the trouble." She pulled the Webley from her coat pocket and raised it to the level of Rachel's head. "Because when she breathes her last, you're next."

Robin's eyes filled with tears. She trembled in Rachel's grip. Martha pinned Rachel with her gaze, letting her see her determination and deadly intent. She didn't want to deal with the fallout from killing Rachel, but she would do what she had to in order to protect her home and family.

Robin stilled. Martha watched Rachel's eyes as her gaze shifted from right to left, looking for an exit. Elaine took a step closer, staying out of Martha's line of sight in case she had to fire the pistol. "And if Martha misses—" She moved the heavy pin from behind her back and held it across her chest like a bat. "I won't."

Rachel let go of Robin and shoved her away. She sprinted across the yard. Millie rushed to tackle her. Rachel stiff-armed her and sent her rolling in the dirt as she fled toward the garage. Millie pushed herself to her feet and ran after her.

"Stop, Millie!" Martha shouted and waved her hand. "Let her go." She placed the pistol back in her coat pocket.

The roar of an engine starting up made Millie take another step toward the garage. "She's stealing the coupe." Millie's voice took on a frenzied tone.

"And how far is she going to go? She's got only what she has on her, a tank of petrol, and it's after five now. Even if she gets to the ferry, or makes the bridge, she's going to be out of luck when her employer finds out how sloppy she's been."

Millie rested her hands on her hips. "Bloody hell." She kicked a stone down the drive.

"Myfanwy!" Lucia called out.

Myfanwy stepped from behind the hedge, a confident smile on her face. "I got it, Miss, all of it."

"Good. We will send the video along to the blackmailers. See if they like it turned around on them."

Robin's harsh sob made Martha turn to look in her direction. Lucia had come and gathered her in her arms. A wave of guilt washed over Martha when she thought about what she had said. She walked over to where they sat. She kneeled on the ground. "Robin. Eyes to me. Please."

Robin lifted her tear-stained face. The fear in her eyes made Martha regret her words. "I didn't mean what I said. I wanted her to believe it. I would never have let her hurt you."

Robin's eyes were wary. "What you said is true. He'll find her." She looked down. "And me."

"No. He won't. Not here." Elaine's voice was loud, and they all turned to stare at her. "I need a good assistant, and you've a talent in the kitchen. No more clients unless you want."

Robin kept her gaze fixed on her hands. "I don't deserve it." She turned and looked at Lucia. "I helped her hurt you."

Lucia hugged Robin's small body to her. "We've all done things we regret. You deserve another chance." She lifted Robin's chin with her finger, her gaze sharp and fixed on her eyes. "Make me proud we gave you one."

Robin stared into her eyes. "Yes, Miss."

Myfanwy came over and held out her hand to Robin. "Come on now."

Robin hesitated.

"I'm not going to hurt you. We need to put the bread in if we want to have any with dinner." Myfanwy passed the cell phone to Lucia. Robin took her hand and stood up. Myfanwy pulled a tissue from her pocket. "Wipe your face. Even if we work in the kitchen, we need to be presentable."

They left the lot, Myfanwy holding on to Robin's hand. Elaine followed after them with her rolling pin on her shoulder.

"What'd you want me to tell the police, Ma'am, about the theft?" Millie opened the door to the car. "Or do you want to call them?"

"I'll call them, Millie, thank you. Are you hurt? You took quite a tumble."

"Only my pride, Ma'am. She dumped me on my ass like I'd never stepped on a rugby pitch." She tapped the top of the car. "I'll park this, Ma'am. Do you want me to bring you the insurance records for the coupe?"

"Just put them on my desk, Millie. I'll call everyone."

"Very good, Ma'am." Millie got in and drove the car slowly around to the garage.

Lucia's hand on her arm drew Martha's attention. She leaned in and pressed a kiss to her cheek. "You were magnificent."

Martha's held Lucia's gaze. "I hated frightening Robin. Her eyes. I don't think I'll ever get it out of my head." She bit her lip.

"You did what you had to do. Rachel believed you when you said what you did." She cupped Martha's face in her hands. "So did I. You are as fierce a protector as Madame said." She kissed Martha, her lips soft and warm, the length of her body pressed against her. "How much time you think we have before dinner?"

Martha wrapped her arms around her and kissed the hollow at the base of her neck. "Enough."

Chapter Twenty

"I'LL CALL WHEN I get there." Lucia smoothed her hands over the front of Martha's shirt. "The next time I see you, you'll be in the black suit I first saw you in." She pressed her cheek against Martha's face.

Martha sensed her sorrow and heard the resignation in Lucia's voice. "I will." She rubbed Lucia's back through the sheer fabric of the gown she wore and held her tight as she kissed along her neck. "But this time I'll wear the tie you bought me the day we visited Portree."

"I'm afraid the shop owner will never get over walking in on us in the dressing room." Lucia turned her head, giving Martha access to the delicate curve of her neck and the space between her shoulder and ear.

Martha moved her hand behind Lucia's neck and cupped it. The give and surrender of Lucia's body against her own set her on fire. Holding her in place, she kissed her, softly at first, her tongue teasing her as she nibbled her lips, then deeper as if drinking from a fountain on a hot day, taking her fill of her mouth.

Lucia raised her eyes to Martha's face and kept her gaze fixed on Martha's eyes as she lowered herself to her knees. "Show me the Mistress of Rowan House. Give me something to hold on to when I'm feeling weak."

Wetness flowed from Martha as she took in Lucia's submission, the way she looked on her knees at her feet. *Mine to command. To cherish.* She gripped Lucia's curls and pulled her head back sharply. With her thumb she traced the thickness of her lip, and slowly pushed into her mouth. The low moan from Lucia brought out the beast in Martha. She reached down with her other hand and rolled Lucia's nipple, squeezing it hard. Lucia sucked on her thumb, her mouth promising delights.

Martha's breath quickened, and she pulled her thumb free. "On your feet." She gripped Lucia's nipples and tugged her forward, leading her to the heavy armchair by the fireplace. She released her and sat in the chair. "Kneel here between my legs."

Lucia sank gracefully to her knees. Martha admired the way the gown flowed and billowed around her before settling over her frame. She pressed her knees against her body, holding her in place as she teased a finger over Lucia's peaked nipple, then flicked it hard. The sharp intake of her breath made Martha smile as she remembered Lucia's challenge to her outside Madame's house. She flicked her other nipple, this time drawing a short groan. The heady scent of sandalwood and cedar mixed with Lucia's desire filled the small space between them, and Martha inhaled deeply. *Heavenly. Exquisite. My angel. Us.*

She tugged the elastic neckline down to frame Lucia's breasts before she lifted a pair of nipple clamps attached with a silver chain from the side table. Lucia's eyes were bright, and she touched her tongue to her lower lip. Martha bent her head and sucked hard, drawing Lucia's nipple deep into her mouth, and Lucia groaned. With firm fingers Martha applied the first clamp. The sharp hiss and short yelp from Lucia's lips as Martha tightened the clamp made her pulse race. She took a deep breath to steady herself before she repeated the process. Lucia's pupils were wide. The chain swung gently as she panted into the pain, and her nipples were a deep claret in the firelight. *So beautiful. Her pain. Her gift to me.*

Salvia pooled in Martha's mouth. She scraped her nail over the tip of Lucia's nipple. *Want her now. Have her now.* "Stand for me. Lift your gown to your hips, show yourself to me."

Lucia obeyed. She stood and set her feet wide, bracing them against the inside of Martha's boots. She gathered the hem of the gown and pulled it up slowly until she was bare. Her thighs glistened and the dark curls between them were wet. She trembled as Martha slid forward in the chair. With one finger she traced a line from Lucia's knee to the damp curls between her legs. She pushed through them and rubbed the pad of her finger over Lucia's clit, drawing a moan from her. "All this from a little kiss? And a bit of rough with your nipples?" Her face was even with Lucia's center. She gripped Lucia's ass with both hands and dug her fingers into the soft flesh as she took her in her mouth. She sucked her clit, savoring her taste and the way it hardened under her tongue. Lucia swayed, and Martha locked her in place, bracing her with her arms and knees as she licked her fill, driving her up and keeping her on the edge. Greedy for her, she was relentless, taking all Lucia offered.

"May I come? Please. Let me come for you." Lucia shook in Martha's arms.

Not ready to hear her surrender, relishing her desire and the taste of her, Martha pulled back. "No." She reached up and snatched the chain free. Lucia's scream as she came echoed in the room. Martha held her tight and laved her nipples with her tongue, triggering another orgasm. Lucia's breath came in short gasps. "Sorry. I couldn't hold back."

Martha pinned her with her gaze. "You're in need of some discipline." She sat back in the chair and patted her lap. "Lay down here."

Lucia's shoulders heaved as she worked to control her breathing and draped herself over Martha's lap. As tall as she was, her hands rested on the floor. "Wrap your hands around my boot. Don't let go." Martha pushed the filmy gown up and exposed Lucia's ass, and the wetness coating her thighs. The catch of Lucia's breath when Martha used her hands to spread Lucia's thighs made Martha want to shove her off her lap and bury herself in her. "So smooth. So soft. I want to see my marks on you." She focused, suppressing own desires, wanting to give Lucia the experience she deserved even as she was desperate to take what she wanted. Lucia's vulnerability and trust sent a wave of heat coursing through Martha. With a gentle touch, she slipped one finger in deep. The soft clutch of Lucia around her finger made her clit swell. "Remind me of your safe word?" Martha added a finger as she talked, pressing deep.

Lucia growled low in her throat and rocked back into Martha's touch. "Peace."

"Peace." Martha added another finger. She moved her other hand below Lucia, and rubbed her clit, drawing a deep groan from her. She pulled her fingers from Lucia, already missing the sensation of possessing her body. Martha raised her hand and brought it down hard across Lucia's ass. The sting of contact and Lucia's sharp intake of breath sent a shock wave of desire through her. She stifled her own groan of response. *This woman. Mine. Hers. Us.*

She leaned over and laid her cheek against Lucia's skin before she kissed the dull red imprint of her hand, cherishing the gift of her surrender, revering the strong woman who sometimes needed to surrender her control just as she did. Martha brought her hand back and slapped the other cheek of Lucia's ass. She worked her clit. Liquid desire dripped from Lucia, coating her fingers. *So wet for this. For me.* Wordless, she began spanking Lucia in earnest, alternating the strength of her blows while she jacked her clit. Lucia moaned and rocked her hips, seeking contact with Martha's fingers before rising up to meet her hand as she was spanked. Lucia begged and pleaded, a litany of need and want pouring from her mouth. Sweat dripped down Martha's face. Lucia's skin was now cherry red from Martha's attentions.

Martha stopped and smoothed her hand over Lucia's ass. The heat of her skin filled her with want. The wet sound of Lucia's quiet tears filled the room. Her fingers were tight around Martha's calf, her face pressed against the soft leather of her boot. She looked down and watched as her tears dripped and traced their way down the leather. Her gaze settled on the delicate curve of Lucia's cheekbone and the way her lips were pulled back, her throat working as she struggled to regain control. *So beautiful. Her surrender. Her tears. Her trust. A gift.*

Martha picked up the bottle of lube she had placed on the table next to the chair. She poured it slowly down the cleft of Lucia's ass, letting it run between her legs and catching it in her hand. She spread the lube over her thick clit before she pushed inside and coated her with the slippery liquid. Lucia's chest rattled against Martha's legs as she moaned. Working quickly, she slicked her fingers and hand to the wrist. Lucia's rough breathing filled the room. The yellow-and-blue flames of the gas log fire sent shadows flicking up the wall of the room. Martha pushed three fingers into Lucia, filling her, while she rubbed her clit slowly. "So tight. Relax, angel. I'm not going to hurt you." She pressed deeper and spread her fingers. "That's it. Open to me."

Lucia's breathing shifted, and she spread her legs and panted as Martha worked another finger deep. She shuddered as Martha curled her fingers over her sweet spot.

"Oh. I'm going to come. Please. I need…" Lucia's voice was rough.

"Shh. Be still. Not yet. I have more for you. So much more." Martha pinched Lucia's clit, and she squealed and bucked her hips. Martha pulled back then pushed forward, adding a finger, and stilled. Lucia panted. Martha rubbed her clit in slow circles. "Slow your breathing. Relax, angel." She worked her fingers slowly. A deep groan from Lucia vibrated against Martha's leg where she lay across her lap. She kept her slow pace, opening Lucia to her, taking her time. Lucia rocked her hips back. "Please. Please." She groaned. "All of you."

Martha shifted in the seat, the pressure on her clit sweet torture. She eased back and tucked her thumb before she pushed forward in a steady forward motion and filled her. Lucia shook and trembled. Martha groaned as Lucia opened to her, taking her deep, the soft fluttering of her body around her hand driving her desire.

Lucia panted. "Please. I'm…I can't."

Martha waited. Waited for the word she wanted to hear more than any other from Lucia's lips.

"Ask properly." She rocked her hand forward, edging Lucia closer but holding back from what she needed.

"Please." Lucia's voice broke. "Mistress. Please let me come for you. Please."

"Come for me, angel. Give me what belongs to me." Martha rocked harder, pressing forward as she squeezed and stroked Lucia's clit. Lucia shattered, soft cries spilling from her mouth as she came shaking, her body clenching around Martha's hand. A surge of liquid silk flowed over

Martha's wrist. She slowed her movements and pressed her fingers over Lucia's clit. She stopped and watched Lucia's face as tears came harder and her sobs broke the quiet of the room. She eased her hand from her gently before she pulled her into her arms. Lucia curled into her, her body shaking with her release. Martha held tight and rubbed her back, a quiet witness to her loss of control.

"Sorry." Lucia sniffed.

Martha caught a tear with her thumb and brought it to her mouth to taste the bitter salt flavor. "Tears are a gift." She pressed her lips to Lucia's mouth in a gentle kiss.

Lucia shivered and pushed closer. She nuzzled the space under Martha's ear, kissing the tender skin there. "I haven't done anything like this in a very long time."

Martha pushed her hand under her curls and rubbed the back of her neck. "You're magnificent. Did I hurt you?"

Lucia gazed into her eyes. "Yes. Perfectly. I see why Myfanwy is devoted to you."

Martha smiled. "Myfanwy has feelings for you too in case you've missed it."

Lucia smiled a soft smile. "No, I hadn't missed it. But I wanted to check in with you."

Martha hugged her close. "Myfanwy has been my touchstone in this world." She pulled back to look in Lucia's eyes. "I don't mind sharing. How about you?"

Lucia quirked her mouth. "With Myfanwy? No. You're her Mistress, even if she won't ask for your collar." She sat up straighter, her voice shifting into a soft command. "As for you." She gripped Martha's chin. "No. I don't want you kneeling to anyone else." She kissed Martha, the sweet submissive gone, hard Mistress in her place. She slid her hand down to Martha's neck, and collared her with her fingers. "Ever." Her eyes glinted in the soft light and her voice was fierce.

Martha smiled and lifted her chin, giving Lucia better access to her throat, signaling her desire. "Yes, Miss."

"COME WITH ME. Elaine can handle the house while you're gone." Lucia placed the folded shirt in her suitcase.

"Madame didn't ask for me. And you know as well as I do she would not be pleased if I appeared without her summons." Martha lay on her side and pillowed her head on her arm. "I need to be here when the new security system is set up. It's too much for Millie to handle by herself."

Lucia firmed her lips. "You're right. I need to do this alone." She tugged the zipper on her suitcase to close it before she moved off the bed. She climbed up and lay next to Martha, mirroring her position. "I never thought when I came here I would be so reluctant to leave."

Martha smiled at her and reached out and tucked a lock of Lucia's hair behind her ear. "I never thought you'd stay."

Lucia caught her hand and kissed her palm. "I'll call you as soon as the arrangements are final." She pressed her face into Martha's palm. "I don't know how long it will be."

"Knowing her, she will wait until she is sure everything is settled. What will you tell her about us? About our arrangement?"

"We have an arrangement?" Lucia raised her head and gazed into Martha's eyes. "I don't recall making an arrangement."

The mischievous look in Lucia's eyes made Martha laugh. She moved across the bed and rolled on top of Lucia, pinning her in place with her body. She kissed her neck and nibbled along her collarbone. "Don't we? Or was it some other woman who lay across my lap while I fisted her?"

Lucia laughed and caught Martha's face with both hands. "It better have just been me or Myfanwy, or there will be hell to pay."

"Just you, angel." Martha looked into Lucia's face. "Just you."

Chapter Twenty-One

THE HEAT FROM the braziers set about the garden kept the chill at bay, and Martha was comfortable in her suit coat. Madame's plain black coffin, surrounded by a mix of white and blood-red roses, occupied the center of the room. Martha watched as Lucia greeted everyone, stunning in a simple black dress. Martha rested her hand on the lid of the coffin, closed per Madame's wishes for the funeral. *Are you watching us, Madame? Chafing at not being able to bend us to your will in person? I wish I had been able to tell you thank you. You were right about Lucia and me. But you knew, didn't you?* She'd arrived at the viewing and spent the morning staring at the frail remains of the most powerful woman she had ever known. Martha wanted to open the coffin to see her face one last time. *You'll never truly be gone. I'll carry your memory on my skin and in the deepest part of my soul forever.*

The folding chairs were arranged in rows as the small group gathered. The time for the funeral approached, and her anxiety increased as she waited for Vivian to arrive. She had come to help Lucia with arrangements. Martha had spoken to Vivian the day before, so she was prepared for the arrival of the trio when they appeared. Vivian walked in flanked by Octavia and Bridget. Vivian's face was a tight mask of sorrow. Martha crossed the room to them. Octavia saw her first, and Martha nodded her head in acknowledgment. Vivian smiled at Martha and reached out to pull her into a tight embrace. The strength in her thin frame surprised Martha. She held tight and waited until Vivian released her.

Vivian reached back and took Octavia's hand. "I know funerals are fraught with emotion, so let's get this over with." She tugged Octavia forward until she stood in front of Martha. Octavia raised her head and looked in Martha's face.

Martha met her gaze. "You are looking well. And happy."

Octavia's broad smile filled her face. "I am, M—" Uncertainty crossed her features as she hesitated.

"Martha. Just Martha."

"You are looking well yourself." Octavia met Martha's gaze. "Thank you for investing for me so well. It made a difference."

"You're welcome. I am glad you were able to put it to good use."

Bridget leaned around Octavia, held out her hand to Martha, and narrowed her eyes. "You here alone?"

Martha clasped Bridget's hand and released it. "Yes. Cook's not here." Martha let the humor show in her eyes.

Bridget quirked her mouth. "I wanted to say thank you. If she hadn't been so... If I hadn't worked at Rowan House, I would have never met Octavia, or Vivian." The realization of what she had said hit her and a blush started at the base of her throat. "I'm sorry. I didn't. I..."

Vivian came over and took Bridget's hand. She smiled at Martha and inclined her head toward Bridget. "Some things don't change."

Martha smiled. "It's fine, Bridget. I'll be sure to tell her."

Lucia appeared at Martha's shoulder and rested her hand on her arm, her demonstration of possession calculated and purposeful. "We need to take our seats." With a smooth slide of her hand along Martha's forearm, she took her hand and turned her away from Vivian before leading her to the front row of chairs.

LUCIA SAT NEXT to Martha, her hand gripping Martha's tightly. Music surrounded them, a blend of Madame's favorite pieces, finishing with the "Flower Duet" from *Lakmé*, reminding Martha of the first time she had watched the opera with Madame at La Scala in Milan. A montage of memories, each more vivid than the last, filled her and she swallowed her tears. *Be strong. For Lucia. For Madame.* Lucia gave her hand a hard squeeze and stood up. She walked to the podium set up beside the coffin. Her hands trembled as she opened the folder holding her notes.

The room fell silent as Lucia started to speak, her voice firm. "Madame was many things, to many people. All of us here have our own memories and precious stories of our experiences with her. She left a letter she wanted me to read to you. Her final command to me was to ensure you all understand she would never have left you if she could have stayed." Her voice broke on the last words. Lucia clenched the side of the podium, pausing before she continued. "These are Madame's words to you." She looked down at the podium and read aloud. "To all who have come here to celebrate my life, thank you. To all of you who have come here to celebrate my death, fuck you." The crowd laughed. "This is a celebration. No tears, or I will haunt you. Celebrate my life. Live every second. Follow my final command, love each other."

Lucia closed the folder and lifted her face to the crowd. "I thank all of you for being here. There is a repast in the formal dining room." She crossed the floor and sat down in the seat next to Martha's. A fine tremor shook her hand, and her eyes were full of unshed tears. Martha hooked her pinkie over the back of her hand. Lucia turned her palm up and Martha clasped her hand. "Well done."

Lucia turned and looked into Martha's eyes. "I need to check on the arrangements."

"Gia and Alicia can handle it. Sit with me." The crowd trickled out through the doors to the dining room until they were left alone with Madame's coffin. Martha tugged Lucia to her feet. "I wanted to do this before, but there wasn't time." She lowered herself to one knee. "I pledge myself to you, Lucia Coruso, for life. I am yours to do with what you will."

Lucia looked down at Martha and quirked her mouth. "Do you think this is the right time for this?"

Martha pointed at Madame's coffin. "She would say yes. And don't think for a minute she didn't plan this. She's probably sitting up there right now with a big glass of wine, crowing she was right."

Lucia looked up at the ceiling before she brought her gaze back to Martha's face. She pressed her lips together, suppressing a smile. "Will you get off your knees before you ruin your suit? And I accept."

Martha rose and held out her arm. Lucia rested her hand on it, as elegant as a queen, and Martha escorted her to the dining room.

Chapter Twenty-Two

MARTHA PACED THE front porch and pulled her phone out to check the time.

"It's one minute since the last time you looked." Elaine tilted her head. "She'll be here when she gets here."

"They're late." Martha shoved her phone back in her pocket. "They should have been here by four."

"A few minutes. Settle down." Elaine went back to examining the dead remains of the perennials in the pots by the front door. "When Jeanine gets back, we need to clean these pots up. They're a mess." She grimaced.

"She's coming back Thursday. Along with a few others. The list is on my desk if you want to start assigning tasks. Why are you out here anyway?"

Elaine smiled. "Keeping you calm. Annoying you enough you'll forget to worry."

Martha opened her mouth to reply and shut it when she saw the car turn in to the drive. She leaped down the two steps and rushed to the end of the walk. The car stopped dead center of the curve. Millie pushed her door open, but before she could get there Martha had yanked Lucia's door wide and held out her hand for Lucia.

"Such service." Lucia smiled as she exited the car.

Martha pulled her into her arms and held fast. "Always, Miss," she whispered into her ear.

Elaine cleared her throat, and Martha let go of Lucia, already missing the shape of her in her arms.

"Good to have you—" she met Lucia's gaze "—home."

"Good to be home." She inclined her head at Elaine.

"See you at dinner?" Elaine raised her chin. "Robin made chocolate tarts for you." She looked into Martha's eyes. "Or should I send Myfanwy up with your food?"

Martha held fast to Lucia's hand and leaned close, her words for Lucia alone. "What is your pleasure, Miss?"

A half smile crossed Lucia's face, and she squeezed Martha's hand. "Have Myfanwy bring us dinner. At eight." She hugged Martha's arm close to her as they crossed the drive and entered the house.

MARTHA PUSHED THE door open to Lucia's room, and Lucia preceded her. She tossed her hat on the bed and unpinned her hair. The loose curls cascaded over her shoulders. Martha stood waiting, watching her, aching to reach out and touch her, to hold her close and not let go.

Lucia placed her large purse on the bed. "I brought a few things back." She crooked her finger at Martha, and she walked to her as if pulled by a string. She stopped inches away. Lucia pulled her in for a long kiss, the heat building between them. With quick movements she unbuttoned Martha's shirt and pushed her hands inside. The warm heat of her palms on Martha's skin made her groan. "I want to feel you. All of you." She stepped back and pointed to a spot on the floor. "Over there. Back to me. Strip."

Martha hurried to obey. The soft sound of fabric moving and the click of the wardrobe opening had her imagining Lucia undressing. The denial of seeing her unclothed ratcheted up her desire. The Mistress in her wanted to turn, to take Lucia in her arms, tear her clothes off, and bend her to her will, yet she wanted to give Lucia her submission, to give her what she needed and craved as much as Martha did. She heard the loud hiss of the purse zipper and the rustle of the sheets as the bed was turned down. Anticipation and the cool air of the room made Martha's nipples hard. She finished stripping off her clothes and placed them in a neat pile in front of her.

"Turn around." Lucia's voice, her command voice, sent a wave of want through Martha, and she pressed her legs together to relieve the pressure between her legs. She wore a bright-blue dressing gown, the color intensifying the blue-green of her eyes and her brown skin. Her hair was now clipped high, the mass of curls swept back and up, exposing her neck and the exquisite lines of her face. Martha groaned softly.

On the bed lay a large hank of pale-brown rope. Martha set her feet wide, clasped her hands behind her back, and lowered her gaze to the floor.

Lucia passed around her in a small circle, stroking her hands over her skin. "I've wanted you since you left Como." She paused and pressed a kiss in the small hollow at the back of Martha's neck, causing her to shiver. "Face the mirror, pet."

Martha turned and faced the full-length mirror. Lucia lit the candles in the antique wood frame. Their yellow flames cast a gauzy light over the room.

"Look at yourself." Lucia leaned against her back. The silk fabric of the robe, and the sensation of her breasts, nipples hard against Martha's back, made her gasp. "Use your hands and expose yourself to me."

She watched in the mirror as Lucia reached around her and passed her hands over Martha's stomach. She moved them up to cup her breasts, pulling her off-balance and forcing her to lean back against Lucia's body. She rolled and pinched Martha's nipples, bringing them to hard points, sending lightning waves of heat to Martha's clit. She moved her hands down and held herself open to Lucia's gaze, the mirror reflecting the deep pink and hard prominence of her clit. She moaned as Lucia tormented her nipples, aching for her to touch her thick clit. Desire flowed, and she squirmed in Lucia's embrace.

A hard squeeze on her breast stopped her movement. "Be still." Lucia's voice was fierce. She continued to torment Martha's nipples. "Can you come this way, pet? For me?"

It was the "for me" that undid her. "I don't know, Miss. Maybe if I touch myself?"

"An honest answer, but not the one I wanted." She kept her attention on Martha's nipples, rolling them softly, then hard, tugging them in a rhythm. She lowered her mouth to Martha's neck. She kissed her and bit down, the sharp bite making Martha cry out. "Shh, pet. They'll hear you," Lucia whispered. She moved one hand down and feathered her fingers over Martha's clit, a whisper of a touch. Bringing her fingers back to her mouth, she licked their glistening tips. Martha's knees gave a little as she watched Lucia's tongue sweep over her fingertips. Her clit was so hard she was dizzy.

Lucia smiled at her as she lowered her wet fingers and continued her assault on Martha's nipples. "I think you need a bit more, pet." She released Martha. "Stay."

She left her there to consider herself in the mirror, trying to slow her rough breathing and aching for her Mistress's touch and approval. Lucia came and stood next to her. She was running the rope through her hands. Martha watched, enthralled, imagining Lucia's hands were passing over her as they fondled the rope. She shifted, trying to relieve the ache between her legs and earning herself a hard look from Lucia. Chastised, she stilled.

Lucia finished preparing the rope. "Clasp your forearms behind your back, pet."

Martha obeyed. The maneuver shifted her shoulders back and thrust her breasts forward. Lucia's hands gripped hers, then the rope caressed her skin. Her fingers twitched, as she wanted to reach out to touch her Mistress's, a small connection to her, but she resisted, remembering her training. The weight of the rope on her arms was soothing. Lucia worked quickly as she tied Martha's hands. She reached around and passed the rope over the top of Martha's breasts, and again below, forming a band.

"Turn to me." Martha obeyed, averting her eyes from Lucia's gaze, watching her hands from under her lashes as she finished her work. "Turn back." And they continued in a steady rhythm. Each time Martha turned back to the mirror, her body was further bound, wrapped in ropes with intricate precision, the knots down the front of her body in a clever purposeful pattern. The knot above her clit shifted each time she moved. The one between her legs pressing against her rim was maddening with the hint of a touch, just enough she wanted to gyrate to increase the effect, to get what she wanted.

"Face the mirror, pet. Do you see how exquisite you are?" Lucia's eyes were intense, a stormy blue, dark with desire. She tugged the end of the rope behind Martha's back, sending a shock wave of pleasure through Maratha as the knots moved against her. Lucia grasped her from behind. With one hand she teased Martha's nipple, engorged from the binding of her breasts. Her skin was exquisitely sensitive, an effect of the pressure of ropes. Lucia's touch sent her spinning toward orgasm.

"Oh. Miss. Please. I'm going to come. Please let. Me. For you. Miss." Martha panted on the edge of her control.

A wicked smile lit Lucia's face. "Not yet, pet." She licked the tip of her finger and touched it to the tip of Martha's nipple, rubbing in slow circles as she tugged the rope. Each swirl of her nipple, each press of the knot over her clit, made Martha groan. She braced herself, panting, lost in the sensations filling her. She kept her gaze fixed on Lucia's face. Her eyes were sharp and her mouth was open as she teased Martha, Lucia's excitement evident. She withdrew her hand from Martha's nipple, making her cry out from the loss of her touch.

Lucia pulled the tie of the dressing gown open. A red leather harness stretched over her hips. Martha's gaze was drawn to the thick phallus jutting out from the harness. Lucia took a small bottle from the pocket of her robe, flipped the cap, and dripped the clear liquid over the toy before she palmed it and smeared lube over the thickness between her legs. Sweat trickled down Martha's back. "On your knees, pet. Head on the floor."

She slid her hand along the rope, giving Martha enough slack to comply, steadying her. Each movement was a sweet torture as she placed her forehead on the floor, her hips in the air. She turned her head to look over her shoulder and met Lucia's gaze. She knelt behind her, the rope leash in one hand, phallus in the other. She set the tip against Martha, dragging it through the wetness between her legs. She held Martha's gaze as she sank into her slowly with a soft murmur of satisfaction. Her lips parted as she pulled back and sank in again. Martha closed her eyes against the pleasure of being filled, and the movement of the soft rope against her clit and her rim.

Lucia gripped her hips. The rope in her hand pressed into Martha's flesh, her fingernails digging into Martha's skin. "Hold on, pet. No coming until I say." And she fucked her, slamming her hips into her, taking every bit Martha had to offer. The sound of Lucia's breathing shifted. Martha clung to her control, waiting for her Mistress, desperate to obey.

"Now, pet, now." Lucia's harsh command as she came, the sound of her Mistress's release, sent Martha spinning into her own orgasm. Waves of pleasure crashed over her as she came hard, her gut clenching, shouting. Lucia continued, and she came again, the pleasure blinding as each shift, each movement caused another avalanche of pleasure to course through her. Finally, Lucia stilled, and withdrew. Martha collapsed to her side. Lucia began unwrapping and untying the ropes. Martha wanted to reach out to stop her. She hated the loss of each turn of the rope as Lucia took her time, moving Martha when she lacked the strength to move herself.

When Lucia was finished, she led her to the bed and made her lie down, covering her with the blanket. Lucia positioned herself so Martha's head was in her lap. She combed her fingers through Martha's hair. Martha kept her eyes closed and let herself sink into Lucia's aftercare. "Well done, pet." Lucia kissed her cheek.

She lost track of what else Lucia said as she drifted. Safe. Cherished. Loved.

"LOOK AT ME."

Martha met Lucia's gaze. On the bed lay her collar, and the sheer gown Madame had commissioned for her. Next to it was a red leather crop, Madame's favorite, the one she kept just for Martha. A second gown of the same cut was set off to the side. The sight of them sent a riot of emotion through her. In Lucia's hand was a pale-blue envelope.

"Madame asked me to give you this. Come." She held out the envelope to Martha.

She took the envelope from Lucia, opened it, and pulled the thin sheet of stationery free. She unfolded it.

If you're reading this I've gone beyond the moon, my most cherished love. Know I love you. I return these items to you. They are yours to keep, or to give as you see fit. Take care of one another in my absence. I will wait for you at the top of the stairs. G.

Lucia came and stood behind Martha. Martha laid the sheet of paper on the bed. Lucia touched her shoulder and turned her into her embrace. She pressed her lips to Martha's temple and wrapped her arms around her. She brought her lips close to her ear. "You've pledged yourself to me. I accept your pledge. Wear my collar when we're together and the gown of Givernay." She pulled back to look into Martha's eyes. "I pledge myself to you. I will protect and keep you. I cherish your service and your obedience."

She loosened her embrace, and Martha stepped back. Lucia lifted the gown and held it out to her. Martha knelt and raised her arms. Lucia fitted the gown over her. The sheer fabric floated down over her skin. Martha lowered her arms and closed her eyes, letting the sensation of the gown settle about her body.

She rose and picked up her collar from the bed. She turned to Lucia and kneeled. Martha held Lucia's gaze as she lifted her worn leather collar, soft with age, the buckle and single loop green with the patina of time, and held it out with both hands to Lucia.

Lucia took it from her and kept her gaze steady as she buckled the collar around her neck. The tug and pull as she fixed the collar in place filled Martha's heart. Lucia hooked her finger through the loop and yanked Martha to her feet to pull her in for a fierce kiss. She nipped her lip and drew blood, sealing their pledge with coppery-flavored kisses. Lucia leaned back to look in Martha's eyes. "Having you as a submissive is like owning a lioness. At any minute you could break free and devour me. You are an exhilarating, terrifying, and intoxicating woman. And mine."

The light in Lucia's eyes made Martha smile. "I would love to devour you, Miss."

Lucia gripped her chin. "I'll consider your request." She kissed Martha again, taking her time. Martha panted and wrapped her hands in the gown she wore to keep from touching her Mistress without permission. *Hers. Mine. Us. We.*

"Permission to ask a question, Miss?" Martha held tight to the seams of her gown.

"Speak." Lucia cupped the back of her neck. "Before I find another use for your lovely mouth."

"The other gown, Miss. Whose is it?"

Lucia smiled a half smile. "Myfanwy's. If she wants it. If you decide to ask her."

Martha swallowed on a dry throat. "Thank you, Miss."

Lucia frowned. "For what?"

"Knowing what I need. For loving me. For your ownership."

Lucia kissed her. "I love you, my lioness."

THE ROOM WAS warm, the bright afternoon sun spilling through the window. Lucia wore her black dressing gown, one of Martha's favorites for the perfect way it draped her curves.

"Do you want me to lay out the teal, or the coral, Miss? I favor the teal myself." Myfanwy held up two dresses for Lucia's consideration.

"I like the teal. It brings out your eyes." Martha finished folding her shirt and placed it on the dresser.

"I see I'm outvoted." Lucia rested her hands on her hips and quirked her mouth. "Myfanwy, I can finish this." She came over and took the teal wrap dress from her and planted a kiss on her lips so sweet it made Martha stop what she was doing to watch.

Myfanwy frowned. "But I like unpacking your things. And I'm almost finished. Millie said the rest of it will be delivered tomorrow."

Lucia held out a small box wrapped in tissue paper. "Well, you can stop long enough to unwrap this."

Martha came and stood next to Lucia. She draped her arm around her waist to watch as Myfanwy opened their gift. She tore the paper and opened the lid. A new collar lay inside, black and red leather woven together. A silver tag with a script *L* and *M* intertwined shone against the white tissue.

Myfanwy blushed. "Oh. It's lovely." She traced her fingers over the edge of the collar. "I don't know what to say."

Martha took her hand. "Say yes, sweet girl. Be ours." She smiled at her and kissed the back of her hand. "Just ours."

Lucia took the other hand. "Be with us. Ours."

Myfanwy's eyes were bright. "Just yours?"

"No more clients. Just us." Martha held her gaze. "And no more clients for us either."

Myfanwy blew out a breath. "Then I accept. The both of you." Lucia pulled her into a hug, and Martha closed her arms about the three of them. She lifted her head and looked at the small black-and-red urn centered on the mantel, wondering if Madame had seen all of this, marveling at her legacy.

Myfanwy kissed the hollow at the base of Martha's throat. "Do we have enough time to celebrate this properly, Mistress?"

"We have a lifetime, sweet girl. If it pleases our Miss." She looked to Lucia, meeting her gaze.

"It pleases me." Lucia lifted their hands palm up and placed a kiss in the center of each of their palms before she raised her gaze, a feral look in her eyes. "Now, where did you put the trunk with my rope?"

Author Note

In the story, Martha quotes the last verse of the beautiful Welsh ballad Myfanwy. Here is the verse with its English translation. If you've never heard it sung there are a number of versions on-line, but I am particularly fond of Beth Anghard's cover. It is this one I listened to and used on my playlist for this book. Enjoy.

Myfanwy boed yr holl o'th fywyd
Dan heulwen disglair canol dydd.
A boed i rosyn gwridog ienctid
I ddawnsio ganmlwydd ar dy rudd.
Aug hofiar oll o'th add ewidion
A wnest i rywun, 'ngeneth ddel,
A rho dy law, Myfanwy dirion
I ddim ond dweud y gair "Ffarwel."

Myfanwy, may you spend your lifetime
Beneath the midday sunshine's glow,
And on your cheeks O may the roses
Dance for a hundred years or so.
Forget now all the words of promise
You made to one who loved you well,
Give me your hand, my sweet Myfanwy,
But one last time, to say "farewell."

About the Author

Brenda Murphy writes short stories and novels. She is a member of Romance Writers of America. When she is not loitering at her local tea shop and writing, she wrangles one dog and an unrepentant parrot. She writes about life, books, photography, and writing on her blog, and guest blogs at Queeromanceink.com

I hope you enjoyed reading this book as much as I enjoyed writing it. Let's connect:

Website: www.brendalmurphy.com

Blog: www.writingwhiledistracted.com

Facebook: www.facebook.com/Writing-While-Distracted

Twitter: @bmurphysideshow

Other books by this author

Dominique and Other Stories

Sum of the Whole

One

Both Ends of the Whip

Also Available from NineStar Press

Connect with NineStar Press

Website: NineStarPress.com

Facebook: NineStarPress

Facebook Reader Group: NineStarNiche

Twitter: @ninestarpress

Tumblr: NineStarPress